ALIEN DIMENSIONS
SPACE FICTION SHORT STORIES
ANTHOLOGY SERIES
#20-#21

DOUBLE ISSUE

Alien Dimensions Series

Edited by Neil A. Hogan

www.AlienDimensions.com

Subscribe to the Space Fiction Books Newsletter

Receive the latest news about Alien Dimensions and other space fiction related titles.

Group giveaways, discounts and more!

Special Offer!

Download Alien Frequency: Stellar Flash Book One for free when you confirm your subscription.

Find out more at
www.AlienDimensions.com

Contents

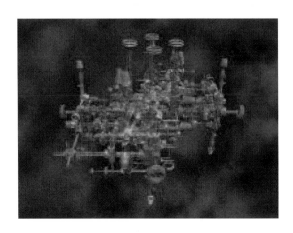

Storm in a Port
By Angèle Gougeon

"Place your weapons in the collection tray and step through the scanner."

The bug's mandibles clicked just a moment quicker than Cal's external auditory translator could keep up, echoing in dual tone from within the canal of his ear. The alien clicked again, impatiently, gesturing at the line behind him, and Cal reluctantly deposited his pistol. A white circle flashed on the dirt and oil-stained floor and he stepped inside, holding still for several claustrophobic moments as the metal grid slid down from the ceiling, scanners flashing bright enough to burn his retinas.

Cal was ushered forward by the next alien, somehow buggier than the last with more antennas than made sense. "Thank you," it clicked. "Welcome to Orbital Station Alpha b 25, the Solar Drifter. Your gun will be held in Administration Section 1-C, ready for pickup upon departure." A small holographic pad was shoved into his hands. "Please retain your ticket. Mass-transit is to the left. Maintenance and repair is to the right. If you are here for medical, please proceed to the elevator and HUB 4. You will find accommodations and the marketplace on HUB 5."

Cal shoved the holo-pad into his pouch and stepped toward the elevator. It was almost distressingly clean compared to the docking bay floor, a dissonance of shining titanium metal and white aluminum walls. Holographic posters flickered to life as soon as he stepped aboard. "Destination?" a tinny, mechanical voice intoned.

"Five."

A harsh cacophony that Cal assumed to be a jingle advertised a cantina on said HUB as he waited with increasing irritation for the door to close.

A lanky alien with tentacles for arms, legs, and face appendages reached him before it could. The alien stared at him for a long moment, with what might have been disgust or shock, before joining him in the small metal tube. With a click, and a flash of lights, the doors finally sealed shut and they began their journey downward. Cal intently stared at an ad for something that looked barely edible, resolutely ignoring the slow drip and steadily growing puddle of mucus beside himself.

The alien stared at him the entire time.

The elevator slid open to a sharp burst of noise and the pungent mix of spices and cooked meats. At their feet, the elevator's cleaning port opened, releasing a small cleaning bot outfitted with a ultrasonic agitator and vacuum. Cal quickly stepped out before it could run over his toes, the alien letting out a gurgle of what might have been affront before it left in a slither.

A wandering peddler saw him standing there, gawking like a tourist, and Cal quickly hurried to the right. A holographic greeter sprung up from the ground, then fizzled as he dashed through it. Long stalls lined the floors from the outsides and insides of the habitat ring, trapping shoppers within the long circumference. The gravity was a little stronger than Cal was used to, grinding his joints down into the hard metal floor, the artificial atmosphere sticking in his lungs.

"A human!" a blue-tinted alien with three eyes, a sucker for a mouth, and iridescent scales shouted. Cal paused, if only to give his translator time to decipher the mess of *"fleshy-tall-topfur-armsnoodles."* The alien waved him over with stubs oddly proportioned to its long body. "Long time since I've seen a human!"

"I'm sure." Cal eyed the alien's shop. It was full of junk. He noticed an old communications system, a broken data pad, and what looked like half of a life support module. Someone could make a fortune cleaning these things up. Someone could spend a fortune, too.

"Knew a Jim," said the alien. Its real voice chittered below the translation, a sound that vaguely reminded Cal of something he'd heard as a kid, listening to those old Earth-that-was holos, ancient recordings all dust and static in his planet's backwater classroom.

"Good Jim," it said. "Good customer. Many, many moons since I saw Jim. Do you know Jim?"

"No, sorry," said Cal. He didn't bother saying that Jim was probably dead. Most alien species lived five times longer than any human, unless the human in question spent most of their time in cryo.

"Too bad. Too bad." the alien said. "You? Name?" The translator futzed, buzzing in his ear. "...make good customer," Cal heard.

"Sorry," Cal said again. He jerked a thumb over his shoulder, and the alien watched his fingers, fascinated, holding up its own two-digit appendage. "I've got business." Cal didn't have business.

The alien nodded. "You come back," it said. "Come look. Good things to buy."

"Yeah, sure."

Cal smiled, without teeth, and stepped back into the chaos of the center aisle. He let the tide carry him forward, ignoring calls and avoiding eyes and the lack of eyes alike. Overhead signs flickered above in increasingly garish colors and brightness, adding unsettling tints to the crowds. To the left, a small sign pointed the way towards the brokerage offices and hiring hall, down in HAB 6 through a small elevator. Finally, there, the elevator to accommodations, of course at the very back of the ringed hall from where he had entered.

Cal sighed, irritated, and waited with a squat little alien with seven feet that only came up to his shin.

The closing doors shut out the din and Cal breathed in, letting the tension in his shoulders relax. All he wanted was a long shower that contained actual water, a good sleep, and a filling meal that wasn't made up of dehydrated supplements.

"Warning. Orbital Station Alpha b 25 is now in lock-down. Please remain in your quarters until the alarm is lifted. Do not panic. Everything is under control. We repeat: Orbital Station..."

Cal raised his head from the sink with a groan, hands dripping with reclaimed water. "I knew I should have stopped in Charris," he muttered. Even Delta 23 A, the planet the Solar Drifter orbited over, would have been a safe bet. It was widely known as a haven, open to any race and free from persecution or embargoes. The pirates loved it. The only reason the planet hadn't been overrun by some opportunistic dictator was because of their strict visitation and weapon laws. No one stepped onto or off the surface without first entering the spaceport and jumping through their multitude of hoops. Cal could have been frisked and long gone by now. Of course, the high gravity and dense CO_2 atmosphere might have been a problem. But that's what personal gravity belts and atmo breathers were for.

"We repeat: Orbital Station Alpha b 25-"

"Mute."

The cold digital voice shut off, leaving his oxygen regulated quarters in unnerving silence. Faintly, the warning continued to play from the hallway. With a low curse, Cal sat on the edge of the sleeper, stiffer than the cot on his skiff, studying the white sterile door to his rooms.

"Query."

The sensor blinked on. A pale, featureless greeter projected itself into the middle of the room, form eerily close to his own. The hologram wavered, mirage-like, "A lock-down is now in effect. Please-"

"Yeah, I got that. Why are we in lock-down? Angry alien with a gun? Pirates? A meteor hit the station?"

"Shields are at maximum percent. Do not worry."

"That's not what I asked."

"Remain in your quarters until the alarm is lifted."

The cold mechanical voice began to play from the ceiling once more. *"Warning. Orbital Station-"*

"Mute! Seriously-"

From within one of the insulated habitation pods, someone began screaming. Loud enough to be heard through the layers of insulating rubber and metal. Cal stared at the door, and then back to the hologram. The scream tapered off.

Cal pushed to his feet, shrugged on his jacket, and re-clipped his pouch.

"Please remain in your quarters until-"

What were the chances they'd been locked inside?

The door slid open with a brush of his hand against the biometric lock and a hiss of compressed air.

"Failure to comply with the rules of Orbital Station b 25 may result in fines and loss of goods," the greeter said behind him.

"Charge it to my docking bay," Cal muttered and stepped into the bright hallway.

"...is lifted. Do not panic. Everything is under control. We rep..."

No one and nothing was in sight. If Cal was in charge of a high-capacity spaceport, the first thing he'd do after securing the oxygen and gravity, was either make sure the elevators were working for fast evacuation, or take them offline to ensure access was restricted. Only one way to find out.

The elevators slid open upon approach. Inside, the holographic ads scrolled red, text a multitude of lines, dashes, and squiggles that Cal couldn't read.

"Destination"

"One," he said, without much hope.

The onboard sensor beeped. "Access denied."

Cal grimaced "Two," he tried.

"Access denied."

"Three?"

"Access-"

"Yeah yeah." *Great.*

"It is not working?"

Cal turned quickly, stepping back to the side of the hallway, heart picking up speed. He hadn't heard the alien approach. It was faintly lilac in color, mostly translucent with the vaguest shape of inner organs and no clear discernible form. Eyeballs sat eerily on its gelatinous face, completely seen through its skin. Humans had once classified them as creature DB 89 f, better known as *blobs*. "No," Cal said, cautiously. "I take it you heard the noise, too?"

"It was a *frt-t-t-t-t-t-t-t-t-t-*"

Cal winced at the feedback, shaking his head to the side. Not for the first time, he wondered if he'd be having this problem if he'd gone for the midbrain chip implanted directly into his brain stem. Not that he'd wanted the third-rate hack of a doctor he'd hired at the time anywhere near his inner soft bits. "What?" he asked, but quickly decided he probably didn't want to know.

"We checked in together." Its form wavered, like a stone thrown into liquid.

"Well-" Cal started to say, but another scream echoed down the hall, so eerily pitched that all of his hairs rose on end. It sounded like a dilloderm, suckers so tough that they could breathe pure radon and no natural material could pierce their hides. "Don't suppose you know another way out of here?" he asked, lowly, vastly unsettled.

"Yes," said the blob. It stared at Cal until he turned back around, his brows and hands raising impatiently. "You have a ship?" it asked, wobbling forward.

"Yeah?" Cal drawled.

"I need a ride. You help me get out. I help you to docking. Deal?"

He wasn't sure how a goopy slime-ball was going to do that but, as Cal listened to the dying gurgles coming from down the hall, he didn't have to give it much thought. "Deal."

The alien bubbled happily, no translation to mask the unsettling sucking noises. It flowed into the elevator, then squished down into the cracks of the cleaning bot's floor port and disappeared. For a few long seconds, Cal stared at the empty elevator, then turned to watch the hallway.

"Please remain in your quarters ..."

"Ready?"

Cal ignored the jump of his heart and, instead, backed up into the elevator. His new friend jiggled impatiently beside him. The doors hung open and Cal glared at the overheard sensor. When they finally closed and the elevator began to rise, Cal could only silently wish that he still had his pistol.

"Where's this?"

Cal stared into the empty, sterile room. An unmanned desk faced the elevator, a reinforced opening built into the wall and protected by a thin lilac plasma shield, fueled by heated argon gas and able to withstand radiation, changes in atmospheric pressure, and the force of a bullet. The inner hallway was clear, but a familiar white ring sat indented into the floor. Cal was pretty sure he didn't want to find out if it contained a simple containment field, or something much more deadly.

"Employee access," the alien said, sounding pleased. "Administration. Much closer to the port."

"How close?"

Cameras were built into the ceilings and walls – high security. So why wasn't anyone around?

"Just up," the alien wobbled taller, as though pointing. "Much closer to the port," it repeated.

"Perfect," he said, without sarcasm. Better than being stuck three floors down with tourists slowly dying around them. Besides, only one elevator connected to the docking bay – security focused on one central point to ensure pirates couldn't board and take over the entire port. The universe had learned from the Alpha a 5 Station fiasco. Better late, than never, Cal supposed.

9

"Anyone there?" he called into the room, peering behind the desk. It was as empty as he'd thought.

"Come," said the alien, rolling towards the hallway.

"Sure that's safe?" The blob stopped and seemed to peer down at the depression in the floor. It gurgled something that didn't translate, then went to the wall, searching for a way in, squelching the whole way. Cal caught the tail-end of a "...doing all the work. Lucky you have a ship."

"Sorry I can't fit into the walls."

"Too rigid," the alien agreed. "And gross."

Cal snorted, amused despite himself. "Excuse me?" This, coming from a ball of goo with a see-through brain and eyeballs. And – yeah, he could even see the alien's translator chip in there, floating in the glass-like organ in its head.

"Human, yes?" it asked. There was a promising dent in the wall, and the alien pried at it with a moist, sucking sound. "You expel waste. And have *bones*. You shed pieces of yourself. Are you not alarmed that you leave pieces of yourself behind? Tiny creatures live on your skin and eyelashes. Humans are disgusting."

Cal opened his mouth. "Fair enough," was all he could say.

The blob finally found something to access, and with little more than a pointed look, slithered in between the walls of the spaceport.

And Cal was left standing there, again.

He hadn't felt this useless since grade school.

From the ceiling, a loud beep sounded. A thick metal slab slid down with a bang inside the scanning circle. Then it rapidly shot back into the ceiling. Faintly, Cal thought he heard a *"Hurry"* from the wall.

Carefully, Cal inched forward. He toed the blinking white band of the circle. When nothing happened, he stepped into it, then out of it, quickly.

"Slow," said the alien, sliding out of a charging port further down the hall. The tiny calf-high robot currently docked let out a vexed beep as it was jostled. With a dim whir, it whipped off down the hall and out of sight before Cal could do much more than blink.

"Sorry."

"Slow and gross," it muttered.

"Hey," Cal objected, "I'm slow, gross, and I have a ship."

The alien peered at him. "And bones," it said, staring at his teeth. "Outside bones," it corrected itself. The surface of its body convulsed with what might have been a shudder.

"Teeth aren't bones."

"Gross," said the alien, again.

Cal rolled his eyes and headed down the hallway. It was just as sterile and brightly lit as everywhere else on the ship. The long curve made it difficult to see too far ahead, and the doors were all locked with signs he couldn't read. His gun was supposed to be in here, somewhere. A juncture forked off perpendicular from the habitat ring but, if patterns held true, the elevator to the docking bay would be all the way around, halfway on the other side of the station. Cal couldn't decide whether it was genius, or lazy planning. The architect of the port had clearly held a masochistic streak.

As if on cue, a door down the juncture flew open. A bug skittered onto the white flooring, slamming into the aluminum plating of the opposite wall. High chittering made Cal's translator ring. Blue ichor was leaking from the alien's eyes. And its mouth and ears. It reached towards them, then collapsed onto the ground. And then its body began to slowly cave in from the inside out.

Cal stepped back. His new alien friend followed, burbling something that couldn't translate. Cal was tempted to say several things that wouldn't translate either.

"Organic-nanites," said his companion.

"Yeah," Cal agreed. Hastily, he stepped further away from the slowly decomposing body, and then began to jog down the hallway that would, hopefully, lead them to the docking bay elevators. He didn't need his pistol that badly.

Cal had seen the aftermath of the Beta c 5 space station – no way was he waiting around for his eyeballs to bleed out of his head and his body to dry up into a dusty husk. Not that there'd even be a husk left. Organic-nanites had been created on planet Phla-7 Z - overpopulation and lack of space for the dead. And the high methane atmosphere ruled out cremation, apparently. Instead of simply creating a controlled methane-free space, one idiot of a genius decided nanites were the answer. Code them to digest organic matter in a controlled environment, and then turn that matter into fuel that also repopulated the nanites that died during the process. Self-sufficiency at its finest. And, it *did* work, Cal supposed ... for a time.

"What kind of idiot creates self-replicating nanobots without a fail-safe?" he muttered.

The alien wobbled a bit as it rolled along, as though shrugging.

"There are rumors," it said. "The mooras were negotiating a contract to mine special resources. The allori refused. Not long after, the nanobots broke loose."

"Sabotage?" Cal had never heard that story before. And, boy, did aliens talk about the nanobot scourge that often left nothing in its wake.

"Very suspicious," the blob agreed. "All organic matter upon Phla-7 Z was destroyed. Once the mooras were sure the nanobots were deactivated, they had much tantalum to mine."

Cal sighed. "Well, that's just great. Nice that they put so much thought into what would happen to the rest of the universe." All it took was one infected voyager stepping off planet and onto a ship. The nanites didn't eat the ship, but they sure ate the crew.

"The mooras only care about what the mooras want."

"Yeah, I've gotten that." Cal stared down at his hands. His fingernails showed no signs of anemia. His heartbeat was fast, but that ought to be the anxiety. He was slightly short of breath, but that was just the space station atmosphere. It had to be.

"Do you think they have any personal energy shields around here?" His tongue felt too thick.

The alien caught up to his right, rolling in that odd way that Cal tried not to think too much about. It made his eyes go funny.

"Security is part of administration," they agreed.

Cal breathed a little easier, relatively speaking of course, with a personal plasma-generation shield in place. Unfortunately, they'd been created for the scarbars, the chitinous race that ran most of the security on the station, and who sported heat-resistant carapaces. A thin gaseous layer of a carbon dioxide and nitrogen mix protected Cal's skin from the boiling hot energy which, of course came with its own problems, mainly the uncomfortable atmo breather shoved into the depths of his nostrils and covering his mouth. Already, Cal's hair was plastered to his skull, sweat dripping. The blob complained that it was drying out.

"Better than being *sucked* dry by a nano-swarm," he reminded them, voice a nasally muffle. "I think the elevator should be up ahead."

"Good," it warbled grumpily. "No more consultations," it said. "No more commercial transport. I quit my job. My boss is a–"

Cal's grimaced as his translator once again broke apart into an incomprehensible clatter. "There it is. Think it'll work?" The doors slid open as they approached.

"Destination?" asked the mechanical voice.

"One," Cal tried, even as the alien popped a disdainful sound and crept right inside the cleaning bot's port without waiting for an answer.

"Access code?" asked the elevator.

"Up yours," Cal muttered.

"Access denied."

Cal almost ran an irritated hand through his hair, before realizing he just might singe it all off. The elevator gave an alarming shudder. "What are you doing?" The alien seeped out from the minuscule cracks in the onboard control panel. The door slammed shut and the elevator began to rise.

"Speeding it up," they said.

Cal patted at his pocket for his port ticket. "We're in Bay 29. A spot near the elevators would be too much to ask for." He jammed the holopad away. "They better have gotten my new fuel cells installed."

"Leave a bad review on their Tourism and Transport Dispatch channel."

Was that a joke? "I'll do more than that."

The dirty floor of the docking bays was a comforting sight. At least until a low gurgle rumbled from the right. "Left it is." Sweat dripped into Cal's eyes. His skin was beginning to feel sunburned. He was going to get a tan without even going surface-side.

He couldn't bring himself to break the silence as they hurried through the abandoned docking bay. An overheated machine ticked quietly overhead. Someone had left their landing lights on, no doubt draining their reserves. Old stains sucked at Cal's boots, ground slightly sticky for reasons he'd rather not speculate on. They sizzled as his companion rolled over it in his plasma shield.

A six-limbed scarbar threw itself to the ground from an overhead walkway and Cal jumped back, hand going for the absent pistol at his hip. His translator squealed in his ear, a panicked voice being picked up piecemeal.

"Didn't think ... alive. So ... blood ... awful!"

"Calm down," said his alien.

Someone else gurgled further into Bay 17 and the bug's dark eyeshine optics rolled with fear. "... got to ... help them," it said.

Cal glanced at the blob, pretty sure it was looking back.

The bug started moaning, grabbing at its undercarriage, and Cal stepped back. "Please," they groaned.

"Medical is on Hub 4," his companion said.

Cal's face twisted. "Thought you were just looking for a ride," he muttered, but he still stepped towards the writhing alien. "Can you stand on your own?" He was willing to help, but he wasn't about to lower his shield.

The alien didn't answer, but they straightened and, stumbling, led them back toward the elevator. Cal couldn't help but think they were all walking to their doom.

*

"Hello?" Cal banged on the sealed doors to medical.

They opened, but a familiar plasma shield flickered into place. The thin asmatodea on the other side stared at them with multiple wide eyes. They blinked intermittently from within a strange, long face.

"The space station is on lock-down."

The scarbar let out a pitiful sound and Cal said, "Pretty sure they need a doctor."

For a moment, the alien remained frozen. Then the plasma shield faded away. "Get into the resonator," they told the worker, abiding no nonsense. They kept their distance until the alien was across the room. "Are you two showing symptoms?"

"No."

"I'm taking blood. Get those shields off."

"Don't trust us?" Cal asked, joking, and got the full force of eight eyes glaring at him. "We were pretty careful."

"No chances," the asmatodea said.

"Of course," the blob soothed. It climbed on top of a chair, an unsettling, jiggling lump. "I do not have blood."

"Your protein fluid will do." To the side of the large clinic, behind another flickering violet plasma grid, a smear ran down the length of one wall.

"Looks like you had problems," Cal said softly.

The asmatodea clicked. The needle jabbed into his arm with far too much force. Cal cursed and shut his mouth. In the silence, the resonator hummed – the machine completely surrounded the bug inside. Cal couldn't tell if he was even still alive in there.

The doctor peered into the enlarged holographic panels in front of its microscope. Cal frowned at the blob's panel – was that hydrochloric acid? That made ... an unsettling amount of sense. "I see nothing," the asmatodea said, a grudging concession. "You are clear."

"The doctors must be busy," said his companion. Cal's eyes roamed the empty clinic. He didn't think he was going to like what the doctor had to say.

The alien clicked in annoyance. "No other doctors," it said. Cal eyed the smear. "Sanbel was in the attached labs. Now he is quite dead. He was attempting to reprogram the nanobots."

Cal straightened. "How'd that go?"

"How does it look?" The doctor waved a long, stick-thin arm through the air, gesturing at the empty clinic.

"And the resonator?" asked Cal. "Can we use that? Some kind of magnetic burst – like an EMP?"

The doctor stared at him, silently.

"He's human," offered the blob, as though in explanation.

"And I was just starting to like you," Cal growled at the blob. "What about Delta 23 A? They've got to be working on a solution."

"The lock-down *was* the solution." The doctor stepped closer to the resonator, tapping at the holographic panel with a two-pincered talon.

"Wait." Cal stood up, running a hand across tired eyes. "You're saying their solution was to wait for everyone on board to die. That's what? At least two thousand aliens? More?"

"They will not risk the swarm getting planet-side."

"I'm not dying here," Cal told them. His companion burbled in agreement. "This is the Beta c 5 space station all over again." The doctor shrugged. "Right, okay." Cal tried to think back on his childhood science classes. "These nanobots, they're messing with the body's enzymes, right? Basically creating rapid cellular decomposition?"

The doctor blinked eight eyes, surprised. "Yes."

"And they're releasing an acidic chemical? Or they're blocking oxygen from the cells, forcing them into autolysis?"

Both his alien companions stared at him. Cal snorted. He was human, but he wasn't stupid.

"Can't you just," he gestured, "and forgive my simple terminology here but just target the so-called mouth of the bot? It can't change any cells if we gag it. Essentially a bot targeting antibody, right?"

The doctor stared at him, then clicked, thinking. "They must have tried." Then, decision reached, eight eyes narrowed at him as it grumbled, "I don't like sleep anyway." The alien pointed to the back room. "You know science. Sonic shower. Go clean up."

"I don't *know* science."

"Then we'll die."

Cal waved his hands. "I can do science!"

"Then maybe we'll live."

Cal crossed the room. "Cross your fingers," he muttered.

"I do not have *fingers,*" said the rolling alien beside him.

Cal glanced down at his hands and had to laugh. "Wish us luck," he tried.

"Good luck."

"You know, I never did get your name."

"Oh," said the blob, pleased. "I am-"

Cal's translator crackled in his ear. "Oh, *come on!*"

Angèle Gougeon is a Canadian speculative author from Manitoba, Canada, with short stories published in several literary magazines, most notably New Quarterly Magazine and Exile Quarterly, as well as several anthologies set to be published this year. She is also the author of a dark Gothic Paranormal novel, Sticks and Stones, published through EDGE Science Fiction and Fantasy Publishing.

facebook.com/artistangelegougeon/

The Resident Sommelier
By Robert M. Walton

Scented steam wafted into my nose, teasing my olfactory receptors.

Dum-de-da, da da-da-da Daaaahhhh! "Space . . . the final frontier . . ."

"Esmeralda, we're not about to watch Star Trek, are we?"

"I've got a new toy to show you. It needed an intro."

I leaned back against the tub's padded rim. "I'm ready."

Space suddenly swirled on the ceiling above our heads like an ebon velvet scarf emblazoned with jewels - beryls, sapphires, topaz. Against this scarf, the Childers-MacCauley transfer hub shone in all its silver and blue splendor. Called Chili-Mac by its residents, its two silver globes, both ten kilometers in diameter, rotated around a seven-kilometer-long shared axis – a fragile-seeming tube only a hundred meters across. Four snowy white concentric rings, two encircling each globe, housed starship docks, warehouse pods, processing bays and repair facilities.

"Nice view. How did you do it?"

"I got a new holographic projector. It compiles feeds from several external web-cams, official and not."

"Nice," I said again and sank lower into bubbly water.

"Relaxed yet, McCabe?" The proprietress and namesake of Esmeralda's Interstellar Hot Tub Cafe nudged me gently with one of her appendages. More famous even than her chili is her reputation for erotic adventurism. She'd never put a move on me, however.

Until now.

I smiled at her. "Not completely, Esmeralda. I'm here on

business."

She frowned. "I don't conduct business while tubbing." Two of her tentacles were draped along the rim of the hot tub. The third was submerged beneath foamy water.

"Sorry."

"That's a good word for you." She sighed.

"I'm a police inspector."

"Please don't remind me!"

"On duty is on duty."

"Maybe another time . . . "

"Maybe."

"Promises, promises." She tickled my big toe with a tentacle tip before rising. Bubbly water splashed everywhere as, dripping prodigiously, she stepped from the tub, her yellow and mauve hide gleaming.

I followed and quickly wrapped myself in an XXL towel. "Want to see the video now?"

"Let's get drinks first."

"I am Mauricio, your sommelier tonight." A rotund man, pink faced with a pencil-thin black moustache bowed from the waist on Esmeralda's outsized 3D video screen.

Esmeralda frowned. "You want me to watch a wine-tasting show?"

"Patience, it's better than a show."

Mauricio, head still inclined in a small bow, offered us goblets of wine.

"You're kidding me."

"Nope. It's an interactive tasting." I took a holo-goblet, held it on my fingertips, studied it. The color was deep ruby without a hint of oxidation. I brought the goblet beneath my nose, allowed the gathered fumes to rise on their own to caress my senses as they could. They did.

Mauricio intoned, "Do you perceive liqueur-like aromas? Plum, roasted meat, mocha, tobacco, truffle and burnished oak? Are you experiencing the fat, lush and smoothly explosive fruit? The powerful underlying backbone - massive but not at all heavy? This is a wonderfully tactile wine, finishing with big, chewy-but-ripe tannins and great persistence."

I took a sip.

"Good?"

I glanced at Esmeralda. "What the guy said - go ahead and try it."

She took the other goblet, held it beneath her slit of a nose and inhaled. All of her eyes popped fully open. "Wow."

Mauricio intoned, "Chateau Beau Latour, 2049."

Esmeralda chugged the glass.

"Hey, you're supposed to savor this stuff, imaginary though it is!"

She inspected the empty, sparkling virtual goblet. "You humans are so primitive. One entire lobe of my brain is devoted to storing and cataloging sensory information. I can replay my favorite experiences in slow motion when I wish. I'll get far more out of this than you will. Sniff away."

"Yeah, yeah." Curious, I checked the net's database for information about Beau Latour '49. "Holy shit!"

"What?"

"A bottle of this stuff costs as much as a small starship!"

"You're kidding."

"I'm not. There are only three known bottles in existence. How did Mauricio get one?"

"Did he have one?"

"Had to - virtual reality has to begin with reality somewhere."

"So, he's rich - what's the problem?"

"He's rich and somebody's trying to kill him. Listen to this . . . "

"McCabe?"

"Yeah?"

"Gonzales here. Are you going to show up any time soon?"

"I'm coming in now." I glanced at the morgue's somber, gray, holographic facade and walked up six steps. Glass doors hissed open for me. I took the drop tube to the left of the entrance and went to the bottom level, passing six well-lit floors on the way. I stepped from the tube into a dingy corridor, the bowels of the morgue. Dr. Elsa Gonzales - a short, compact woman - awaited me in her tiny lab at the end of the hall. As usual, she was hunched over her electron microscope view screen.

"Still just a sub-assistant coroner?"

She looked up and stared at me with eyes that would make a shark shiver. "Don't be silly, McCabe. I run things around here. It's useful that only a few people know that. You know that."

"Yeah, yeah, just pulling your chain a little bit."

19

"Don't."

"Why did you call me?"

"I have a private practice."

"I didn't know that."

"There's a lot you don't know."

"Hey, my neck has been bothering me. Maybe you could give me a checkup sometime?

Gonzalez smiled. Nothing could have shocked me more. "McCabe, McCabe . . . my services are far above your pay grade."

"Right."

"I've got a virtual vid that I'd like you to watch, also far above your pay grade."

"Right."

"When you've seen it, go visit the dude. He's a patient of mine and he wants me to put him under stage four station quarantine - confined to quarters with drone monitors, alarms and a security force guarding him."

"He's that sick?"

"If being scared witless counts as being sick, he's at death's door."

"Extortion?"

"That or worse." Gonzalez turned away. "I'll count it as a big favor if you can look into it. Here's his personal info." She handed me a data chip.

"Sure. I've got nothing big going today."

Gonzalez looked at me. "One more thing - it would be a good idea if you took Esmeralda with you."

"Esmeralda?"

Esmeralda frowned. "Gonzalez wants me to go with you to see this Mauricio?"

"That's what she said."

"Why?"

"Let's find out."

Beyond Chili-Mac's twin globes rose the glowing aquamarine transfer arch from dozens of cometary-ice processing plants to the Hub's axis. Water – both for reaction mass and atmosphere – was the station's lifeblood. Farther out, I knew, great clusters of giant water balloons shielded Chili-Mac from bursts of radiation and served as life insurance in case of ultimate accidents. This shining vista inspired thoughts of human greatness: genius, courage, perseverance, shared purpose and a dozen other positive qualities that were needed to create Chili-Mac and make it an ongoing endeavor.

I glanced at Esmeralda. She was looking through the rear window at a spider's nightmare of tubes, pods, girders, cables, derelict spaceships, and less reputable structural members. The Cubicles - slum, skid row and red-light district all rolled into one - raised thoughts opposite to the ones I'd just had.

"Worried about your place while you're gone?" I asked.

"Always. I need a new bouncer."

"What happened to Bob?"

"He's on sick leave, a reproductive problem."

"A reproductive problem? Bob?"

"It's time for him to lay his eggs. He's a single parent and won't be off his nest for a couple of months."

"Will you give him a shower?"

"Funny, McCabe, funny."

I shrugged. "Just asking."

Our shuttle slowed. Green lights flashed ahead of us as we closed in on an open docking ring near habitat globe Mac II. Esmeralda gripped a handhold with one tentacle. "So where are we going?"

"Mauricio has rooms in the Beverly Balconies."

"So, this is Beverly Balconies?"

Five slender fingers arching, spreading, cascading, became five waterfalls above and to either side of us. Billowing like dream-clouds in Chili Mac's seventy percent gravity, they curved between emerald arches of glass and fell, trailing silken feathers of mist. The arches supported groves of hanging trees and ferns. Interspersed among them were shining globes, luxurious habitats constructed of smart glass. Each globe could vary configuration and transparency at its owner's whim.

"Like the view?"

"Amazing!"

"Never been here before?"

"Are you kidding? I only got in because I'm here with you and you only got in because you're a cop."

"This way." We stepped onto a magnetic levitation walkway. I

21

waved the chip Gonzalez gave me in front of a sensor. The walkway lifted us and carried us upwards through mists and hanging boughs until we reached a discreet blue glass doorway.

I reached into my jacket's inner pocket and pulled out my favorite piece of cop equipment.

"What's that for?"

"SOP - I always deploy a surveillance mini-drone when I'm going to be indoors with a victim or possible perp."

Esmeralda looked uneasily at our placid surroundings. I again flashed the data chip at a sensor next to the front door. It slid open.

"After you." I offered Esmeralda an ironic bow.

She stepped through the entrance, squawked and crashed to a halt.

I peered around her lower, right side tentacle and saw a three-eyed, three-tentacled, mauve-mottled being exactly like her - though less than half her size - standing in an elegant living room.

"Henry!" she squawked again.

"You're mistaken." He waved all of its tentacles at once. "I'm Mauricio."

"Mauricio! My grandmother's sacred orifice! You're my cousin Henry!"

Henry's tentacles drooped. "Esmeralda, good to see you again. What brings you here?"

"She's with me. I'm Inspector McCabe of the Chili-Mac habitat patrol."

"You are welcome, Inspector, but I do not need your services."

"Dr. Gonzalez thinks otherwise. She sent me to speak with you."

A bar laden with glasses and expensive bottles rose from the floor near the window. Henry walked to it. "Drinks?"

"No, thanks. Esmeralda?"

"Not a chance."

"I'll have one." Henry poured himself a tumbler full of what looked like scotch, drained half of it and then held the tumbler in front of one eye for inspection.

Esmeralda took a step toward him. "What are you doing here, Henry?"

Henry tilted his head back so that if he had a nose he'd be looking down it. "This is my place. I've come up in the world, cousin."

"Over how many dead bodies, you leech?"

"By the sweat of my brow, cousin. I am Mauricio, famed sommelier and producer of the seventh most popular virtual vid in the known galaxy." Henry sipped scotch.

"Uh, Henry?"

"Yes, Inspector?"

"Just why do you need protective quarantine?"

Henry put his empty glass on the bar. "I recently suffered an amorous misadventure - more of a misunderstanding, really. A young female's relatives wish to harm me as a result."

"An amorous misunderstanding?"

The lights dimmed. A chime tinkled, stopped and tinkled again. Henry's eyes darted in independent directions. "That's odd. All the house's systems just shut down."

I checked the drone's feed on my smart watch. "Well, well."

"What?"

"We have company, three dudes in black. They move like a professional hit team. Have you got any weapons, Es?"

"Inspector McCabe, you know that's against the law."

"Have you got any weapons?"

Esmeralda pulled out a blue-steel .44 magnum. "I like the Dirty Harry movies."

"Holy Clint Eastwood, Es! That cannon would put a slug through all three bad guys and then kill the cat."

"What cat?"

"Anything else?"

She produced a Marine KA-BAR 2319, its matt black composition blade promising lethal damage to any and all. "In case somebody gets too close to shoot."

"And?"

Her third tentacle reached into another hidden pocket and pulled out a sonic grenade. "Only this. It's good for stopping bar fights."

"That's what I want." I reached for it. "Into the bathroom, everybody!"

"I beg your pardon?"

Esmeralda gripped her cousin with a tentacle and plucked him off the smart carpet. "Shut up, Henry, those boys mean business!" She tucked him next to what might be her bosom and carried him into the bathroom. I followed, pulling the door nearly shut behind me.

"Cover your earholes, folks." I wrapped my head in a bath towel, crouched by the door and peeked through the crack.

Glass cracked, crashed and tinkled. The three men in black entered simultaneously, one through the jimmied front door and two through the shattered patio door.

I glanced over my shoulder. Esmeralda had wrapped Henry in a fuzzy, pink bathmat. She wore a red towel like a turban. I pulled the grenade's pin and rolled it into the living room. I had time to open my mouth and cup my hands over my towel-wrapped ears before a giant punched me in the gut, knocking me into the sunken bath.

I lay breathless and stunned until Esmeralda prodded me with a tentacle. "Alive?"

"Barely."

"What's next?"

"Let's see what happened." I staggered to my feet and opened the bathroom door.

All three intruders lay unconscious on Henry's plush, violet carpet with blood trickling from their ears.

"Good grenade, Es - better than police issue."

"Military grade."

"Aren't you going to arrest them?" Henry squeaked.

"They'll have back-up. I guess we've got less than three minutes to get out of here."

Esmeralda poked Henry. "Let's go."

"Henry?" I touched a tab on the shuttle's console, putting it into hover mode.

"Yes, Inspector."

"What was that all about?"

"I told you. It's a dreadful overreaction to an amorous parting."

I stared at him. "Your girlfriend's relatives are professional assassins?"

Esmeralda wrapped a tentacle loosely around Henry's neck. "Cut the crap, cousin. I recognized one of those boys. He works for the Betelgeuse Cartel. What did you steal from them?"

"I assure you, Es . . . " Henry gurgled, "I have nothing owned by that cartel."

Esmeralda squeezed. "Okay, what did they steal that you stole from them?"

Henry's face went from pale rose to passionate purple. "Wine! Just a few cases of wine!"

"How many?"

"Twelve."

Esmeralda relaxed her grip. "Tell us about it, all about it."

"There were one hundred and forty-four bottles of the rarest, most exquisite wines from Earth's 21st Century."

I leaned closer. "Were?"

"I've consumed nine bottles while producing the first nine episodes of my Mauricio virtual-vids. There are one hundred and thirty-five remaining."

Esmeralda's eyes narrowed. "How much are these bottles worth and how did you get them?"

"The least expensive is worth something more than a hundred and fifty thousand credits. The most expensive are priceless - I'm saving them for the later episodes, of course."

I nodded. "Of course. These wines are three hundred years old?"

"The oldest is three hundred and fifty-two."

"Right - so why are they still any good?"

Henry brightened. "A connoisseur and collector - one Vlad Putin - purchased these bottles. To protect his investment, he had a very special wine vault constructed. Equipped with molecular scrubbers, micron filtration, temperature-controlled inert gas and an independent nuclear power source, it was guaranteed to keep the wines in perfect condition."

Esmeralda frowned. "So why didn't he drink them?"

Henry made puppy-dog eyes. "Sadly, Mr. Putin passed away shortly after the vault was completed and stocked."

"Tragic."

"Very."

"And then?"

"Disposition of his effects was disputed for decades and the wine vault was overlooked - until five years ago. Its discovery in a Moscow warehouse in pristine condition caused quite a stir - if you'll pardon the expression - in the culinary arts world."

"I remember now. There was a heist - lots of art and other artifacts."

"The wine vault among them. As you know, the Betelgeuse Cartel runs an extensive interstellar fencing operation. They acquired the vault."

"How did you get it?"

"I undertook some work - entirely legal, I assure you! - for the Cartel and had access to the vault. Unfortunately, the Cartel's boss and I disagreed on its ultimate use."

"So you boosted it."

Henry slumped. "In a word, yes." He looked up, pleading. "They were going to drink it!"

"Amazing."

"I couldn't allow such a travesty. As you must realize, I have superlative acting skills."

"You're modest, too."

Henry ignored Esmeralda's jibe and continued. "My copyrighted holographic persona is syndicated for at least forty more shows."

"How much have you made?"

"Two and a half million credits, with some endorsement payments still due."

I did some rough arithmetic in my head. "So, you get about two hundred and fifty thousand credits for drinking an irreplaceable bottle of wine every three weeks or so?"

Henry stiffened. "I consider my work to be a public service."

"Sure."

"Millions of viewers get to virtually taste these rarest of tipples, a wonderful experience they would not otherwise have."

"But they have to listen to you." Esmeralda sighed. "Still, you've got a point."

"Where's the vault, Henry?"

"I took the precaution of storing several dozen large items in several dozen of Chili-Mac's bonded warehouses. Most of those items are empty crates. One is the precious vault."

"I see."

A gleam came into Esmeralda's eyes, all three. "Do you have guarded storage for evidence, McCabe?"

"Sure."

"I've got an idea. Let's go get the box."

"That's it." Esmeralda plopped a case of wine on the seat behind Henry.

Henry moaned, "Each bottle should be handled - if handled at all! - like a newborn, like the rarest crystal vase, not tossed about like cans of tuna!"

"Shut the pie-hole, cousin. McCabe? You've contacted headquarters about picking up the vault?"

"They're on the way."

"We want the cartel's boys to see this."

"Lights, cameras, action, Es - a squad from the swat team will provide security and forensics will give the warehouse the full treatment. You didn't leave any tentacle prints, did you?"

"Henry's the only one who touched anything and he's the owner of record."

Henry sniffled. "My wines, my babies, what will happen to them now?"

Esmeralda patted a bottle of Domaine de la Romanee-Conti Montrachet Grand Cru.

"Nothing bad, cousin, nothing bad."

I didn't trust the smug look on Esmeralda's face, but I decided not to quibble about the grape juice just yet. "What do we do about Henry?"

"Let's head back to my place and talk about it there."

Some minutes later, I looked out of our shuttle's front window. Mares' tails of smoke and steam sprouted from various places in the cubicles maze. I shook my head. "Damned place leaks like a sieve."

Esmeralda looked up. "Like a what?"

"Never mind. The place leaks."

The shuttle's autopilot snugged us up against an airlock in what used to be a bulk cargo container, now just another appendage to the Cubicles.

"This is the back way into my place, through the basement. Grab a case of wine, McCabe."

I did and followed Esmeralda through the lock, down a passageway, through a second lock and into a storage room beneath the bar. An old-fashioned wooden wine barrel two meters in diameter rested at the room's far end. Esmeralda stopped in front of it, put down the two cases she was carrying and winked at me. "Watch this."

All three of her tentacles felt around the rim of the barrel and then pressed down simultaneously. The front of the barrel swung out on concealed hinges. "Pretty nifty, huh? Pull on the spout and it dispenses wine, too."

I nodded. "Yeah. What do you keep in there usually?"

"None of your business."

We stowed the rest of the wine in the faux barrel. Esmeralda closed its hinged front and then touched its antique wooden spout. The spout bled a few red drops onto her tentacle. She licked them off. "It's the house wine - Esmeralda's blend - not bad."

"What's in it?"

"None of your business. Let's go upstairs."

Esmeralda's bar and dining room could seat a hundred comfortably, or a hundred and fifty even more comfortably. About twenty customers lounged at tables or held the bar down with their elbows. Sam the cook was busy behind the grill.

"I didn't know you served breakfast."

"Sundays only - Sam makes killer huevos rancheros."

"What's that?"

"Deep-fried homemade tortillas topped with ghost peppers, cheese and two eggs, sunny-side up - habañero sauce on the side."

"Sounds deadly."

"You have no idea."

A chair scraped as somebody stood. I took a second look at the clientele. Half a dozen were obviously locals - thin, slouched over their huevos and wearing threadbare work overalls. Another half dozen were dressed stylishly - Chili-Mac idlers, slumming for sure. The rest were thugs wearing chinos and sports shirts in pastel colors. The one who had just risen glared at me. Half a dozen more pushed through the front door.

The bar regulars slid to the corners of the room. Sam, a weary look on his face, crouched behind the grill. The young idlers stared like deer caught in headlights and then ran for the restrooms. Esmeralda sighed. "Betelgeuse Boys. Showtime, McCabe."

The standing thug stared daggers at me and then at Esmeralda. His neck tapered down from his head into weightlifter's shoulders. "Give us the rat and we'll leave without trashing the place."

"Who?"

No-neck pointed at Henry. "The rat."

Henry quivered and gibbered. Esmeralda smiled. "Nobody comes into my place and molests one of my customers, sport. Leave."

No-neck shrugged. "Have it your way."

I glanced at Esmeralda. "It's the two of us against all fourteen of them?"

The kitchen doors swung open and a seven-foot tall, broad-shouldered figure covered with blue fur stooped as he stepped into the room. He held a serving plate heaped with huevos rancheros.

Esmeralda brightened. "Bob's here."

A bartender, a bouncer and a middle-aged cop against a pack of trained killers? They never had a chance.

Bob glanced at Esmeralda. She nodded to him. He carefully put his plate down on a bus cart.

No-neck snarled at Bob. "Stay where you are, you walking carpet."

Bob surged forward, fangs bared, seized two thugs, crashed their heads together and let them fall limply to the floor. Six more pulled out shock rods, spread into a half circle and advanced on him warily.

Esmeralda catapulted into action, plucking up a thug with two tentacles and flinging him into the group advancing on Bob. Shock rods popped and hissed. Thugs screamed.

Sam ducked behind his grill. Henry dove beneath a table. Customers cowered in corners.

One thug, in search of a soft target, jumped over the counter and went for Sam. Sam flung a pitcher of habañero sauce in his face. He clutched his eyes and howled.

Two Betelgeuse bangers, including No-neck, came for me. No-neck moved to my left. The other guy came in first from my right. I flicked my right hand. My wrist taser shot a dart into his chest, shocked him rigid and dropped him straight to the floor. No-neck slashed at me with a knife the twin of Esmeralda's. My work suit-coat is woven of fifth generation kevlon, proof against anything that's not armor piercing. The blade glanced off my left sleeve and I zapped him with my taser's second dart. He hit the deck and groaned.

"Amazing! Down but not out."

Esmeralda wrapped a tentacle around his head and thumped it on the floor, hard. "Out."

I glanced around to see how we were doing.

Bob was wiping up the floor with the last two thugs - really wiping it. He pushed their flattened faces across Esmeralda's checkered linoleum like a couple of sponges. The guy behind the counter had stopped screaming. Sam held his mallet ready for additional tenderizing, if needed.

"Shall I call in the meat wagon?"

Esmeralda frowned. "No need for official help. I hire Cubicles folks to take out the trash."

"You often have bodies to remove?"

"Sometimes. This is like a bad Saturday night, only it's Sunday morning."

I sat at the counter, nursing a cup of coffee and hoping that I was a safe distance from the huevos rancheros. Henry sat at a back table, looking nervously in three directions at once. Bob sat at the other end of the counter from me, stashing away his second plateful of huevos. Esmeralda entered from the kitchen.

"Well, that takes care of that."

I raised an eyebrow. "Do I want to know the details?"

She shrugged. "Nothing terrible - only four of them needed medical transport. We dumped the rest in various alleys and trash bins."

"Won't Betelgeuse want payback?"

"Nope. We had a right to play defense. I've got a reputation, too."

"So I noticed."

"Besides, the bosses will think you Chili-Mac cops have impounded the wine. They'll be trying to find somebody to bribe so they can get it back."

I nodded toward Henry. "What about him?"

"We'll get rid of him this afternoon."

"You wouldn't . . . ?"

"Nah! We'll put him on a tramp freighter. You can come with me and wave good-bye, if you want."

Bob burped.

"I thought you said he was out sick."

"He was pregnant, not sick."

"What about his eggs?"

"He must have found an egg-sitter. Complaining?"

"Why did he come in?"

"He likes Sam's huevos rancheros. He came for breakfast."

"Thank God for ghost peppers."

Bob held his empty plate out to Sam. Sam shook his head mournfully. "More?"

Bob nodded.

"You're going to regret this."

*

We watched as the starship Billie Holiday floated into a clear spot in Chili-Mac's crowded skies.

I glanced at Esmeralda. "Henry's on there?"

"Yep."

"I didn't see him board."

"You did. You just didn't recognize him."

"Where's he going?"

"Tau Ceti Six. After that, we don't need to know."

"The Betelgeuse bosses will eventually find out that the wine isn't in police custody."

Esmeralda smirked. "Sooner than you think."

"Won't they go after him?"

"They'd like to, but Henry's got six different aliases and bank accounts strewn across the known galaxy. Don't worry about him. Besides, he's not in the wine business anymore."

I turned to her. "Speaking of which, what are you going to do with the wine?"

"You know, McCabe . . . " She paused for effect. "The secret of success is knowing when you've got it made." She smiled at me. "I make a good living with my cafe. I've got it made."

"You didn't answer my question."

"Médecins des etoiles sans frontières."

"What?"

"I'm going to keep on producing Henry's wine show here in the Cubicles and give the profits to the Star Doctors."

I thought about that. "Good idea. Those docs help lots of out of the way places. How will you replace Henry?"

"I've already hired an actor."

"Who?"

"Bob."

"Bob? You're kidding me!"

"He's got an amazing voice. You should hear him read Jane Austen! He's a wine connoisseur, too."

"What kind of sewer?"

"It's French."

"So?"

"It means expert."

"Right."

Esmeralda rubbed her chin with a tentacle tip. "We'll subtract a few thousand credits to pay for damages to my place, of course."

"Of course."

"And I'll get to dispose of the open bottles."

"Of course."

"Speaking of which, care to tub?

I swallowed. "Still on the job, Es. I've got to explain at least some of this to the powers that be."

"Well, you know where I'll be."

Robert M. Walton's novel Dawn Drums was awarded first place in the 2014 Arizona Authors Association's literary contest and also won the 2014 Tony Hillerman Best Fiction Award. He and Barry Malzburg wrote "The Man Who Murdered Mozart", published by Fantasy & SF in 2011. Most recently, his "Duck Plucking Time" received a first place in the Saturday Writers short fiction contest.

chaosgatebook.wordpress.com/ and amazon.com/Robert-M-Walton/e/B001KMNLJY

The Sixth Animal
Elana Gomel

"They never come back," Lila said.

Arvid looked over her shoulder at the holo which showed the abandoned city licked by the green tongues of the jungle. The crumbling buildings looked almost familiar: narrow grey spikes stabbing into the perpetually overcast skies of Draconis-3. His brain automatically classified them by analogy: a little like Gothic spires, a little like Mayan pyramids. But he knew that from close up, the analogy would fall apart.

The walls were not stone but some weird composite which they still could not analyze properly. The sharp peaks sagged to the side instead of rising in a straight line. What appeared to be slit-like windows were narrow gouges in the walls that did not penetrate all the way into the hollow interior – provided there even *was* an interior. They were not sure about it. They were not sure about anything except the fact that builders of the city were nowhere to be found.

"They look alike to me. Maybe it's the same set every day."

Arvid tried to keep frustration out of his voice. Their surveillance technology was cheap knockoffs – the best they could afford with the stingy academic grant. Supposed to investigate yet another set of ruins on yet another earthlike planet, they were an afterthought at best, a PR exercise at worst. The X-web Coordinating Council was only interested in tangible results, while Arvid and Lila were not equipped to bring in anything but knowledge. And it seemed pure knowledge had few buyers.

"No way," Lila said. "Let's watch it again. Look at them!"

They saw the animals come into the clearing in front of the building which Lila irreverently called "The Popsicle". It appeared to be half-melted, leaning to the side, its top hanging down in slicks of the composite which had a slight pink tinge to its elephant-skin grey. They could not be sure whether this was the result of some sort of weaponized hit or just the alien taste in architecture.

The clearing was a plaza, round in shape, free of vegetation, and paved with rectangular slabs of the composite. And while The Popsicle, along with all the other structures in the city, had no visible means of ingress, there was a circular hatch in the middle of the plaza. Arvid and Lila had tried to open it, but the hatch did not respond to tugging and pulling. They had planned to come back with such tools as their rattling X-web-enabled LMV contained but it turned out there was no need. The animals had done it for them.

Arvid knew he should be happy for Lila. It had been his idea to apply for an archeological grant; she had been willing to play the second fiddle by doing some zoological research on the side. And yet, in an ironic twist, he had discovered nothing about the Builders, while she had a readymade biological mystery on her hands. He should be happy for her…but he was not.

How fair was it that xeno-psychology remained a languishing academic discipline, while xeno-biology was bringing in big bucks and tenured positions? It had seemed the other way round when the X-web was discovered: a quantum tunneling network, clearly of artificial origin, that linked dozens of earthlike exoplanets, some of them littered by ruins. Arvid still remembered the excitement of his first year of PhD in xeno-psychology when contact with intelligent aliens appeared within reach.

But it all fizzled out pretty quickly. The ruins held few clues; the origin of the X-web was obscure; and the practical fruits of being able to navigate multiple solar systems with nothing more expensive than a quantum key and a shoddy LMV had ushered in a new Gold Rush, with the gold being biologicals. The X-web-linked planets all had life but no intelligence, or at least none that was current. Finding the secret of life extension in some alien plant took precedence over poking through enigmatic ruins.

He forced his mind away from the bitter thoughts of his dwindling career and turned his attention back to the recording. On screen, the emerald algae-like vegetation fencing in the plaza was

34

pushed aside by animal bodies as they entered, paying no attention to each other. Arvid was reminded of the wildlife in the African savannah approaching a waterhole. But there was no waterhole here. There was nothing that should have attracted five different creatures of unrelated species. And nothing that should have made these animals – both carnivores and herbivores – just stand, lie, or loll around the plaza as if they were paparazzi awaiting the arrival of a celebrity. And absolutely nothing that should have prompted the repetition of this scene every day for the two planetary weeks they had been on Draconis-3.

The animals did not always arrive in the same order. This time, the first one to show up was a large pale creature that looked like a hairless bear with no eyes and an elongated muzzle fringed with sharp fangs. It walked on two legs, as did a surprising number of Draconis-3 animals, but its hind paws, hanging loosely by its sides, were clearly those of a predator: long, powerful, and tipped with wicked claws. Its grub-like skin and blind muzzle revolted Arvid, while Lila was fascinated by how it hunted by smell only. Its single huge nostril was located on top of its flat skull, and it twitched and drooled. Lila had dubbed it the Bald Bear.

The second creature was a small skittering thing like an armadillo with multiple legs. Its carapace was beautiful bright purple.

The third animal seemed to be lost in its own loose skin. Lila had explained to Arvid that it was a grazer-equivalent, the local version of wild cattle, but to him it looked like a rolling half-empty sack of piebald hide with some something thrashing inside. Occasionally a tiny head with huge eyes and a proboscis would poke out, snatch a leaf or a branch, and disappear back into the sack.

The fourth animal was a slinky catlike thing that Arvid liked because it looked reassuringly normal, like an Earth carnivore – apart from the fact that its four legs were so short that it appeared to slither through the vegetation on its striped belly. But it did have four legs – an exception on this planet; and a long snout; and even mangy fur. Lila insisted it was a nocturnal insectivore but Arvid thought of it as a short-legged cat.

The fifth animal, though, was the one that unnerved Arvid the most. It walked on two legs like the Bald Bear, and there was something humanlike in its erect posture and lithe stride. Its body was also humanlike in its proportions: a cylindrical trunk, narrow hips, long legs and arms, the latter equipped with prehensile fingers.

35

But that was where the similarity ended. The creature had no head. Its shoulders curved into a shallow featureless arc. There were no eyes, mouth, or ears. It was just a walking headless mannikin, its skin greasy and pink like that of a piglet.

The five animals surrounded the plaza in a rough circle, waiting. And then with a sharp click the hatch in the middle of the plaza rose, disclosing a black hole. There was a spiral staircase leading into the darkness, its treads gleaming in the rain. The animals filed down: the Bald Bear first, the Purple Armadillo second, and so on. The Headless Man brought up the rear. The two upright walkers navigated the stairs with ease; the rest managed somehow. When the Headless Man's shoulders disappeared into the hole, the hatch fell back.

"There may be an exit somewhere in this wet salad," Arvid muttered, nodding at tangled fronds of the jungle, its hues of green washed into fluorescent brightness by the drizzle.

"Maybe," Lila did not sound convinced. "But these are not the same as showed up the day before."

"Couldn't tell the difference."

"The same species, yes, but not the same *individuals*. Animals are individuals too, just so you know! Look!"

Lila played back part of another recording. Reluctantly, Arvid could see that the Purple Armadillo there was smaller and lighter-colored than the one they had just seen.

"So, every day five individuals of totally unrelated species walk into the city, dive into some sort of underground tunnel, and disappear. We don't see them coming back. But next day five more show up – and so it goes. Right?"

"Right," she sounded angry.

"Can there be a signal from the city? Something we have missed?"

"The city is an empty shell. There is no EM, as you know perfectly well. This is a *biological* mystery, Arvid. It has nothing to do with your theoretical sentients."

"Except our remit here is to explore the city and write a report for the Archeological Society, remember?"

"When you can get inside The Popsicle, let's talk about it!"

The conversation went downhill from there.

Lila stopped under a squat sprawling tree, letting drip fall onto her upturned face. The trees of Draconis-3 were more like giant moss, lacking the central trunk and separate leaves. A clutch of juicy fronds, exhaling the aroma of sea mist and amber, rustled above her. The drip was warm, and the air was filled with gentle vapors. She could feel her skin drinking the moisture in.

"Better than a spa," she muttered.

A long trill sounded in the canopy. Draconis-3 did not have birds; the only flying creatures were insect equivalents. But many ground dwellers communicated in songs, so the jungle was filled with natural music. Lila smiled but the smile slipped off her face when she remembered the five animals who right now would be wending their way from their different habitats to converge on that damned hatch. There was something profoundly unnatural about this behavior, and that bothered Lila. She recalled the conversation she had had with Arvid after they observed the five-animal ritual for the first time. She had tried to explain why the set of the five was so weird.

"These animals are natural enemies," she had said. "The Bald Bear preys on anything that moves; and the Cow Sack is eaten by all the large carnivores in the jungle. I have recordings. You can see that they roll away as fast as they can when they smell a predator. The Purple Armadillo lives in the marshland, and the Snake-Cat is a nocturnal solitary insectivore. What the hell are they doing together? And why are they going down into the tunnel? Wild animals are afraid of artificial structures."

"What about the...headless thing?" he had asked. "Could it be...one of the city Builders? Degenerate or something?"

"This is not a fucking Eloi! Come on, Arvid, that's not how evolution works! This thing has no more intelligence than a cockroach. The reason it has no head is because it has no central brain, just a handful of neurons in the spinal cord. It's a scavenger. It's not a man who has forgotten his head at home!"

Symbiosis existed on this planet; she was sure of it. But could these alien lambs and lions really be natural collaborators? Maybe not; but Arvid's stubborn conviction that the putative Builders were somehow involved made no sense either.

The truth was that Lila was a little afraid of the very idea of alien intelligence. Animals were the same, whether on Earth or anywhere else in the Galaxy, driven by the biological imperatives of survival and reproduction, which she understood in her gut. But sentients, whether humans, the extinct Builders, or the anonymous creators of the X-web, could break the evolutionary chains. They were free and therefore dangerous.

She squinted through the ever-present watery veil. The sagging towers of the city loomed above the jungle, dissolving into the clouds.

"Fuck you!" she muttered. "Leave my animals alone!"

Arvid puttered around in the LMV, going over the data from the city, still smarting from the latest fight with Lila. She was in the jungle with her beasties, of course. He still remembered the time when her fierce love for life in all its endless variety was one of the things that had attracted him to her. Now....

Was it because he was jealous of her professional success? She had a position waiting for her back on Earth. He did not. It was as simple as that. The Archeological Society grant was his last bid for a tenure track somewhere, and it was not working out. Could they continue their trial marriage with her career blossoming and his in the doldrums? The fact that he had to ask this question of himself was the answer, and the answer was no.

He poked his head out. The jungle closed around him like a sodden noose: a bubbling mass of formless protoplasm. Without intelligence, alien life had no interest for him. And there *was* intelligence on this planet: he could feel it in his bones. Lila could say whatever she wanted about alien ruins being the same everywhere. She was wrong. There was a genuine mystery here: large cities but no obvious factories or manufacturing sites; buildings still standing but no remains of the Builders; and most of all, that bizarre five-animal ritual performed daily. *Something* must be functioning in the ruins to open and close the hatch and to attract new animals every day. Were they a food source for the Builders hiding in some underground facility? But why these five animals? Arvid could not imagine an intelligent entity that found the Bald Bear and the Headless Man appetizing.

A religious ritual, then? A sacrifice? That was more likely. Ancient Earth cultures had practiced animal sacrifices of endless bizarre varieties: hecatombs of lambs and slaughter of bulls, not to mention massacres of their own kind to appease the gods, the burnt children of the Phoenicians and the flayed captives of the Aztecs. If there was some sort of religious ritual performed daily in the subterranean catacombs of the city, it would make sense that only specific animals were selected.

But how were they induced to go down? There must have been a call or a signal of some kind, even though their trashy equipment could not detect it. Everything they had was subpar. They had managed to send a mini drone into the tunnel once, following that day's batch of five animals. It had disappeared into the darkness as thoroughly as the animals themselves, transmitting nothing. They tried to recall it with no results.

Well, the great archeologists of the past did not rely on drones.

Lila bent down to pick up a brightly colored creature that looked like a cross between a frog and a dragonfly when she felt a gaze on her back of her head. Somebody was looking at her with malevolent intent. Even though she knew that local predators were deterred by the unfamiliar human smell, Lila felt a chill travel down her spine. Cautiously, she straightened up and turned around.

A Headless Man was standing just behind a curtain of vines, looking at her.

Lila swallowed. The species' bare skin was photosensitive, so in effect, its entire body was one giant eye. But it was truly brainless: she had dissected one specimen and found only rudimentary ganglia, not more than required for zooming in on rotting carcasses. Its mouth was tucked between its legs and also served as its reproductive apparatus. All in all, despite its bizarre appearance, a Headless Man was a common scavenger, occupying the same ecological niche as terrestrial cockroaches.

So why did it feel as if it were watching her?

"What do you want?" Lila asked, feeling like an idiot.

The creature raised the vines with its supple fingers in a strangely graceful gesture. She tensed as it moved toward her.

And then she realized it was backing off. There was no difference between its front and rear; it could move in any direction without turning around. It disappeared into the green.

Lila released the breath she did not know she was holding in.

Arvid stood shivering in the rain under the sky the color of murky glass. He was not cold: the planet's cloud-swaddled surface was balmy all year round. Perhaps it was the excitement of discovery. And perhaps fear.

A Bald Bear stepped out. Arvid's fingers involuntarily clenched around his small taser and he forced them to relax. He stood still, allowing the beast to approach. Unfiltered by the screen, its alienness was palpable: the skin the color of damp paper; the wet flap of the nostril on top of its head, and most of all, its smell: sharp and vinegary like old salad dressing.

The animal stopped some distance away, and then dropped down to its haunches; its eyeless muzzle tucked into its chest.

"Hello," Arvid said inanely and got no reaction.

The rest of them followed in a quick succession: a Purple Armadillo, which today was lavender-colored; a Snake-Cat slithering through the mossy undergrowth so quietly that Arvid fairly jumped when it almost touched his shoe with its narrow snout; a large Cow Sack, hopping along with an asthmatic wheeze; and finally, when Arvid was getting impatient, afraid Lila would come back from the jungle and figure out where he was, a Headless Man.

That was a larger specimen than the ones they had seen before, towering above Arvid. Its rounded shoulders heaved occasionally as if the creature was trying to lift some invisible burden, and its pinkish-brown skin looked peeling and weirdly, sunburnt. It stepped closer.

Was it intelligent? Was any of them?

Arvid looked around and felt only the dumb indifference of animals, not the curiosity of a self-aware mind. He was alone, he realized. Surrounded by overabundant life, he was truly alone.

"Well, boys," Arvid croaked, "we are all here, so let's do it!"

The "boys" did not react but something else did. In the middle of the plaza, a hatch swung open.

Lila came back to the LMV tired and dispirited. After the encounter with the Headless Man, she had been making one mistake after another. She dropped a sensitive probe that instantly went on a blink; she inadvertently released a swarm of trapped bog-lizards; she entered wrong data into the day log. It was as if she was sabotaging her own work. She felt as if Arvid was looking over her shoulder, the familiar grimace of discontent on his face.

She knew their marriage was over but did not know whether Arvid was aware of it or not. In truth, she did not know anything about her trial husband anymore. It was as if they were standing on two sides of a chasm, shouting at each other, their voices reduced to an inaudible whisper by the distance. She was not angry. She just could not hear him.

But when she stepped into the LMV, the silence that greeted her was literal. Lila called out for Arvid and looked for a message telling her he went back into the city, even though it was useless. They had already established that there were no alien artefacts lying around. No stone axes, or scrolls, or rusty machines, or painted murals helpfully illustrating the entire history of the vanished race. The city was as unnaturally sterile as the jungle was teeming with life. Perhaps the artefacts were all neatly stored inside the half-melted towers. Perhaps the Popsicle was the equivalent of the Library of Alexandria. But since they had no means of getting inside, the speculations were moot. Which did not mean Arvid would give them up any time soon.

There was no message left on their comm system, and their cheap AI had all the smarts of a lobotomized chimp and could provide no information on Arvid's whereabouts. Lila took a shower and heated a single-portion dinner. By this time, her rehearsed speech about the amicable discontinuing of their trial, and how they should remain friends and colleagues, and how she had enjoyed every moment they had spent together had run several times in her head. Now faint regret was supplanted by real anger. What was he thinking; didn't he realize they were on an alien planet; there were explicit rules and regulations, the most important of which was that nobody should go away on their own without informing the rest of the crew, and yes, they *were* a crew, even if they were no longer husband and wife, and how could he be so irresponsible…

When she exhausted her entire stock of resentment, night had already fallen, and Lila realized that Arvid was not coming back.

When the pale dawn dripped into the darkness like milk into coffee, Lila was ready. Draconis-3 had no satellite, and its nights were pitch-black and populated with a particularly nasty biome of nocturnal predators. She had walked around the LMV, shining the flashlight and shouting Arvid's name to no avail. A chorus of chittering and whistling in the dark was not reassuring but Lila forced herself to be rational. Rushing around blindly would not help. If Arvid was injured, he could be lying under a moss-tree ten meters away and she would never find him. Breaking a leg would maroon both of them on Draconis-3. She had to wait for daylight, and hope that Arvid's unfamiliar smell would deter predators and scavengers.

Lila managed to doze off and when she woke up, she suddenly knew where he would be. She had no way to open the hatch, but it would open by itself when the next batch of five animals showed up. All she had to do was wait.

She was at the plaza when the sky lightened to its usual sullen grey. Her hunch was correct: lying by the closed hatch was Arvid's i-strap.

"What an idiot!" she muttered, and after a couple of futile kicks at the hatch cover, she sat under the dripping fronds of the moss-trees surrounding the plaza and waited for the five animals of the day to show up.

And waited. And waited.

It was only when the gloom was so thick that she could barely read the numbers on her own i-strap that Lila accepted the five animals would not come.

That was impossible. For the duration of their entire stay on the planet, five animals appeared at the plaza as regular as clockwork. The mystery of this ritual was only matched by its dependability. Like a savage who did not know anything about the lunar orbit but knew with full certainty what phase the moon would be in on any given night, Lila counted on the five animals of that day to be there. But they were not.

Biting her lips to stop herself from crying, Lila walked back to the LMV. Night had fallen, filled with whispers and cries.

She pulled short when the black mass of the LMV loomed ahead, blending with the jungle. This was not right! No matter how imbecile their AI was, it should have turned on the perimeter lights.

A purposeful stir in the tangle of shadows. There was something large by the LMV, something multi-limbed and indistinct: a crawl of unseen forms, a knot of movement.

Lila pulled out her taser, regretting that the charter of the Archeological Society prohibited deadly ammunition.

"Lila!"

Arvid's voice.

The relief was so great it made her giddy. She rushed forward. And stopped.

The perimeter lights were still off, and Arvid retreated deeper into the slithering shadows. And wasn't he, or whatever spoke with his voice, somehow…too big? Too…complicated?

"Lila…"

The word was overlaid with…echoes? Sonar refractions? Like prism-broken light but in sound. A multitude of voices trying to sound like one, a chorus of ventriloquists…

"Light!" Lila yelled, and the idiot AI finally obeyed.

Lights sprung all around the vehicle, and in their brightness, Lila saw what Arvid had become.

His face was still there, under the shock of familiar black hair, but it was attached to the naked torso of a Headless Man, sunk into its broad shoulders, and sitting askew because it was crowded by other heads, also sprouting from the same fleshy matrix: the narrow twitching snout of a Snake Cat and the blind muzzle of a Bald Bear, leaning to the right because there was not enough room for it there. The pink glistening skin of the chest merged imperceptibly with the lavender scales of a Purple Armadillo whose small triangular head poked from where the creature's bellybutton would be if it had one. Below its narrow hips, its body broadened into a shapeless rolling pad of a Cow Sack. And while one arm was not simply human-like but actually human, with an opposable thumb and a sprinkling of black hair, the other one was a hefty, clawed limb of a predator.

Lila must have screamed. Or maybe not. Some things transcend shock, propelling their witnesses into a realm of icy lucidity.

"Please listen," Arvid's lips were moving but the voice – voices – were coming from random places of the composite body. "I don't think it was supposed to work this way. But they were missing one…and so, no matter how they tried, they could not put together a Builder…"

"Symbionts," Lila said, her lips icy cold and dry, even though they were wetted by the gentle drizzle. "They were symbionts."

"Yes, exactly. Not one intelligent species. Not even many. But different species, coming together, blending…I think each city had its own set. But there was always one…"

"The sixth animal."

"Yes. The catalyst. It went…extinct? I don't know. Disease, maybe? But this was why the cities were abandoned…"

"But here we are."

"Yes," the Arvid-thing said. "*We* are the sixth animal."

A multitude of simultaneous impulses paralyzed Lila. She wanted to laugh at the irony of it all. She wanted to reassure Arvid that they would stay together. She wanted to scream.

But she said nothing because precisely at that moment, the

drooping towers of the city, lost in the night rain, blazed forth with a multitude of lights, flooding the jungle with artificial luminescence.

The city awoke, sensing the arrival of the Builders.

Elana Gomel *has five non-fiction books published by Routledge, Macmillan and others, of and numerous articles on subjects ranging from science fiction and fantasy to posthumanism and Victorian literature. She has more than 30 fantasy and science fiction stories published in New Horizons, Bewildering Stories, Timeless Tales, The Singularity, New Realm, Mythic, The Fantasist and other magazines; and in anthologies The Apex Book of World SF, People of the Book, Twelve Days of Christmas, Ink Stains and others.*

amazon.com/Elana-Gomel/e/B001KHVFCE

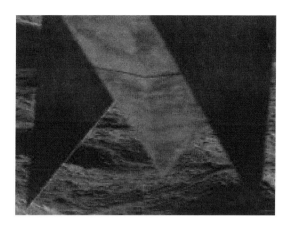

Lines of Descent
By Conor Powers-Smith

There was no mistaking the landscape for anything but what it was, an utterly and unalterably alien environment in whose shaping earthly life had played no part, and upon which humanity could hope to have only the most trivial and transient influence.

From a distance, the sprawling region most resembled a cave system with its roof somehow removed, countless titanic stalagmites rising from the ashy soil like the gnarled fingers of an army of corpses struggling to escape interment. They were all gray, but no two were of an identical shade, each tower and canopy tinted red or brown or green or some other color based on the precise chemical composition of its gaseous diet.

The great slender towers, the tallest of which stretched well over a kilometer toward the perpetual green-gray cloud cover, were more akin to gigantic petrified trees than anything else, except that they were very much alive, in fact animate; the vast cones of their canopies moved of their own accord, shifting imperceptibly during the course of the day to follow the arc of the small, dim smudge that passed for a sun, occasionally pivoting with alarming quickness to guzzle passing currents of methane or sulfur.

Viewed from within, the region struck the human mind most resonantly as a jungle. The cloud-towers rose up on all sides, making progress in a straight line impossible for more than a few meters at a time, imparting a strange mixture of claustrophobia and agoraphobia. Countless other species grew on and between them at every level, as vast and complex a labyrinth of life as in any known ecosystem in the galaxy.

"Damn it!" muttered Huxley, slapping the back of his sweat-drenched neck and coming away with a handful of lumpy black goo. He might've saved the energy; the little parasites that buzzed through the air here died immediately upon ingesting human blood, though this didn't stop them from trying.

Behind him on the winding trail, Brodeur chuckled, while Simmons and Cassidy, bored with the joke after so many repetitions, made no sound save for labored breathing and the scuffing of boots.

Ahead, the little expedition's guide made no sound at all, its silence all the eerier when juxtaposed with the violence of its movements. It swung the shallow, inverted pyramid of its main body forward by planting and pivoting two thinner, more sharply angled triangles projecting from the pyramid's high base. Since the Strattons stood over seven feet tall, every inch of which appeared to be solid rock, one expected the sound of an avalanche to accompany their progress, but the thickly cushioned pads at each point of contact did a remarkable job of muffling the sound of their movement.

There was debate among the mission's anthropologists as to whether the Strattons' pads were an adaptation against predators, or their own kind. Huxley favored the latter supposition, since in his eighteen months on Stratton Five he'd never seen one of the natives evince the least concern about animal attack, while they were constantly on guard against members of their own species.

That was especially true when Strattons ventured out of their rigidly defined home ranges, as their guide was doing now. A kind of taboo attached to far travel, and with good reason. Strattons were fiercely territorial, and their many tribes were arranged in a complex and constantly shifting network of rivalries and alliances that made it impossible to know from one day to the next whether you could expect hospitality from the neighboring group, or a swift and violent death.

Like so many sentient creatures, though, they could generally be persuaded to bend their codes of conduct for the right price. In this case, Murph—whose native name was unpronounceable, and on whom the group had bestowed the nickname in a drunken joke the significance of which Huxley had long since forgotten—would earn a crate of the marshmallows the Strattons prized so highly if he could escort the team safely to the survey area and back. The pronoun "he," too, was a misnomer of convenience, since the

Strattons were genderless.

Huxley knew Murph would gain inestimably in status among his immediate kin group, and the widening spiral of relations of which it was a part, if he secured this bounty. Still it was amusing to think of Murph risking his life for the simple love of marshmallows. God only knew what the things did to the Strattons' insides; *probably no worse than what they do to us*, went the joke in the human enclave.

"Damn it to *hell*," Huxley breathed, the last two words lost to him as he momentarily deafened himself with a hard slap to his right ear. Even when his hearing returned, it was muffled until he dug the twitching black mess that had so recently been a living, bloodsucking creature out of his ear.

"They love you, Huxley," Brodeur called. "Must be cause you're so sweet."

Simmons and Cassidy snickered, and Huxley turned to glare at the three of them, balding Brodeur with his toothy grin, fresh-faced Simmons shyly trying to hide her smile, seasoned Cassidy making no such attempt, openly eager for anything resembling entertainment on this slog.

"Too bad they're not dung beetles, or they'd be all over your head," Huxley called back, gratified this time by the laughter that followed; louder, he was sure, or at least more genuine. His eyes lingered on Simmons, sweat sticking her shirt to her long, lithe body, then shifted to Cassidy, shorter and less noticeably proportioned, but with a no-nonsense femininity that was every bit as attractive.

He turned and came to a sudden, stumbling stop, about two steps short of walking into Murph. The Stratton was standing perfectly still in the middle of the path, his unsubtle way of telling the humans they were making too much noise.

It made more sense than telling them to quiet down, as most humans would've done, but the very logic of it was somehow irritating. It was silly to resent being treated like a noisy child, when they'd hired Murph as much to keep them safe as to guide them. Recognizing that it was silly did nothing to dispel the irritation, which also had on its side the heat, the bugs, the three miles they'd already walked, the four left to go, and the persistent anxiety of wandering through an alien and potentially hostile environment. And Brodeur.

Huxley turned to see Cassidy come to a stop within six inches of him. Her scent arrived just as she did, fresh sweat overlaying a subtly sweet cleanliness. She held one finger up to her lips in a shushing gesture, partially covering a little smile Huxley liked very much.

He wasn't sure what it meant, but found a theory in his own answering smile, which felt frankly suggestive, and which Cassidy seemed to take in stride. It wasn't a promise, but it was promising. Happy encounters on expeditions like this weren't unknown. A delicate bud of excitement began to blossom in his belly.

Simmons had stopped a few feet behind Cassidy, and as Brodeur caught up he walked into her, gently but with what Huxley interpreted as obvious intent. The hands he put on her back, ostensibly to steady her, lingered longer than necessary, too. Worse, Simmons didn't draw away, and the smile she gave Brodeur seemed to communicate more than forgiveness for his supposed mistake.

Huxley faced forward again with a sour feeling. His belly was empty. He hadn't eaten since before setting out. He had yet to figure out how to communicate the necessity for regular meals to the Strattons, who aggregated their nutrients from the air and soil while resting.

He didn't want to admit his inability to make Murph understand the seemingly simple concept of food; his only purpose on the trip was to communicate with Murph, which he felt already gave Brodeur an advantage, as he and the two women were all biologists on a mission, while Huxley was a glorified interpreter. He was hoping nobody suggested a lunch break, although he would've welcomed one if he'd been able to accomplish it. Now that he'd acknowledged his hunger, it was impossible to ignore, a wet rope twisting in his belly.

Though the humans remained obediently silent, Murph stood motionless for some thirty seconds. Huxley was about to ask a frustrated question when, with the same eerie silence with which Murph moved, three others Strattons slid into view ahead.

Glancing right and left, Huxley found another on each side, the broad, flat slabs of their bodies disconcertingly unmarked by eyes, mouths, or other recognizable features. He knew there'd be more behind them, but he looked anyway. Two of them stood like unfinished statues a few yards behind Simmons and Brodeur.

A sound like wind rushing through a cave broke the silence. It was impossible to tell which of the newly arrived Strattons was speaking; they had no mouths, but adjusted a network of internal passages roughly equivalent to microscopic throats to produce their language, which emanated not from a single opening but from thousands of tiny holes like pores in their rocky skin.

"What's it saying?" asked Brodeur.

"Introducing himself," Huxley said.

The wind rushed on, modulating constantly, its gusts and wails sounding to the human ear like an eerie blend of undirected natural phenomenon and conscious communication, the stuff of ancient ghost stories.

Brodeur said in a tense whisper, "That's a long name."

Huxley didn't bother to explain that the Strattons were speaking in turn, the next picking up the moment the last had finished. Each individual introduction was indeed lengthy.

"It's not just names," Huxley said. The humans had instinctively drawn together, so his low voice was audible to all of them despite the continuing storm of talk from the Strattons. "It's places, events, ancestors. It's complicated."

"This is the stranger ritual, isn't it?" said Cassidy. "Are we okay here?"

"We should be," Huxley said, glad for the chance to reassure her, though not as confident as he tried to make himself sound. "They're almost done, let's see how Murph does."

Murph did fine. When the last of the other Strattons had finished, a pause of a few seconds passed, after which Murph began his own introduction. He gave his true name—a dry, lilting breeze Huxley always found peculiarly haunting—and proceeded to describe his village, its several clans, finally his own family line, beginning with the three parents who'd contributed his hereditary material, then tracing each of their lineages.

The Strattons placed no significance on the individual who contributed the initial small offshoot of his own body to the reproduction process, burying it in a few inches of loose soil before taking no further part. Instead they traced their parentage by the three individuals who later injected into the spot a paste consisting of chemical catalysts and the molecule that served the same basic function for them as DNA did for Earth life. All three of those parents were necessary for what could be loosely termed fertilization.

They were astute enough to have recognized that the initial donor contributed no genetic material, his offshoot serving only as a

49

latticework upon which the new organism built and sustained itself. Whether they'd arrived at this knowledge through long observation or formal scientific study was another open question in the human enclave.

They were also fantastically accurate chroniclers of ancestry, memorizing minute details by an early age despite the spiraling complexity of tripartite parentage. They had good reason to be so meticulous.

Each of the other Strattons had traced his ancestry back two generations, naming a total of twelve parents and grandparents. When Murph reached this point, he paused for a moment, and, when there was no response, continued on to the third generation, naming twenty-seven great-grandparents as the other Strattons listened attentively.

This time when Murph paused, one of the other Strattons began to speak. He traced one line of descent only, back through the two previously elucidated generations to the third, which included the sweetly whistling name of an ancestor he'd shared in common with Murph. The Strattons, Murph included, burst out in a veritable cyclone of talk.

"We're okay," Huxley told the others. "Kinship has been established. They'll give us any help we need or leave us alone if we prefer."

"I think we prefer," Brodeur said. In the biologist's grin, Huxley saw a reflection of his own relief, only realizing when the danger had passed just how nervous he'd been.

Considering the proximity of their territories, the fact that Murph and one of the other Strattons had shared a great-grandparent wasn't surprising. The stakes of the exchange had been dire, though; had the ritual gone on to the limits of their ancestral knowledge without revealing such a link, the other Strattons would've fallen on Murph and beaten him to death as a stranger and interloper. Huxley could only assume the same fate would've awaited himself and the other humans.

Certain traditional societies on Earth had practiced similar rituals within the last few centuries, a fascinating piece of convergent evolution that had produced any number of scholarly papers. There was always room for one more, though, Huxley assured himself, especially one written in the first-person.

The ritual had been observed exactly twice, both times by

anthropologists studying the Central civilization, the network of clans and villages with which the human mission to Stratton Five had first made contact, and among which it was still embedded. Huxley was the first human to witness the ritual from the other side, or at least the first who'd get the chance to report on it; more than one human had disappeared along the fringes of the territory where they were known and tolerated.

Huxley was contemplating the buzz his paper would generate when Brodeur broke in on his thoughts by asking, "Now what's going on?"

Huxley returned his attention to the present to see Murph standing among the other Strattons, having moved away from the humans with typical noiselessness. The shift went further than mere proximity; Murph had clearly left one group and joined another. The noise the Strattons made had changed, too, and with a sinking stomach Huxley realized why.

The excited welcoming of a relative had ceased, and the formal recitation of ancestry had resumed. They'd begun the ritual again. And the only possible audience was the four humans.

"Huxley?" prodded Brodeur. "What're they saying? Are they gonna have us for *lunch*, or are they gonna have *us* for lunch?"

"Oh, God," Huxley breathed. "They're doing us." He'd assumed Murph's kinship status would carry over to all of them. How did the Strattons expect to establish a common ancestry with members of a species that had evolved light-years away?

But of course, they need not expect any such thing. They had their own moral code, alien in many ways but in others perfectly comprehensible. It was wrong to kill a stranger without first trying to establish kinship; after trying and failing, it was not only acceptable, but mandatory. Even if there was no possibility of kinship, as surely here there was none, their natural impulse would be to go through the ritual for form's sake, so they could massacre the group with a clear conscience.

It was an interesting anthropological detail, and Huxley automatically stored it away for use in his paper. A moment later he realized he wasn't going to be writing any paper. He was going to die instead.

"Huxley," Cassidy said. "You can talk us out of this, right?"

"I...no." It was an effort to speak even those few words. It was strange how lifeless he could feel while his heart raced in panic.

"What's the plan then?" asked Brodeur. "Run? Fight?"

Huxley shrugged, listening to the wind of the Strattons' recitation slowly shift as the speakers changed. He didn't bother to answer Brodeur aloud. There was no escaping a pursuer that could've run down a horse without exerting itself. They could fight if they wanted; Huxley doubted the Strattons would notice.

"Can you stall them?" said Brodeur. "We can call back to the settlement for help."

Huxley shook his head. If the human settlement had been equipped with vehicles capable of navigating this tortuous landscape, the party would've been using them. It would take hours for anyone to reach them on foot, which would be too late to do anything but collect their remains. "Remains" was being generous; when the Strattons were done with them, the humans would be a red smear.

Murph's names fluted out, followed by the second recitation of his ancestry. He'd joined the other Strattons to the extent that he was now part of the ritual on the interrogative side, though he acknowledged his low status in that group by going last. Another anthropological tidbit Huxley would be unable to pass on.

Of greater immediate interest was his own impending death. He watched the other Strattons for signs of eagerness, but they stood perfectly still, patient as stones. He wondered idly which would be the first to move, and whether this privilege too would be tied to status.

The wind died, and there was silence. Huxley forced a breath into his clenched lungs. He could die now, or in a few minutes. He stepped forward.

"My mother was named Theresa, my father was Thomas," Huxley said. "My mother's mother was Beth, my mother's father was Samuel."

He stopped as the wind returned, Murph telling the others that the human was responding in its own language. Murph explained that the humans had only two parents, a fact Huxley hadn't known he was aware of, and that the other Strattons took in stride, judging by their continued stillness. Murph made no attempt to translate the alien names.

When Murph was finished, Huxley continued, "My father's mother was Sandra. My father's father was Daniel." He thought the names were right but wasn't sure. It couldn't matter.

52

The only names that could save his life would not be forthcoming; there were no Strattons in his family tree. As he listed his great-grandparents, all invented, he briefly considered slipping a Stratton name into the mix. If he could even remember one of their ancestors' names, though, he'd never be able to pronounce it, and if somehow he could, they were far too smart to believe it.

All at once he hated them. In their own way they were intelligent, inquisitive, inventive. Yet they were so bound by their social system, by the instincts of tribalism and defensiveness that shaped it, that their natural reaction to meeting four alien beings was to brutally murder them for failing to share a common ancestry.

He would fight when they came for him, he decided. He would try his best to hurt or kill them, whether they noticed or not.

When Huxley had finished with his supposed great-grandparents, the Strattons were silent for a moment, then one began to speak, and the ritual went on. One after another, each named his twenty-seven great-grandparents.

Twenty-seven names went by amazingly fast when each marked another step toward death. In what seemed like no more than a minute or two, Murph, again the last to speak, had finished his litany, and the Strattons waited in silence for the response.

Huxley spoke slowly, stretching these last few moments of life as far as he could. "My great-grandfather Patrick's father was Mickey Mouse, and his mother was Queen Victoria," he said, filling in names at random. "My great-grandmother's father was George Washington, and her mother was the Mona Lisa."

Almost before he'd begun, it seemed, he'd reached the end of his meager list of sixteen imaginary ancestors. He braced himself. The silence seemed to last much longer than his recitation had, though it could only have been a few seconds.

The wind began again, and Huxley let out the breath he'd been unconsciously holding. He would live a few minutes more, however long it took for however many of them remembered their fourth-generation ancestors to detail them.

Eighty-one names apiece, and they went by like hurried introductions at a not-very-large dinner party. Only five recited this time, and Huxley knew he was lucky it was that many. Their ancestral knowledge was deep, but not indefinite. This could be the last round of names they'd be able to provide. Again Murph was the last to speak, and again he was followed by a waiting silence.

"Albert Einstein," Huxley said, inspired perhaps by how relative his perception of time had become. "And he was married to Sally Ride."

Since this was the closest thing to an epitaph he was likely to receive, he might as well use the opportunity to enunciate his heroes, some of the intellectual giants on whose shoulders he and the rest of the human mission had been carried to Stratton Five; and off whose shoulders he and the other three humans in this ill-fated party were about to plummet.

"Charles Darwin," he went on, "and his wife Margaret Mead. Watson was married to Crick. Marie and Pierre Curie actually were married. Also Carl Sagan and Ann Druyan."

There he stopped, struck suddenly by an inspiration suggested by his last pair of intellectual ancestors. It wouldn't work. It couldn't. But the most it would cost him was a few seconds of life. The real damage, the uncontrollable rising of his hopes prior to certain and violent disappointment, had already occurred.

"All my ancestors," he began, "and all the species mine evolved from, and all their ancestral species, too, back to the earliest origins of life on my planet—" He paused, relieved to hear the low breeze of Murph's translation; they were at least listening to this deviation from the formula.

"All the chemical elements that each was built from, except hydrogen and helium, were created in the cauldrons of ancient stars, or in the massive explosions with which they died. Nuclear fusion forced the lighter elements together to form the heavier ones, and when the reactions reached their end the elements were ejected into space.

"Carbon, oxygen, calcium, iron, silicon, all the elements from which life was formed and on which it still depends, share the same parents, stars that burned billions of years before your people or mine, or our earliest ancestral species, or the planets on which we evolved, even existed.

"All my people, every creature on Earth, shares the same last name, which is Star-Stuff. You and I are part of the same lineage. Our planets are separated by only a few dozen lightyears. The atoms in your bodies were created in some of the same stars as those in mine. So, I claim kinship with you. I am your cousin far-removed. We are children of the same stars."

He stopped, and a few seconds later Murph went quiet too. The silence stretched on, and Huxley had nothing else to break it with. He waited, heart hammering in his chest, mind strangely calm.

Then the wind blew, a rattling gust that meant, "This is true?"

"It's true," Huxley said. "I swear it's true. You're welcome to kill me if it's not."

After Murph translated, the matter-of-fact reply came, "Yes, we will crush you if it is a lie." Then, not missing a beat, "Welcome, kin. Walk our land in peace."

The strength went out of his legs, and Huxley found himself sitting in the gray dust. "Thank you," he murmured. But they were already retreating, vanishing into the alien jungle as silently as they'd emerged. Murph remained, standing in place without comment.

A hand came to rest on his shoulder, and he looked up to see Cassidy standing over him. "You okay?" she asked.

Her hand felt good there. All at once he felt human again. He didn't know if that was better or worse than whatever nameless state he'd entered for a moment. It was certainly more comfortable.

"Yeah," he said. "I'm good."

Five minutes later they were moving again, Murph no longer making any effort to keep them quiet.

###

Conor Powers-Smith has had stories appear in AE, Analog, Daily Science Fiction, Nature, and other magazines, as well as several anthologies.

amazon.com/s?i=digital-text&rh=p_27%3AConor+Powers-Smith

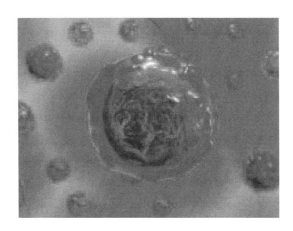

We Can Wait But No Longer Want To
By Mary Jo Rabe

Emma sighed. It had been a dismal couple of weeks. She ran her swollen fingers aimlessly through her short, white, curls, having freed them from the tight cap she always wore while baking. She was a little relieved that she could finally free up her thoughts.

She knew that Mars was a dangerous place for Earth-born human beings, and she had gotten used to all the accidental deaths. However, the death toll of the past weeks had saddened her. She couldn't get rid of the feeling that she should have found a way to prevent them. Yet, now there was certainly nothing more she could do here.

The community stirred and sloshed around joyously. The elders had long since insisted that they shouldn't note the passage of time, as that might discourage them. Martian microbes functioned most efficiently together when a forward-looking attitude of optimism prevailed. However, a group mind also ensured that emotions remained at a balanced level. One microbe's frantic outburst was quickly diluted by the equanimity of the rest.

At this point in time, though, every individual microbe and therefore the entire community — bonded as they were together in the group mind — couldn't deny that much time had passed since they fled underground.

Their retreat had been necessary. Mars had lost its atmosphere. Low temperatures, even lower air pressure, and lethal cosmic radiation made life on the surface no longer practical. Microbes were sturdy but not impervious to external environmental conditions.

So the group mind agreed that the microbes needed to wait in safety until things changed again. Patience ensured survival.

Obviously, though, much time had passed; suddenly they were no longer alone! The microbe group mind sensed communications on the surface. They came from somewhat intelligent life forms that hadn't been on Mars before.

To their genuine surprise, the microbes recognized that these new life forms didn't share a group mind. Each creature depended on its own individual thought resources, making it, of course, intellectually inferior to the microbe group mind. Still, they were fellow intelligent life forms, and they were here!

Many microbes immediately began to fantasize about contacting these creatures and, with their help, leaving the underground premises. Maybe they could even combine with them to create hybrid life forms that contained the best qualities of each. There was a whole universe to explore, and the microbes had spent enough time underground.

It was dark outside, but Emma could still see the silhouette of Olympus Mons off in the dusty distance, today not as comforting a sight as usual. It was good to have the cafeteria up on the surface of Mars. Its circular structure, complete with a panorama view through clear, but radiation-resistant, plastic, floor-to-ceiling windows was perfect. It may have been costly, but the cafeteria gave the settlers a place to gather and remember why they all had wanted to come to Mars.

It took a number of planetary revolutions around the star before the group mind developed translation algorithms to understand the new life forms completely. This simplified discussions since the microbes could agree on designations. The creatures came from the planet next closest to the star which they called their "sun". They called their home planet "Earth".

Groups of microbes joined together to analyze and interpret manageable segments of communications. Then they loaded their data and hypotheses into the group mind's examination center where they could be analyzed, parsed, and reassembled.

The fact that the "Earthlings" had no group mind might have been the reason that they indulged in the use of so many different languages, which, of course, caused numerous ambiguities. It took some time before the microbes could rise to this challenge of understanding them. The group mind was stretched to its limits.

The Earthlings on Mars communicated with each other and with creatures on their home planet via electronic transmissions that the microbes could access easily. The creatures communicated more interesting bits of conversation to each other via sound waves inside the artificial structures that they built.

In addition, there were the purely mental conversations the creatures had with themselves. These turned out to be most fruitful. Fortunately, during their lengthy existence, the microbes had developed telepathic skills, both as individuals and together in the group mind.

Occasionally Emma felt a little old at forty-some Martian years (one advantage of relocating to Mars — your age sounded younger). She couldn't move her short and stocky bulk around as quickly or gracefully as she once did. However, without fail, one glance out the cafeteria window, and the dusty, red surface would energize her and persuade her that second chance at life was just beginning.

That only made it even more distressing that settlers so much younger than she now had no more chances for any kind of life on Mars.

What the Earthlings defined as emotions or feelings remained fairly incomprehensible to the microbes. Microbes, both individually and as a group, were an ebullient bunch, always celebrating the present and looking forward to the future. It was difficult to understand the often pessimistic, unhappy mindsets of the Earthlings. The microbes did the only thing they could do; they continued to collect data in the hopes of making sense of it all.

The cafeteria was open day and night. Emma prepared the food every morning, then let her capable staff take care of the customers in the afternoon while she took a needed nap.

Generally, she stayed in the cafeteria the rest of the time when all the scientists and engineers showed up. They liked to brainstorm while they ate. Emma was always glad that they liked her food, but what she really enjoyed was listening to them talk shop.

Emma loved the astronomers. She was, however, skeptical about SETI projects. Until any alien life forms showed themselves, she assumed that Earthlings had to make sense out of the universe on their own.

Emma was convinced that scientists could only do serious research by leaving their home planet. You had to get away from familiar ideas and prejudices in order to think beyond the limitations of human brainpower. That's why she worshipped the engineers who made it possible for human beings to survive on Mars. Emma did what she could to keep the colonists fed, but it was the engineers who gave them breathable air and usable water.

Opinions in the group mind were seldom unanimous. Some microbes just enjoyed being contrary. Nonetheless, eventually a consensus emerged about the Earthlings. Limited by their individual consciousness, they weren't all that bright. However, their physical forms did enable them to build impressive structures which let them survive in more variable settings than the microbes could.

The group mind decided to attempt contact, as soon as the Earthlings made it possible. The microbes themselves didn't want to risk leaving their underground bodies of water. There was a risk of losing some individual microbes during the process of a first contact, but their essence was stored in the group mind and could be inserted at any time into new microbe bodies that could be produced by controlled mitosis whenever desirable.

Two weeks ago, Emma's friend Dr. Ruth Sandcorn had showed up in the cafeteria with her engineering team and wanted to celebrate. They had discovered an additional, huge, underground source of water. Emma brought them the best she had to offer, pasta with tomato sauce and garlic toast, everything raised in the greenhouses and tent-covered fields.

Ruthie was popular, young, and enthusiastic, a tall, chubby woman with obviously well-developed muscles. With her habitat nickname of Ruthless Ruthie, she had a certain reputation for asserting herself. Emma treasured her as a loyal and reliable friend.

"Do you have anything suitable to drink on a great occasion?" Ruthie asked.

Emma smiled. "Martian wine gets better every year," she said. "Just like the work you engineers do."

"We do what we can," Ruthie said. "And it is not always safe or easy. We have just sent a sample of the water we just discovered to the clinic for testing. As soon as the doc gives his okay, we'll start laying pipes. And then the habitats will have all the water they could ever need."

First came the violent vibrations and the clouds of mildly radioactive dust. A quick analysis showed that neither occurrence threatened the well-being of the microbes in their frosty, underground lake.

Then the group mind detected mindless, mechanical machines that crawled through the holes in the rock walls and submerged themselves in the half-frozen, microbe home waters. They quickly realized that there was no use talking to the stupid machines but hoped that the intelligent life forms that created these machines would arrive soon.

Indeed, the intelligent life forms entered the microbes' home soon after their machines. However, said life forms were encased in individual, little impenetrable habitats, and the microbes couldn't initiate physical contact. One-sided telepathy functioned well but showed that the Earthlings themselves lacked any telepathic powers.

The good news, however, was that the creatures planned to transport water from the lake to all the habitat structures on and below the surface. The creatures wanted to "use" the water, to submerge the sustenance they grew in it, to imbibe it themselves, to splash it across the surfaces of their physical bodies. They planned to do everything the microbes needed in order to establish physical contact.

The microbes celebrated by entering joyous, optimistic data into the group mind, all the more ecstatic when the mechanical creatures placed a receptacle into the lake and scooped up some water. The microbes remaining in the lake experienced a twinge of jealousy for the first time in their existence. Every single microbe wanted to be among those collected by the Earthlings.

A week after Ruthie's announcement, Emma was getting ready to bake some desserts when she thought she heard someone out in the cafeteria. She tried to recognize the voice and then wished she hadn't. Barbara Cohan, the young, constantly whining astrobiologist was there. She was a high-maintenance time-sink, but Emma often felt sorry for her.

Emma thought Barbara was borderline paranoid, in any case difficult to take seriously. Still, Emma always tried to make everyone feel at home on Mars. She went into the cafeteria reluctantly.

Barbara yelled, "I found them. They're here, just like I predicted."

"Who do you mean, dear?" Emma asked. "Who's here?"

"Martian life forms," Barbara yelled. "They found microbes in that new underground lake. I saw them under the microscope, myself."

"I did a quick evaluation of one of them, and its DNA is alien. We have found extraterrestrial life."

The lucky microbes that the mechanical machines transported to the quarters on the surface squirmed and gyrated with pleasure and transmitted all their impressions back to the lake where the others waited. In one bright room an Earthling poured the water into a different container and then flashed it with low-grade radiation that tickled but didn't do any harm to the microbes.

Unfortunately, the Earthling, while not encased in a dense structure, still prevented any physical contact with the microbes. A few microbes jumped up at the creature's appendages but merely bounced back into the water.

Time passed. Then a second Earthling came and poured the water through various devices while shining radiation on them and dousing them with chemicals. A quick telepathic consultation with the group mind, and all the microbes uploaded their data. This proved to be a sensible precaution. Suddenly one microbe, Thrub as it called itself, was separated from the others and quickly lost its ability to function.

"Yep, this body is dead," Thrub broadcasted from the group mind. "When do I get my new body?"

However, no one paid any attention to him because of the excited, though thoroughly confusing thoughts from the second Earthling who had caused Thrub's merely physical demise.

The Earthling was astonished to discover that there were life forms on Mars and that they weren't identical to those from her home planet. The microbes could only conclude that such nonsense came from the fact that these creatures lacked a group mind to analyze such hypotheses.

The microbes were willing to tolerate such mental ineptitude, but the Earthling's hysterical ramblings were cause for concern. The unreasonable creature wanted to prevent any contact between the microbes and the Earthlings. Worse, the frantic creature wanted all the Earthlings to return to the home planet and abandon the microbes.

Microbes, by their nature, individually and in the group mind, couldn't be depressed, but they weren't enthusiastic about the idea of having to wait again to leave their underground habitat and come into contact with new life forms.

The first Earthling then enclosed the water in the original receptacle and ordered one of the mechanical creatures to return it to the underground lake. The microbes then engaged in extensive brainstorming.

The mood in the Martian habitats was unpleasant after Dr. Brach and Barbara Cohan announced that there were Martian life forms in the underground lake. Barbara Cohan insisted that they must abandon the settlement on Mars and return to Earth. Others, naturally, said they could just filter out the microbes and use the water anyway.

Barbara said that was much too risky. The microbes could kill the human beings and vice versa. She invoked the ancient Murphy's Law, but most people disagreed with her.

The microbes had a good laugh about filters. They quickly figured out a way to decrease their size to make them both undetectable to the Earthlings and able to pass through any filter. Staying alive on Mars for billions of revolutions around the star had taught the microbes how to adapt.

The group mind theorized and all agreed that they needed more information about the Earthlings. They intensified their telepathic investigations and developed hypotheses about the physiology of the Earthlings. How these creatures functioned turned out to be fairly straightforward. Trying to understand the mental processes of the chaotic, individual creatures remained nearly impossible. They were basically illogical and unpredictable.

Emma couldn't ever forget that horrible day when Barbara Cohan killed Ruthie Sandcorn and her engineering team. Everyone in the habitats saw the video message from Barbara Cohan, wearing a surface suit and standing at the top of Olympus Mons.

"I did it," she shouted. "I saved the microbes. There are bombs all over Mars. They have already exploded and killed everyone at the underground lake and will soon kill everyone else."

Martian security forces, directed expertly by Sheriff Curtis Long, were able to overwhelm Barbara and disable the bombs before they could do any further harm, but Ruthie was gone.

Emma tried to mourn Ruthie, one of the nicest people ever to come to Mars, a generous and charitable soul. However, her rage at Barbara for killing Ruthie and her rage at herself for not preventing the whole fiasco somehow made her incapable of any action or feeling. She just felt an overwhelming, all-encompassing sadness.

The microbes didn't know what to make of the telepathic mayhem they picked up on from the Earthlings. These creatures were truly mysterious. Their emotions controlled them and prevented them from thinking rationally. One theory the microbes quickly developed was that living creatures would simply always go crazy without the calming influence of belonging to a group mind.

Some of the Earthlings had died which made the others inconsolable. This was understandable, since the dead Earthlings were gone forever, and their essence not preserved in a group mind. Thrub joked that he was glad the demise of his former physical body didn't cause such consternation in their group mind.

Unlike the Earthlings, however, the microbes were sensible and pragmatic life forms. Connecting with the Earthlings offered advantages, and so the microbes did what they could to encourage the Earthlings to get physical contact with the lake water.

"The water from the lake is flowing," Doc Brach told Emma as he took another chocolate chip cookie from the stack on his plate. "And they're thinking of putting up a plaque to Ruthless Ruthie and her crew where they died at the underground lake. This water will make it possible for human beings to settle the whole planet."

"The plaque won't bring Ruthie back," Emma said sadly. Doc Brach was a kind, no longer young man. His short, muscular stature revealed his Earth origins. The settlers born on Mars were all tall, slender, and almost frail-looking, though of course strong enough for the lower Martian gravity.

"No," Doc Brach said. "In the final analysis Dr. Sandcorn and her associates were victims of mental instability. Barbara Cohan was basically insane, completely dominated by her obsessions. We have all kinds of nanobots that can repair purely physical damage in human bodies but so far they can't repair thought processes that no longer function correctly. The human brain is just too complicated."

"Ruthie would have been glad to know that her project was completed," Emma said. "She was so happy when they discovered the underground lake because she knew how to get the water to the habitats, how to make it a reliable resource for human life on Mars."

"Are you sure the water is completely safe to use?" Emma asked.

"Yes," Doc Brach said. "The water from the lake has to be filtered and desalinized, but the engineers have installed the necessary machinery and nanobots inside the pipes. I have done every possible test, and the water that comes out of the faucets in the habitats is safe."

The microbes slid through the filters easily and darted out of the way of all the nanobots; it was truly no problem to avoid such dull-witted, primitive, little machines. The water that then emerged from the pipes the creatures connected was abysmally bland and no longer contained the minerals the microbes needed, but the microbes were certain that the fluids in the bodies of the Earthlings would have more taste.

Having had enough time to think through their strategy and come to a consensus, the microbes aimed to find a way to join the Earthlings, not as parasites but rather as symbiotes.

It wasn't so much that they were tired of their pleasant life in the lake. However, it was restrictive and more than a little dull. They wanted to return to the surface, to be an active participant of the workings of the entire universe.

Their microbe bodies weren't flexible enough to survive on Mars outside the underground lake. However, they were certain that the advanced mental capabilities their group mind afforded them would be sufficient to meet all challenges.

They stayed in the water and came into contact with the Earthlings' bodies, entering the surface tissue during cleansing activity, clinging to water droplets that the creatures inhaled, and riding along on top of substances the creatures consumed for energy.

Everything was fine until the microbes tried to merge with the alien cellular tissue. Suddenly they found themselves attacked from all directions by cells that the creatures' bodies produced. The temperatures inside the creatures' bodies rose to a level quite uncomfortable for the microbes and which made them somewhat lethargic. Then nanobots arrived in monstrous numbers and began hacking away at the microbes' membranes.

A quick consultation with the microbes still in the lake and the conclusion was unavoidable. They couldn't merge with the Earthlings. The alien physiology was too strongly programmed to ward off any invaders. Self-preservation demanded that the microbes withdraw from all cellular structures and merely paddle around in the fluids.

Emma didn't feel good. This was odd. Her whole life she had been healthy as a horse, never counting or paying any attention to various aches and pains. She felt feverish and dizzy. She left the kitchen area, walked into the cafeteria, and collapsed on the floor.

When she woke up, she was lying on an uncomfortable bed in the infirmary and Doc Brach was injecting her with nanobots. She felt better, just confused.

"What was that?" she asked.

"I wish I knew," Doc Brach admitted. "Almost everyone has been having these fainting spells, often combined with fever or nausea or cardiac issues. But they don't last long, and one dose of nanobots seems to eliminate whatever the cause is. As soon as I saw what was happening, I gave myself a couple of extra doses."

"Did it come from the water?" Emma asked.

"People didn't get sick until we started using the water from the underground lake," Doc Brach admitted. "But you know as well as I do, correlation doesn't prove causation. I'm puzzled but relieved that the whole thing seems to be temporary. You are the last one to get sick and then to recover."

"So we're going to continue to use the water?" Emma asked.

"We don't have many alternatives," Doc Brach admitted. "I have tested the water over and over again. There just isn't anything in it that should affect human beings."

The microbes had to reassess the situation. The bad news was that it wasn't possible to merge with the Earthlings and create a new, hybrid creature. The basis for life in the Martian life forms wasn't compatible with that of the Earthlings.

The good news was that if the microbes stayed small enough, they could hide in the body fluids of the Earthlings without causing the Earthlings to combat them as invaders. This meant that the microbes could leave their frosty underground lake and go wherever the Earthlings went. The telepathic bond of the group mind remained strong.

With some navigational trial and error, the microbes managed to enter the cerebrospinal fluid of the Earthlings and explore their brains more thoroughly. While individual minds couldn't even come close to the accomplishments of a group mind, the brains of the Earthlings were impressively complicated. It took some time for the microbes to explore them sufficiently.

The next step was obvious. While being careful not to invade any cells, the microbes began to encourage the production of chemicals that influenced brain activity. This didn't damage the creatures; on the contrary, they began to use their minds more efficiently.

Soon the Earthlings began to respond to mental nudges from the microbes. The microbes were overjoyed when they picked up on the plans to explore and settle the Oort Cloud.

Emma shook her head as she took the chocolate chip cookies out of the oven. She never told Doc Brach about the funny itching she sometimes felt behind her eyes. She didn't want him to think she was losing her mind.

Maybe it was part of the aging process, but Emma felt more optimistic. The sadness of the past seemed like a vague discomfort, no longer an unbearable agony. She was definitely looking forward to joining the settlement on Pluto where they needed a cafeteria lady. She liked the other crew members. Sometimes she even had the impression that they were all of one mind.

Mary Jo Rabe has published "Blue Sunset", inspired by Spoon River Anthology and The Martian Chronicles, and has had poems and stories published in Fiction River, Pulphouse, Space Opera Mashup, Rocketpack Adventures, Whispers from the Universe, Future Earth Tech, Blaze Ward Presents Cloak and Dagger, Alternate Hilarities, Pandora, Stygian Articles, The Martian Wave, Astropoetica, The Sword Review, Raven Electrick, Mindflights, Star*Line, and Space and Time.

maryjorabe.wordpress.com/
amazon.com/Mary-Jo-Rabe/e/B007MMFCPM

The Preparations
By Larry Lefkowitz

The ambassador peered through the telescope toward Earth. When he became fatigued or lonely, he found the sight of his planet comforting. The telescope was a gift of the Government of Nestaria; with typical thoughtfulness, the Nestarians had placed it in the building given him as his embassy-residence, in the proper position for viewing Earth.

How like the Nestarians, he thought, his appreciation tempered with a touch of envy. The telescope as instrument and gift symbolized the twin aspects of this people that awed him: their advanced development and their compassion. The tremendous magnifying power of the telescope which on Earth would have required a lens half a mile in diameter they had compacted into a small instrument supported by a tripod. It allowed the view to reach the ambassador with but a few minutes' delay. Such an achievement was a tribute to their scientific genius, but the unobtrusive manner in which it had been made available to him was a tribute to their tact.

He smiled ruefully – despite the disparity in power and influence that existed between their planet and his own, he was never patronized. He was made always to feel the ambassador.

Through the telescope, Earth appeared as a small disc of light, so far away it was impossible to discern its features. Yet the Nestarians had understood that the view of it alone would be reassuring to him.

Tonight, the sight aroused mixed feelings. Longing, as always. But shame, too. Today, again, the Nestarians had raised the matter of Earth's "preparations," as they called them. The way they avoided the phrase "preparations for war" amused him – but because they and he both knew this was what the word meant, it had taken on a meaning more sinister than if the whole phrase were used. The threat to peace posed by these preparations had been made clear to him by the Nestarians, gently, tactfully, as if he were a child at their knee.

Their forbearance was the more impressive in light of the absolute horror he knew they felt at even the concept of killing. They had left war behind eons ago, or had never resorted to it – this was not clear: Nestarian legends hinted that they had once engaged in wars, but whether they were based on prehistoric events or were completely invented was unknown; the Nestarians discouraged inquiry about them. He could well imagine if the inhabitants of Earth had never practiced war or only done so in antiquity and were suddenly confronted with another planet's threat to resort to it, how repugnant the idea would be. How primitive! The inhabitants of such a planet would seem the cavemen of the universe. He doubted that his people would then have been willing to maintain diplomatic relations with such a people, let alone treat them as equals.

He marveled at the tolerance of the Nestarians – this large-headed people with their dark velvety skins; the former attribute ungainly in Earthite eyes, the other so appealing. The large heads contained their tremendously developed brains, a principal contribution to their civilization's advanced development. In the pond of the universe, he thought helplessly, they are frogs and we are tadpoles -- underdeveloped Nestarians -- and we must swim in the same pond.

Yet it is we who threaten them! Why did they not strike? Had they learned wisdom or were they merely tolerating a lesser form of life?

The ambassador took his eye from the telescope and the view of Earth. He walked slowly, weighed down by these thoughts, to the padded chair specially designed to gently support the Nestarians' soft-skinned bodies, and still more delightful for an Earthite body to sit in. It made him feel as if he were suspended in liquid silk; but tonight it could not ease his depression.

He sensed that the Nestarians realized he was uncomfortable about his planet's preparations, and he felt their sympathy with his individual dilemma. Voltar, the Nestarian official responsible for the sector that included Earth, and who he later learned, had suggested the gift of the telescope, had averted to this once. They had become friends, and it was at the last of their dinners together, before diplomatic relations had worsened. On parting, Voltar had said, "If things . . . get worse . . . on Earth, you are welcome to stay with us."

He had not replied, his first reaction being one of indignation. He resented the invitation -- it had the suggestion of disloyalty about it, of having to seek political asylum -- but this feeling yielded to gratitude as he realized it was motivated by concern for his well-being. And he was secretly pleased by the awareness that the Nestarians considered him civilized enough to stay on their planet. Most of all, he was touched that this superior being considered him a friend.

But was he really any different than the rest of his species? True, he was an ambassador, more educated than the majority of his planet's inhabitants, more sophisticated, more experienced. He knew that aggression was a waste of resources, that war was irrational.

With the Nestarians, however, it seemed more than knowledge -- not merely knowing that war was wrong but *intuition* that it was wrong. Nor was this awareness limited to the ambassadors among them; all Nestarians felt it. He sensed a growing, disconcerting belief on his part that the difference between Earth and Nestaria was therefore fundamental. For one planet, it was instinctual to live in peace and the other instinctual to practice war.

He had hinted this to Voltar once after a savory dinner of Nestarian seasnails washed down with ample amounts of vintage Nestarian wine. The effect of the wine and food had freed the conversation of the usual pleasantries, to politics, and Voltar had expressed his incredulity at the "preparations."

"You must understand, Voltar," he had replied, "that events sometimes determine activity with a will of their own." The ambassador noticed that he was unconsciously drumming on the table, as if supplying an increasing rhythm reflecting the increased pace of such events. He stopped at once, embarrassed.

Voltar didn't notice – or pretended not to notice. "Yes, but with such dire possibilities?"

"I should have said events plus individuals. There are certain individuals who feel it necessary to protect . . ." He had let the sentence trail off.

"Protect from whom? From what? There is no threat to Earth."

He knew this to be true. He groped for an explanation. "There is also technological determinism, gearing up industry . . . all these factors . . . " He saw Voltar's puzzled expression.

"But don't they realize what it will mean? How wrong it is to want to destroy, to kill? How can they contemplate it? And as policy?"

"Perhaps it is something within us. I often think about it, that maybe it is inborn, like chlorophyll in plants."

He would never forget Voltar's expression. It lasted only an instant – a look of horror. He couldn't remember ever seeing a Nestarian lose control like that, even for a moment. Then Voltar had turned the conversation away from the direction it was taking. Or on looking back, it had seemed he had, for he began to comment on the beauty of the purple sunset spreading out from the base of the Nestarian sky. But then he had paused before adding, "Twilights are always sad, they would be unbearable if one did not know a new day would dawn. They are only part of the whole cycle. Days end but years continue."

There was something sad, almost helpless, in the tone in which this was said, and it affected the ambassador in a curious way, so that although he hadn't had time to dwell on the statement then, it had stayed with him. What did it mean? Was it merely a philosophical utterance, or was it more significant? A symbolic reference to what would happen to Earth if it persisted in preparing for war -- that if it had to be destroyed, a greater good would be served: the peace of the universe?

The rest of the evening, they had reverted to talk of pleasantries. But at one point, about an hour after the lengthy Nestarian sunset began, when the purple had almost turned to black, the ambassador had tried to raise the matter again -- the thing that was troubling him. Both had been concentrating on the terminal stage of the sunset and were silent, caught by its beauty, when he said softly to Voltar, "Do you believe that evil can be . . . intrinsic . . . to some civilizations?"

Voltar sat for a moment without saying anything, his huge head silhouetted against the purple-black background like an ancient Easter island totem, and then the head inclined forward slightly as though it were a load too heavy to bear, "We Nestarians do not believe in evil, it is alien to us."

The words seemed to remain suspended, something physical, an evanescent extension of the curtain of descending darkness. "Evil" and "alien" stood out in the ambassador's mind like the allegations of an indictment.

"But maybe it is because with you good is inborn," he replied.

Voltar said nothing. He simply touched the ambassador's hand with his own, saying in a voice that was almost a whisper, as if talking to himself, "I don't know . . ."

And then on parting, Voltar has said again the words that kept coming back to the ambassador: "If things … get worse … on Earth, you are welcome to stay with us."

He didn't see Voltar in the days that followed, which made him wonder what the Nestarians were up to. How would they cope with the threat? For their problem was, in some ways, the converse of his. They had never been to war -- or if they had, it was so long ago, in their pre-history, they had forgotten what it meant; they hadn't had to kill, to destroy life. Now they were faced with the choice: kill or risk being killed.

He could only imagine what they were going through -- a conflict that went to the essence of the meaningfulness of their existence. Unlike Earth, whose history had so often posed this choice between kill or be killed so that over the centuries, the fact of having to make a choice was no longer remarkable -- had in fact become secondary to determination of the method most successful for effecting the killing

Unlike Earth, Nestaria had never experienced the choice, had never become acclimated to making it by history. Vague legends were one thing, the glorification of warfare by patriotism, chivalry, holy war and other guises was another. The concept of warfare, which on Earth had been institutionalized to a way of life as much present as absent, would appear to the Nestarians as nothing less than murder.

Although the existence of his planet depended on the result, the ambassador found himself nonetheless fascinated by the effect of the choice on the Nestarians. He had the feeling he was watching a laboratory experiment where organisms were being subjected to totally new stimuli. Except that these organisms were the most highly developed encountered in the universe so far, and it was his task to ascertain what they would do.

He began to walk around his spacious quarters, barely conscious of his movements, all his energy committed to speculating on what the Nestarians would do. Would they commit the ultimate dishonor in their own eyes and strike first? The decision-makers on Earth they were gambling that they would not. The fly taunting the elephant, but an elephant with the soul of a saint. He thought of the cartoon in the last news transmission that had been sent to him. It showed a figure with a halo, arms raised in horror, looking down the barrel of a cannon which extended from Earth. The arms were raised in horror, but the manner in which the picture was drawn made it clear they were also raised in surrender.

And it was his duty to represent such a planet. In truth, he hoped another government would come to power on Earth, but there was little possibility of that happening in time. The oligarchs were clever, gambling that the Nestarians wouldn't – couldn't – act out of war. That they would not interfere in Earth's efforts to increase its influence in the universe through belligerency -- an increase in power that would not be lost on other planets. That, if necessary, the Nestarians would allow themselves to be destroyed by Earth before they would destroy Earth. The ambassador shut his eyes and shook his head from side to side, attempting to grasp the concept of such total self-sacrifice, at their refusal to bring their scientific and technological superiority to bear.

Sometimes, secretly, one part of him wished that the Nestarians *would* destroy Earth, root out this abnormal cell before it could spread its toxin throughout the body of the universe: -- necessary surgery. At other times he could not bear the thought, and in a fit of pique – or was it atavism – sensed within himself a buried primitive impulse that Earth should conquer. That Nestaria might be the most civilized planet, but that Earth would be the most powerful.

It was easy to throw up his hands and surrender to fatalism, or to comfort himself with the belief that there was a manifest destiny that Earth should expand throughout the universe, carrying *his* species, providing a kind of immortality. Such feelings would be followed by revulsion. A world based on animal force was evil enough; an infinitely greater evil would be a universe based on it.

When the invitation to dinner arrived from Voltar, the ambassador knew that something crucial was about to happen. At dinner, Voltar's greeting was cordial, without a hint of urgency, although his subsequent conversation, while amiable, was somewhat strained. This forced quality puzzled the ambassador, because it was unlike him. He attributed it to Voltar's haste to reveal the reason he had asked for the meeting, and expected him to speak of it shortly, but his conversation continued to be the pleasant, innocuous conversation typical of a leisurely dinner with a friend, of the kind they once enjoyed together.

After a time Voltar turned the conversation to the laws of science with such deftness that it seemed not a change in subject, but a natural extension of the direction of the conversation. Still, the ambassador sensed an underlying agitation, an imperceptible hurrying of pace.

"Every action causes a reaction," Voltar was saying. "Not only on the object upon which it acts, but also in itself, it being changed in the process. Sometimes this self-change is beneficial, sometimes harmful." Then he hesitated ever so slightly, looking closely at the ambassador. "Nestaria, too, is subject to such laws of science, and the processes that we undergo are similarly governed. In our case the process will be harmful. We will be changed for the worse, if we decided to take preventive steps. If we build the machine."

So that was the message. Its abruptness, despite Voltar's careful attempts, struck the ambassador full force: now it was the Nestarians who made preparations. Even before he could grasp its full portent, the ambassador was frightened by Voltar's last words. "The machine?" he asked with foreboding, yet curiosity.

"The terrible machine. That is how we refer to it. We do not know what else to call it. It is capable of immense destruction – no planet would survive it. Immense destruction," he repeated, not as warning, but in awe at the machine's power. His lips formed a slight smile that did not go undetected by the ambassador, who thought: he is embarrassed by talking about such things.

"Although the machine is not intended for us," Voltar continued, "by the very act of building it, we will begin the process of our own destruction. And if we use it, our inner destruction will be irreversible."

The ambassador realized the smile had not been one of embarrassment but of helplessness. He hesitated to ask the question that had to be asked, and which he knew Voltar could not answer. "Will you . . . will it be used?"

The smile faded and the face of the Nestarian appeared to lose its smoothness, to become desiccated and wrinkled, as if, punctured by the question, it had physically drained of its contents and shriveled. In a dry and rasping voice that seemed to have undergone a similar transformation, now unrecognizable to the ambassador, Voltar replied, "I do not know. If we do, it is your planet that forces us."

The Nestarian's words jolted the ambassador. More horrifying than their abrasive sound, which the ambassador attributed to the emotion with which they had been uttered, was his realization that it was the first time Voltar had abandoned the use of impersonal expressions such as "preparations" in referring to Earth's activities. Until this moment, Voltar had been careful to avoid personal references, he surmised, both because the activities were too painful to contemplate, and out of deference to avoid linking him with those activities. The ambassador was astonished and offended at how accusatory and condescending the words "your planet" sounded. That Voltar had used them was an indication of the desperation he and his planet were beginning to feel.

Although the transformation in Voltar's face when he had been asked about the machine had been abrupt, the ambassador realized, without having noticed it before, that its withered, collapsed appearance had not suddenly occurred. It had, in a less pronounced form, become a permanent aspect of his features, as if his face had come to reflect on a miniature scale what was at the same time happening to Nestaria. Not so much aging alone as – the ambassador could think of no other way to describe it – a loss of innocence.

The tense silence that had settled over the meal continued. Each pretended to concentrate on eating, absorbed with his own thoughts, until Voltar said quietly, "I feel whatever happens Nestaria will lose. You see . . . we are beginning to hate."

Thinking of those in power on Earth over whom he had no control, the ambassador was about to reply, "I am not my brother's keeper," but knew this denial would be foreign to Voltar, and so he said nothing.

The rest of the meal was a denouement: a few meaningless comments that both of them seized on to break the tension, followed by their mutual, albeit self-conscious, discovery that each had work to do, whereupon the evening ended.

The machine was being built. Its site was a park within view of his study window. The Nestarians were making sure he would be able to mark its progress, yet had placed it at a distance where it wasn't flaunted in his face. They weren't building the gallows in the condemned man's yard; their desperation hadn't yet eroded millennia of culture. Nonetheless, slowly, inevitably, their tactfulness, like their control of the situation, was dwindling.

Notwithstanding the Nestarians' balanced attempts with respect to the location of the machine, it held the ambassador's attention as gallows would its victim. He watched its progress with morbid fascination.

To the Nestarian people, the device sitting placidly and inconspicuously in a corner of the park among the flowers would look like a decorative piece of sculpture – its cannon-like shape without meaning to them. An attempt, he assumed, to disguise its presence and lessen its horror to the people, who were only gradually being told about Earth's preparation and the machine, and only in the briefest terms. The ambassador noted that on the street, people whispered to each other, especially if they recognized him as the Earth ambassador, and he was sometimes the recipient of hostile looks – something he had not experienced before. They rushed from place to place rather than walking in their usual stately fashion.

Government officials had taken to preparing the people by openly citing the Nestarian legends! The fearful tales of battles with axes used for killing instead of building, of destroying villages with fire, of making slaves of captives. Such consciousness-raising of previously buried tales was an ominous step indeed. It would be easy enough to make the transformation from citation to recitation to glorification. The whole process was beginning. How familiar it all seemed.

Despite their obvious reluctance, the Nestarians continued to build the machine. With their large heads, the workers surrounding it seemed like knights on a chessboard clustering to protect their queen. And, in a sense, they *were* part of a gigantic chess match, as was he. He wondered if they would be miraculously confounded like the builders of the Tower of Babel, though this was a bit anthropocentric. If God existed, it was more likely the Nestrians rather than the Earthites who were created in his image. The thought made him uneasy.

He moved away from the window to escape the sight of the machine, yet he could not eliminate it from his mind. Would it be used or was it a bluff, a Trojan horse in reverse?

He wandered aimlessly through the embassy, unaware of his path, absorbed in thought. It was that time of day just before twilight, when the Nestarian air was at its calmest, and soft light suffused everything in an ethereal radiance. A time of peacefulness, when he was best able to think.

Soon the sunset would come, the sunset which had ceased to give him peace, and which of late he had come more and more to dread. Its symbolism was obvious, but still he could not shed the melancholia that came upon him as it descended. It struck him now as primeval, with its deepening purples and blacks, evoking the Nestarian legends of warfare and strife.

From his study of the beginnings of Nestarian history – a study that, unlike the Nestarians, he was not reluctant to undertake for fear of their past – he believed they had once resorted to warfare among themselves. He sensed that Voltar, too, was tormented by the legends, and at such times he would feel once more a kinship with the Nestarian that defied the physiological and evolutionary differences between them.

If the legends had a basis in truth, the Nestarians, in approaching war, risked recalling to life their buried past. Whatever long-dormant ingredient within them that had allowed fratricidal warfare would surface under the impetus of preparing for war with Earth and would send them reeling toward the past, a regression that would be as fatal as it was inevitable.

Perhaps it was this atavism Voltar feared as much as anything. This was the reason the idea of war, of killing – the ultimate evil -- being intrinsic had so affected him. If his people resorted to war, however brief, to destroy Earth, they would leave themselves vulnerable to reviving the past, a past of evil, and being devoured by it. The legends might then become reality. And if Earth's destruction were thus to serve as the force to liberate their atavistic urges, they would have only replaced one form of the evil with another: Earth's belligerency with their own. They would end up doing the very thing they were attempting to get Earth to avoid. Yet if they didn't act, Earth would continue to spread its aggressive ways throughout the universe.

As the days passed, he watched the machine near completion. Although it was small, the Nestarians worked slowly, as if loathe to finish it. Or maybe they were being deliberate, to give him time to convince the Earthites to change their minds. He was aware they expected him to report about the device, but he was unable to tell Earth whether they would actually use it. Everything he knew about the Nestrians told him they wouldn't – but then, they had never been faced with this challenge before. And if they did not use it, they might be committing suicide. This was reason enough to cause them to act, but there existed a more important reason, one that, in wrestling with the problem, he had come to believe would be determinative.

Even if they would rather perish themselves, their fear of the future virulent influence of this aggressive planet, which was now threatening them, on the universe might cause them to act. Refusing to act would leave the universe to the mercy of a planet whose methods would become endemic, even if the planet itself should someday be defeated.

Altruism was what the ambassador feared most – more than saving themselves, although risking destruction in the sense Voltar feared, they would save the universe. He dreaded the Nestarians would consider this; but knew it would be the very thing they would consider. How difficult it was to try to fathom the thoughts of a people so advanced; it seemed almost presumptuous to attempt to anticipate how they would resolve their dilemma.

His own dilemma went beyond whether he should warn Earth or let it be destroyed for the greater good. He knew within himself that he *would* warn Earth, but what was to be the nature of the warning? *Cease what you are doing or they will destroy you,* or *They can never destroy you without destroying themselves, and that is decisive.*

After days of weighing the choices, he decided what he would do: simply state the facts in the impersonal diplomatic language of his profession and point out the possible courses of action and their consequences, without himself making a judgment. Earth had brought about the crisis, he reasoned petulantly. Let Earth live with it, a despairing voice within him answered.

One morning he saw from his window that no workmen surrounded the machine, and he knew it was finished. The machine appeared so small and ineffectual, incapable of destroying Earth. Then he remembered the telescope and its power. He appreciated the irony: both instruments pointed toward Earth, one to gather its light, the other to extinguish it.

But the destructive device did not threaten Earth alone. As Voltar had recognized, even if the Nestarians did not use it, in constructing it, they were destroying something in themselves. The beginning of

77

that destruction he had seen for himself – a week before, Voltar had passed him on the street and pretended not to see him. That good man was learning to be dishonest with himself. The same man who chided him humorously when they first met, before the crisis, "You know, I am glad that Earth was included in my sector; it is the only planet that gives me any challenges." To which the ambassador had replied, "It is the only one that gives me any, too!" and from that moment, they had been friends.

He wondered if Voltar remembered his words now. How different from the ones he had spoken at their last meeting: ". . . we are beginning to hate."

The Ambassador informed Earth of the Nestarian preparations but was equivocal about whether the machine would be used. It was impossible for him to know if this information would be enough to deter Earth from continuing with its preparations.

However, he soon learned it was having some effect. The position of the anti-war group had been aided by the information, and the oligarchs were on the defensive. Between the lines of the diplomatic messages, he could decipher that a struggle was occurring. He began to hope. He learned that the preparations had been halted while "discussions" were taking place. For a month echoes of the battle reached him through items in the news and diplomatic reports he received. News headlines such as "Doomsday Looms" versus "Earth's Manifest Destiny," the articles reflecting the opposing stances. The diplomatic reports were couched in more diplomatic language, but their conflicting positions were clear.

He requested permission to come home to give a personal report on the Nestarian situation, though equally interested in getting a close look how the struggle was going. If able, he would lend his assistance to the anti-war group. Permission was denied. He was alone, as he had been alone since the beginning of the crisis, when Earth had ordered his staff home. The ambassador knew that the only reason he wasn't replaced was that earth knew the Nestarians trusted him. The idea that he was being used to put the Nestarians at ease while Earth readied for war disgusted him.

Then he received a diplomatic report that made him despair. It contained one sentence buried in the middle of the last page: "Defense preparations have been resumed." There was little time remaining. Nestaria would be forced to decide soon. Events were out of control, onrushing with a force of their own. It all seemed somehow *determined*. Irrevocable.

He paced back and forth in the embassy study. Through the window he could see the Nestarian device looking like a toy cannon that kids on Earth played with, though on Nestaria there were no toy cannons, only a solitary one that was real. The incredulity the ambassador felt over what was happening was overwhelming. Beyond comprehension.

And then one evening as the sunset descended, he was filled with an uneasiness that deepened into a foreboding as the purple shadows lengthened and thickened, until he was enveloped in a blanket of purple so pervasive he felt himself inhaling the vapor. Then a figure approached, object in hand, as if an executioner synergized out of the vision and mist to summon him. But the object was a scroll, and the Nestarian a messenger who, upon handing the scroll to him, slipped back into the haze without waiting for him to read it. The message was in Voltar's script, but not his usual elegant script, and showed the haste with which it had been written. That, and the almost insulting fact that it contained only two words -- but they froze his blood: "Don't watch."

He had been warned. In a final act of friendship, Voltar had sneaked the message to him. Don't watch through the telescope. The time for maneuvering had ended. He was suddenly aware that the purple had turned to black. What surprised him was the calm he felt. Perhaps because he knew it was too late to warn Earth, andtoo late for Earth to act on the warning -- there was nothing more he could do.

Despite Voltar's message, he felt compelled to watch through the telescope. The sight was familiar: bright Earth, behind which a few stars glowed dimly. The whiteness of the planet hypnotized him as he stared at it. All his powers of concentration were needed to keep his mind from wandering while his eyes remained fixed on his planet. At times, it would blur from his intense focusing upon it, and he would quickly blink until the image was clear.

So absorbed was he in gazing at it that he lost all sense of time. He did not know whether he had been watching for minutes or hours until, in an instant, the round disc of light that was Earth turned from white to red. That was all. The stars behind it looked the same as they had before. He had difficulty grasping that anything had changed. He continued to look through the telescope without seeing, numb, until he heard a noise behind him.

Voltar had entered and was standing awkwardly in the doorway. The two stared at one another.

The Earthite understood from the Nestarian's expression that he had come to comfort him.

"I am sorry," Voltar said, his huge head bowed, his velvet features pained.

"I am sorry, too," the ambassador replied weakly, "for all of us."

"I realize this isn't the time . . . but I want you to know . . . you are welcome here . . ."

Again, the offer. But now, the circumstances in which it was made had change. What had previously been merely a possibility had now occurred. A sudden realization struck him. *He was the last of his kind – the last Earthite.* The last of the primitive men.

He looked at Voltar. He hated this Nestarian standing in front of him, hated him as a member of the race that destroyed Earth. But most of all, he hated him because Voltar was not the end – *his* species would continue. His history hadn't ended. He had a future. The ambassador's jaw tightened.

Voltar noticed it and guessed his thoughts. "Please do not hate me," he said.

The Nestarian's words had a curious effect upon the ambassador. Before they were uttered, he had wanted to push in the velvet face of Voltar. But when he heard his words, he realized he had learned nothing by Earth's destruction. That is why we were destroyed, he thought, because of our hatred. It was his planet's fault, the fault of *his* species. His anger subsided. He smiled wearily. "I do not mean to hate you. I told you once that it is inborn with us . . . was inborn with us." He paused, then said, "May I ask a favor of you?"

"Of course."

"I want to go back."

"Back?"

"To Earth."

"But . . ."

"I know. I want to go back. To be with them."

Voltar understood.

"A small ship, enough to hold one person."

Voltar nodded. "There is one at spaceport four . . . Do you want me to accompany you to the ship?"

"No . . . Thank you."

The two looked at one another. Neither knew what to say. The ambassador fingered the telescope -- Voltar's gift. He let go of it and walked to the doorway. He paused before going through it and started to say good-bye, but couldn't bring himself to finish the word. "Remember me," he said instead.

His last view of the room was not of Voltar, but of the telescope behind him. He wondered if it would be too small to show his ship headed for the red disc, an impotent sperm plunging toward a dead egg. He wondered, too, if Voltar would watch.

Larry Lefkowitz *has written across a wide variety of genres. You can find more of his works here:*

amazon.com/s?i=digital-text&rh=p_27%3ALarry+Lefkowitz

Day One Day
By David Castlewitz

Every agent in the Department of Morals and Ethics had to visit North Colony at least once. Noland hoped this assignment would be his one and only venture to the warm climes, where males and females wore little clothing, covering neither their forelegs nor their forearms. Only the hindquarters were clad, a practice that Noland found disturbing.

In the transit hub's main lobby, he squatted on a cold floor, his front legs folded beneath his body, his forearms lying across the lower part of his neck. Others – merchants, students, police officers -- waited in this corner reserved for southern citizens. He hoped to finish his assignment and get home in time for the Day One festival, which commemorated when Sarryn first came to this planet. He didn't want to spend the holiday with strangers.

Overhead, the vaulted ceiling displayed graphics depicting stylized scenes from the war fought with the planet's biped natives. The mural paid tribute to the fierce Sarryn warriors who defeated a primitive foe, matching clubs and stone swords against explosive bullets and devastating grenades. The aboriginals that survived the carnage fled into the wilderness. Prisoners were enslaved.

Once the transit center was cleared of northern citizens, a guard waved a stubby forearm in a "Stand up" gesture. Noland bristled. He disliked being treated like a herd-dweller, little better than the nomads of the home world.

Once processed, Noland emerged from the transit hub. His full-body wool garment made him itch. The midday heat engulfed him.

82

He looked around at the dusty street. A few self-drive carts rattled down the middle. Overhead, auto-sentries hovered, buzzing. When he trained for this assignment, the virtual reality rendition of the transit hub sparkled with glass and steel. Crowded moving sidewalks carried half-nude smiling workers. He chuckled at the reality. Dust and prefab buildings. Nothing sparkled.

"You from Morals?"

Noland turned to the male who'd sidled up to him, a droopy-eyed elder with a long silky mane of white and gray hairs.

"The clan sent me. I'm Franz."

"Are you in the family?" Noland asked. He hadn't expected cooperation. He'd been told, blood relatives protected one another. Families helped miscreants, even to the extent of engineering an escape. The culprit he'd come to investigate was a minor. He expected her family to interfere at every opportunity.

"I've got a cart reserved. I'll take you to the ranch."

"What's your relationship to the child?" Noland scoured his memory for the seven-year-old's name.

"I'm an uncle," Franz said.

"Jenile," Noland blurted, remembering the name. "You're the child's uncle?"

"I'm a clan uncle," Franz said, his large front teeth clacking. His nostrils flared. "I reported the filly."

Noland let this new knowledge sink in. He didn't need to know why Franz turned in a child for a misdemeanor that should've earned the culprit nothing more than detention or a sound smack on the rump.

The cart stopped at a fence made of thin slats, some drilled with large holes for easy handling. The simple barrier meandered to Noland's left and right, disappearing into the hazy distance to surround the ranch,

Carefully, Noland stepped onto the ribbed plank that had lowered itself from the back of the cart, his cloven hooves finding purchase that helped him keep his balance. He extended his forearms for additional support, as though he could grasp the air.

"What're we waiting on?" he asked.

Franz' pointed at a low rise on the other side of the fence. A figure appeared. Then another. And, soon, more. They lined up, the youngest members of the clan at either end, the family leaders, females and males, side-by-side in the center. Greeters, Noland realized. The North kept old traditions alive.

When Franz touched his ear, a section of the fence parted, and Franz trotted through the gap, his wiry tail swishing back and forth. Noland followed. He didn't think he should wait for an invitation.

"Wait here," Franz said, and proceeded up the gentle slope to confer with the greeters. He stopped in front of a male with a massive mane that spilled over his shoulders. Not someone Noland would want to meet in a fight. He hadn't engaged in mock combat in thirty years. He wasn't a colt anymore.

"You can interview the filly," Franz said when he returned, his long face betraying his concern. "And the parents. The immediate family. Only. Nobody else in the clan. Do you agree to these terms?"

Noland bristled, the minute hairs across his back tingling. Limitations to the scope of his investigation should've been decided before he came. But objecting now wouldn't help anyone. If he galloped away, he'd have a long and arduous trip ahead of him. He and Franz had traveled for half a day in that cart. How long would it take him to reach the transit hub if he went by hoof?

"I want to put this matter behind us as rapidly as possible," Noland said.

Franz nodded, his long snout making an exaggerated up and down motion. "Spoken like the diplomat that you are."

Noland followed Franz up the hill. Across the crest, the greeting party had already dispersed. In the distance, robots worked in the fields. Huge, wheeled contraptions, the machines slowly maneuvered between rows of corn and some green and leafy plant Nolan didn't recognize. Elsewhere, smaller robots off-loaded rolled sheets of metal from a flatbed truck. Some bipeds worked alongside the automatons, under the supervision of Sarryn overseers.

"Did Jenile let one of the workers loose?" Noland asked, trying to better understand the crime.

"No," Franz said. "Mister Huggs – that was his name – was my personal pet. Since he was a boy. She freed him. Just let him go. She's a criminal. She deserves to be punished. I don't care if she's just seven-years-old."

The female had the typical sagging pouch where her teats – or, rather, the remnants of those organs because this Sarryn was beyond mating age – lay hidden beneath a flimsy hind-quarters garment.

Naked forelegs drew Noland's attention, but he averted his eyes and looked, instead, at the female's long neck and decorative yellow mane. She'd been a beauty in her youth, he decided.

"I'm her mother, so you better talk to me before you see her."

Noland tapped the informational device embedded behind his ear. "Hallie," he said when the female's name floated in front of him. He blinked away the rest of the information that followed. He didn't want to know too much about the parents.

"Hal-Lay," the female corrected. "They write it as 'Hallie,' but I prefer – "

"Hal-Lay then. Fine. What do you want? I don't have you – "

"I want my daughter released to my custody."

"If she is released," Noland said in a slow and willful tone of voice, "what will you do to her?"

Hal-Lay snorted, her dark nostrils flaring. She parted her thick lips and showed a row of large white teeth. "Nothing. She's a child. She thought she was – "

"Franz seems to think – "

"That old thing? He meddles too much. He doesn't know what he's talking about."

"Wasn't it his pet biped that your daughter stole and let loose?"

Hal-Lay thick lips vibrated.

"I'll conduct a fair investigation," Noland added.

Hal-Lay backed out of the cottage. Far behind her, a blue-eyed stallion stood staring. Noland didn't like soldiers and this male's long straight horns growing straight up near his ears looked like a killer. Curled tusks jutting from the side of a wide mouth added to the effect. Tusks and horns. Dangerous weapons.

Noland watched Hal-Lay rub her long neck against the large male's. The pair swayed in unison as they walked away, side-by-side, bodies touching.

The detention center stood behind a high fence of corrugated metal peppered with tiny holes and topped by barbed wire. Tall posts overlooked the interior grounds. Sensors atop the posts gave evidence of someone watching who came and went. As Noland approached, his nostrils twitched from the smell of bipeds and the squealing slippery animals kept in nearby pens. He guessed the building on the other side of the fence served a dual purpose, housing workers as well as detainees.

The swung open, its hinges creaking. Several guards stood on the grounds, stamping the dust, stirring up the grit and gravel. A female approached, her slender tusks giving away her sex more readily than the immodest girdle wrapping her rump. Like her male counterparts, she wore her mane unadorned. No necklace dangled across the boney intersection where forelegs met body. No streaks of henna or bits of shiny metal anywhere across her back.

She carried a flat stick in her hand and she softly tapped her open palm with it. A harder smack might leave a mark, Noland surmised. Back home, guards used shockers and other weapons to keep prisoners in line. No old-fashioned sticks or straps. No lethal clubs, either.

"They said you'd be along," the guard said, and waved Noland in with a nod of her long snout.

An acrid smell filled the air. It was what Noland first noted when he stepped into the detention center, at the lip of a wide corridor lined on both sides with tall and narrow windowless doors. Narrow troughs on both sides of the corridor gurgled with water carrying away waste in a swift moving current. Soon, the cell doors gave way to open stalls enclosed by thick wire woven into a hexagonal pattern.

Only one of the stalls was occupied. By a naked filly. Noland didn't like that. It smacked of abuse. As did the straw heaped in a corner. She didn't even have a decent toilet. Just a large hole in the floor. A cement trough provided noxious smelling water. Remnants of a recent meal sat in a wooden plate.

Jenile displayed no signs of physical abuse. No welts. No tears in her skin. "I know who you are," she said when Noland introduced himself. "They told me you'd be coming."

Noland didn't think she sounded like a seven-year-old. No childish excitement in her soft brown eyes. Her tail didn't swish back and forth. Maybe confinement had matured her. Maybe she knew that her childish prank might warrant an adult's punishment.

But then Jenile rubbed her face against a rough wooden post and shut her eyes. Tears dripped into a crevice leading to her nostrils, which puffed as she let loose a sigh. Gurgling erupted from deep in her throat.

"Do you understand what you did?" Noland asked, and watched the child for signs of remorse. Regret. Or vulgar pride. How did she feel deep inside? Although he'd never before investigated a crime in North Colony, Noland was certain his skills wouldn't fail him.

Criminals were criminals. Inside, they hid behind their hubris, knew how to feign an apology, held authority in disregard.

"I've done it before," Jenile said, her coarse tongue licking her lips.

Noland blinked. "You have?"

"I mean, I've let a biped ride on my back. I've played with their kids. We all do. I mean, juveniles do. It isn't bad."

"It's not proper," Noland said as a vision of young Sarryn cavorting with equally young bipeds, all of them naked and glistening with sweat, danced in front of his eyes.

"I asked Uncle Franz if I could play with Mr. Huggs."

Noland took a moment to digest this. Most bipeds had numbers burnt into their backs. Few had names.

"I didn't think he'd run away."

"Did he?" Noland asked as a quick follow-up, ready to catch the child in a lie. She was charged with letting the animal loose. Letting this pet run off. She'd helped him escape. That was her crime, even though Noland considered the mere idea of playing with a biped as evil a trespass. Down south, no child would even think of such a thing. Bipeds weren't playmates.

But northern society was different, he reminded himself. He couldn't say that it was better. He'd grown up amongst strangers who became fast friends, and teachers he learned to love. An idyllic place, that school where he'd been educated. It lacked family ties. No clan or tribal loyalties. Just strangers thrown together.

"Yes," Jenile said after a long silence. "He ran. He climbed over the fence and ran into the meadow. The grass was so tall, I couldn't see him. That's how he got away."

"You didn't pursue him?"

"I couldn't. He got swallowed up by the flowers."

Noland flashed on a mental image of the surrounding fields. Many were cultivated, with robots working the cropland. Westward, beyond the fence, mowed grassland loomed in the distance. Nothing quite matched Jenile's description of where she'd played with the biped.

"Can you show me where this happened?" Noland asked.

"No. Uncle Franz said I can't leave detention until the family decides what to do with me. Or until you decide. Until somebody makes up their mind. Somebody decides."

Noland sensed movement behind him. He looked back over his

shoulder, moving so quickly that he danced sideways on his forelegs and had to plant his rear hooves firm against the floor to keep his balance. The elderly uncle stood on the other side of the stall.

"Do you have what you need?" Franz asked.

Noland trotted past Franz and outside into the fresh air. He slowed, his hooves kicking up dust clouds. He stopped before reaching the fence. He felt the guards' eyes on him. He shook off the sweat running along his neck. Specks of foam dribbled from his mouth. He waited for Franz to join him, but the old uncle didn't move from the detention center's open doorway.

Reluctantly, Noland walked back.

"She told me the biped escaped on its own. Ran into a field of tall grass." Noland mentally reviewed his few minutes with Jenile to be sure he remembered everything she'd said. "She claims you allowed her to play with your biped."

Franz snorted. "I didn't tell her to open the gate and let him run away. She did that on her own."

"She claims the biped climbed the fence."

"What difference does that make?" Franz retorted.

"All the difference that's needed!" someone said in a booming voice. Noland turned in the direction of that voice, his vision absorbing the image of a massive stallion. Long straight horns with deadly points, and thick curled tusks growing from the edges of his mouth marked the intruder as a soldier.

"And you are?" Noland struggled not to feel intimidated by the stallion's size and angry demeanor.

"Vinders," Franz said, nodding at the soldier.

"Jenile's father," Vinders said. "And if the filly didn't open a gate, if this biped took advantage of her, then there's been no crime committed. If anything, she's a victim. And you, Old Uncle, are as much to blame as anyone. You let your pet cavort with the child."

Noland stepped back, head shaking, his mane bouncing across the length of his long neck.

"What do you think happened?" Noland asked in a calm voice. He struggled now to retreat in the face of this angry parent. He knew he shouldn't feel intimidated.

Vinders shook his head and smacked his lips with his tongue. "Something this old one has been trying to make happen for years. The filly didn't do anything wrong."

Franz neither shied away nor attempted to come close.

"This Uncle," Vinders continued, "doesn't want me to be elected tribal chief. Ask him. You're so skilled at ferreting the truth? Ask him."

"This has nothing to do with politics," Franz said.

Vinders raised his arms, his massive hands clenched into lethal fists. He backed up, head down. Ready to charge, Noland feared, and took a few steps backwards himself, his thin black tail swishing between his legs, betraying his fear.

Neither Franz nor Vinders showed fright. Franz didn't pound the ground or let his hindquarters bounce back and forth in an involuntary shimmy. He didn't snort and bow his head, preparing to receive the stallion's charge.

Vinders lowered his fists, his blue eyes unblinking, his glare as solid and deadly as before. But the moment for attack had passed.

On the other side of the surrounding fence, several male Sarryn massed. Like Vinders, they sported deadly tusks and lethal horns.

"I have just as many supporters," Franz said.

Noland half expected to see the old uncle's own army line up at the fence. But that didn't happen. Instead, silently, Vinders walked away. Two guards opened the gate for him, and he trotted out. He whinnied and cantered away, his followers lined up behind him, heads held high.

"Do you want to explain this to me?" Noland asked, a sense of unease in his gut.

"You're smart," Franz said. "Explain it to yourself." The old uncle trotted away. The gate was still open. He left the compound.

Noland stifled an urge to shout at him to stop. He let a dozen explanations roll through his mind. There was just one answer that held up under scrutiny. It was a sad explanation for what had transpired, for why a juvenile was held in detention, and why the child's father found it necessary to present a show of strength.

It was why everything about North Colony always seemed so wrong to Noland. Their tribal ways, passed down over the centuries by the families that settled this continent would lead to ruination. In the south, where cadres ruled, and family ties were non-existent, intra-tribal war was impossible.

Sad, but Jenile was in the middle of it all, and rescue meant leaving home for long years of detention in the south.

The link to his office surfaced for only a moment. Eyes closed,

Noland waited for his surrogate to wake and transcribe his thoughts. But the Action Writer Personification System fired up only briefly. Disappointed, Noland paced the floor of his one-room cottage. Outside, the sun peeked between the tops of the surrounding trees. Dozens of clan leaders had arrived during the night. According to Franz, the election of a new chief for a ten-year term, along with other tribal affairs, would occupy the settlement for the next few days. Now, the morning showed Noland rows of white tents neatly lined up, each with a clan pennant atop a tall flagpole.

The tribal conference would stretch past the Day One festivities, Noland surmised. Good. Everyone would be too busy to take notice of him. There'd be no opposition when he led Jenile from the detention center to the ranch's main gate, where he intended to place her in a cage aboard an auto-cart.

He again tried to link to his office surrogate, tapping the inter-communicator behind his ear, as though it needed physical assistance to wake up.

A knock on the door to his cottage interrupted him. Someone called his name, adding, "Old Uncle sent me."

Noland pushed open the door with his snout. A juvenile stood at the threshold. He couldn't tell if it was male or female. So many young Sarryn possessed features of both sexes at this age. Soft manes. Large luminous eyes. Lean backs.

"They're taking Jenile out of her cell," the juvenile said.

Noland squinted at the young Sarryn. "Is it Vinders? Her father? "

"They'll kill her if you don't stop them." The messenger's long face implored Noland to follow before turning and dashing away.

Noland followed. The uneven ground beneath him fought him and he stopped to get his bearings as well as to adjust his balance. A wave of dizziness ran through him. An intoxicating smell drifted past. Incense burned in large metal saucers set on tripods arranged in a rough circle.

Noland drew in a deep breath. The aroma stung his nostrils, brought tears to his eyes, and confusion to his brain. He hastened his pace. An overturned log sent sparks into the air. Naked Sarryn danced in a circle, some of them engaging in pantomimed sex acts.

Cymbals and drums and flutes supplied a musical accompaniment. Acrobats performed in the meadow, near the rows of tents. Noland pushed past a mental haze as strong as the smoke from the bonfires. He tore himself away from the intoxicating aroma of burning incense. He stumbled into cleaner air.

A herd congregated at the gate in the fence around the detention center. A small figure walked with its head down emerged from the open gate. Behind it, a huge figure bumped the smaller one's rump, as though to urge it forward. Noland drew close enough to make out faces. Two were familiar. Franz and Vinders.

And the small figure was Jenile.

Shouts and barks, along with fierce whimpers of protest, filled in the air. The huge mass at the gate split in two. Most of the Sarryn males sported the pointed horns and sharp tucks of young warriors. Opposing them, Franz pranced back and forth in front of a small group. Elders, Noland realized, judging them by their gray spotted manes or dark-tipped horns, the latter obviously fighters of a past age.

"Let her be!" Noland rushed between the mobs, his hooves digging into the soft ground. His shouts had no effect. Vinders and others – Noland looked for Jenile's mother, but didn't see her – pushed the youngster along, forcing her uphill. Franz protested. He stumbled, his rump hitting the turf a few times. His supporters helped him to his feet and fended off attackers.

Noland pushed his way through the thick crowd, head-butting those who got in his way, using his hands to shove others out of his path. He shouted, "I represent the legitimate authority of the Department for Morals and Ethics."

Derisive laughter greeted him, along with blank stares. Sharp horns left shallow bruises on his rump. Two young warriors crushed him, one on either side. They parted only when Vinders barked an order at them. Slowly, Noland stumbled uphill, until he drew abreast of Jenile and her father.

"She's my prisoner," Noland said to Vinders. "You've no authority to take her."

Hal-Lay suddenly appeared alongside Vinders, her snout pressed into his thick neck. He turned on her and struck her with one of his tusks. He didn't draw blood, but he did make her yelp. She melted back into the crowd. Franz trotted up the hill, his small band of followers at his back.

"I want an end to this," Vinders said. "No one in the tribe wants her punished more than me."

"It's not up to you," Franz said. "That's why Noland is here."

Vinders snorted. "This puny piece of nothing?" He poked

Noland's forehead with an extended finger.

Noland slapped the hand away. He stood stock still, wary of Vinders' blood-filled eyes.

"I've the authority of the Department," Noland said, his voice deliberately soft. It was a tactic designed to force opponents to listen. That seemed to calm Vinders. This time, when Hal-Lay came to his side, Vinders didn't fight her off.

"I've every right to lead the tribe," Vinders said.

"No one doubts that," Noland said.

Vinders looked at Franz and those massed around him, most of them elderly, many of them old soldiers with scars to remind them of battle tales. Not so long ago, every tribe in the north seemed to be at war with every other tribe.

"We don't want a chief whose family deals in deceit," Franz said.

Jenile whimpered. She sat, forelegs folded beneath her, rear legs extended, arms tucked in.

"You don't have to kill this child to prove anything," Franz said.

Vinders turned to his own followers, who had slowly coalesced behind him. "Are you with me?"

They shouted and pumped the air with closed fists.

"Let Noland take her south," Franz said. "They'll deal with her."

Vinders bumped Franz with a shoulder. "She's my daughter. I'll deal with her. I'll do what must be done."

Noland felt himself suddenly separated from the front of the herd. Long snouts pushed him sideways and backwards. Hands pulled at his mane. He felt as though he were sinking into a mass of flesh.

Vinders and Jenile disappeared into the hazy distance. They descended the other side of the hill, the filly stumbling on her spindly legs, her father pulled on the rope looped around her slender neck.

By the time Noland struggled free of the warriors surrounding him, Vinders and Jenile were too far off for shouting to stop them, as if words along could do the job. Several of Vinders' supporters body slammed Noland the moment he took a step forward. They growled. One, on his hind legs, pawed at the air. Hal-Lay stood nearby, head down, tears streaming from her large dark eyes.

Not until Jenile and her father had disappeared from view did the herd dispersed. And, though he feared it was too late, Noland did what duty told him he should do. He broke into a gallop, intent on catching up to Vinders and Jenile and putting a stop to this travesty.

Jenile didn't deserve to die in exile. Or die under the hooves of her punishing father. She should be cared for, kept in prison, perhaps until she matured, Noland thought, and no longer harbored peculiar feelings for bipeds.

Where? Alone on the plain, with fields of tall grass facing him and woods on either side, the ranch at his back, Noland pondered which direction to take in pursuit of Jenile. The sound of hooves pounding the hard ground made him turn his head, his long neck twisting, to watch Franz struggling to catch up. He'd forgotten about the old Sarryn in his haste to pursue Vinders and Jenile.

"Which way?" he asked when Franz caught up. The elderly uncle hung his head. Foam formed around his mouth. Sweat drenched his gray mane. He gulped the air. Audibly. Loudly. Noland waited for a reply.

"Straight on," Franz said. "Don't get so far ahead."

"Keep up," Noland seethed, and pounced in the direction Franz had indicated. Straight ahead. Into the field of wild grass, across vast patches of colorful flowers, keeping the woods on either side as visual cues that he headed in the right direction.

When he reached a low rise, he looked back at Franz, who labored in the distance, emerging from the field of grass and flowers, moving at a steady walk, and then a trot. Looking ahead, Noland saw a group of Sarryn standing in a loose circle. He stepped carefully down an incline, careful not to lose his footing in the soft ground.

Eyes turned in his direction. Noland wondered what had alerted them. He kept going, wary of these one-time warriors, especially their leader, Vinders. He spied Jenile. Hal-Lay stood beside her. Other youngsters came into view. More Sarryn appeared. More than Noland had initially realized.

Jenile rubbed faces with old and young alike. Appalled, Noland tried to increase his speed, but nearly stumbled because of the soft ground. Was this the way of the North? Bring friends and relatives to the execution?

Several Sarryn broke away from the herd and trotted to intercept Noland. He came to a halt when they reached him. Franz sidled up alongside him.

"It's too late," Franz said.

"They haven't killed her yet. I can still save her." Noland sidestepped to get around the three old warriors facing him.

"Vinders has their vote," Franz said. "It's too late to change – "

"Vote?" Noland hissed. "Is that what this is about? They're going to kill Jenile."

"No," Franz said.

One of the three Sarryn blocking Noland's way spoke up. "You southerners don't know anything."

"She's to be exiled," Franz said.

"Which is as good as killing her," Noland said. He looked for Jenile, but didn't see her. The loose circle in the near distance broke up, with old and young lining up on either side of Hal-Lay and Vinders. Noland pushed past the three warriors blocking his progress. They gave him no resistance. He knew why. It was too late to do anything. He couldn't save Jenile now.

Noland trotted on. Without hope of helping the filly, but unable to stop himself from making the attempt. When he reached the line stretched out across the prairie, he nosed his way into a place beside Vinders.

"Is this what you want for your daughter?" he asked.

Vinders nodded. "It's what she deserves."

Jenile walked across the flat terrain. From beyond a far tree line, other Sarryn appeared. They surrounded Jenile, as though welcoming her into their herd. Soon, bipeds emerged from between the trees. Some mounted the backs of the wild Sarryn. Noland wondered if Franz' pet, that Mr. Huggs, was among them. He watched Jenile until she merged with the mass of bipeds and Sarryn. Until she disappeared among them, a biped riding on her back.

Those to his left and to his right dispersed, leaving Noland alone with Franz atop the low hill overlooking the now-empty field.

"She's gone," Noland muttered, and glared at Franz. The old uncle had lost his bid to lead the tribe. Noland thought he knew why. The elders were on their way out. And he didn't care. Whatever happened to Franz was of little consequence compared to what had happened to Jenile.

Was this what Jenile wanted? Noland wondered. Though he'd often heard of the North's inclination to exile criminals, he knew he'd never really understood the practice. Barbaric. Worse than outright execution. Did these northern tribes think exile more desirable than imprisonment in the south?

A thought crossed his mind. Had Jenile found the home she wanted? Franz' pet biped had his home as well. He imagined that

that was who rode atop the filly's back when the herd ran for the woods.

Noland harbored a grudging happiness for them. Those feelings blossomed into well-wishing, even if this wasn't the outcome he'd imagined when he first ventured north. He didn't understand these Sarryn very well, he told himself. Even though they were all descendants of ancestors who conquered this planet, wresting it from the once-ruling bipeds.

*After a long and successful career as a software developer and technical architect, **David Castlewitz** has turned to a first love: writing in all its many forms, especially SF and fantasy. He's published stories in Future Syndicates II, Farther Stars Than These, SciFan, Martian Wave, Bonfires and Vanities, Summer of Speculation: Catastrophe, as well as other online and print magazines.*

amazon.com/s?i=stripbooks&rh=p_27%3ADavid+Castlewitz

Heritage from the Stars
By Derek Spohn

Gurlag held his breath as a pair of Zuma guards trotted past him. He struggled to make them out beneath the faint light of the world's twin moons. There was no telling how many other guards Medigo, Gurlag's master, had sent after him. He couldn't allow them to drag him back to Medigo. Not after he had learned that there were others like him. He had suspected it since he was a child, but now he knew for certain that he wasn't alone. Gurlag would find out who he was and where he came from.

Where was the vessel the others had travelled in?

"Where are you, you filthy beast?"

Gurlag was hooked back into the present by the arrival of more Zuma guards.

What should he do? They were only a short distance away from the bush he hid behind. He didn't stand a chance at outrunning them. The Zuma had four legs versus his two. Nor could he outfight them. They were shorter than he was, but they each had four arms.

One of the Zuma guards kicked the bushes Gurlag hid in. Gurlag bit his knuckles to keep from screaming.

"Medigo will have our wings if we go back empty-handed." The guard said. Its companion clacked its mandibles together in its version of laughter.

As soon as the Zuma guard turned away from the bush, Gurlag made a line for the nearest tree.

"Catch him!" One of the guards called out. Gurlag didn't understand why the idiot didn't chase him down himself. It couldn't have been that big of a surprise to the guard.

Gurlag jumped a few feet into the air and wrapped his arms and legs about the tree. He climbed. It was only a couple of seconds before a guard dug its claws into the soft flesh of his ankle.

"I got the little devil!"

Gurlag clung to the tree until the bark drove beneath his fingernails. A bird fluttered its wings and drew his gaze upwards. With a final heave, he reached for a small branch. The branch snapped off in his hand and he lost his grip on the tree.

The guard flung Gurlag against the ground. Panting, Gurlag bolted upright and jabbed at the guard's compound eyes with the stick. The guard screeched and raised its arms to its injured eyes in time to catch a drop of green blood.

Gurlag hurled the stick at the second guard. The guard slowed to dodge the projectile. Gurlag scrambled up the tree.

He didn't stop until he reached the top.

Gurlag watched in satisfaction as Medigo followed his guards to the base of the tree that he was in. He waved at the Zuma. Medigo ignored him.

Medigo wasn't as rich or influential as he made himself out to be. When it came to anywhere after the next town over, Medigo's money and power was no more than a speck of dust on a beach. Medigo had enough self-insight to understand this. After all, it seemed that Gurlag's purpose was to give his master an outlet for his insecurity.

Medigo chatted with the four guards in a voice too low for Gurlag to make sense of. Gurlag swung his legs about the branch he straddled. Medigo craned his neck up to meet Gurlag's gaze. "Gurlag, come down now and your punishment will not be too severe."

"Tell me more about the ship that landed near the capital the other night." Gurlag said.

Gurlag had awoken the day before to the sound of Medigo arguing with one of his guards. Growing up, the Zuma told Gurlag that, after the gods scraped him together from mud, they rejected him for looking too bizarre. But the conversation Gurlag overheard sent a shiver down his spine.

The gods didn't cast Gurlag away. The Zuma stole him from his people after his ship arrived from the heavens. Medigo had said his people were back for him. Gurlag had to find them.

At last, Medigo spoke up. "If I tell you then will you climb down from there?"

Gurlag paused to think it over. "Yes, of course."

"How do I know you're not lying?"

"How do you know I'm not telling the truth?"

Medigo threw his upper arms into the air in a gesture of exasperation. "If you hadn't been such a struggle for me to get ahold of, I'd have my guards chop down this tree right here and now." Then, as if he remembered the guards were still there, Medigo turned to them. "I want at least one of you here at all times until that thing decides to come down from there. You can work out the shifts yourselves."

Medigo weaved through the trees towards the village.

The guard's snoring woke Gurlag about midday. He thought about dropping a shoe on the Zuma's head to get it to shut up but decided to spare his feet.

A pair of two-legged creatures stepped into view. They had clothes wrapped about them from their ankles to their shoulders. The Zuma only wore clothes to protect themselves from the elements. Save for the worst weather, Gurlag was only ever given rags to wrap about his waist.

Then Gurlag saw past their clothes and realized they were the same species he was. He would have noticed it sooner except he couldn't remember having ever seen anyone who looked like him. They must have been from the ship that landed near the capital. Gurlag fidgeted on his branch. He was growing too eager to stay put any longer.

"Hey!" He called to the pair. He was beyond caring how the Zuma guard might react.

The two figures looked up at Gurlag and, for the first time, Gurlag met the gaze of another member of his species. The man's face was pale as snow. He had dark hair and a beard speckled with white. His cheek bones were high, stretching his face in a way Gurlag never believed possible.

The woman reminded Gurlag of a beautiful sunrise. Her skin was tanned as gold as her hair was. His heart skipped a beat as she looked back at him. He had an urge to ignore the Zuma guard and climb down to greet her.

The pair seemed nowhere near as excited to see him as he was to see them.

Gurlag was too eager to wait any longer. He shimmied down the tree's trunk.

"Stay where you are." The voice sounded higher in pitch than his. It must have been the woman. Her voice sounded as majestic as a bird's music. There was hesitation in her voice, as if she didn't have full command of the language she used.

"What?" Gurlag looked down in time to see the guard stir. It craned its head about in the direction of the newcomers. Once it saw them, it raised its sword over its head and rushed at them.

A flash of light spewed from a device in the man's hand. The guard stopped in its tracks and collapsed in a heap.

Gurlag dropped the rest of the way to the ground and ambled over to the pair. His smile gave way to a frown as soon as he saw the woman's expression.

"You idiot," she said. "You could have gotten us killed."

Gurlag couldn't meet her eyes. "I'm sorry."

"Yeah, I bet you are."

"Rosa," the man said, "Drop it."

She rolled her eyes.

The man stretched out an arm to Gurlag. What was Gurlag supposed to do with it?

The man shook his head and pulled his hand back to his side. "Right. Alien culture and all that." He said. "Anyway, I'm Isaac and this here nuisance is Rosa."

"Are you from the ship that landed near the capital?"

"No, but we're friends of theirs." Rosa said. She pointed to the sky. "We come from way up there and it's time to blow your freakin' mind away, kiddo, because that's where you're from, too. It's time to take you home."

Gurlag felt lightheaded. He raised a hand to steady his head. It didn't help much.

"Rosa, we talked about this." Isaac said. "You can't keep breaking the news to them like this. You have to be gentle."

"But it's fun to watch the look in their eyes."

Isaac put a hand around Gurlag's shoulder and led him away. "We need to get away from here before the guard wakes up. I had my gun set to stun when I shot him."

Rosa tugged at a sac on her back. Her hand came back with a

bottle in it. She handed it to Gurlag. He gulped it down until it was empty.

"Rosa, I'm surprised." Isaac said. "That's the first practical thing you've done since we met Gurlag."

"I can be helpful when I want to." Rosa said, a hint of a smile on her face.

"How do you know my name?" Gurlag asked. He felt better already.

Isaac reached into a pocket and pulled out an instrument with a reflective screen on it. He tapped the screen and it lit up. Isaac pointed to a red light on the screen. "That's you." He pointed to a green light next to the first one. "This is me. Your mother wanted an easy way to track you and the others in case you wandered away while you were still kids. You all outnumbered her a few dozen to one. So, she put tracking chips in each of you. When she realized she couldn't protect you all from the Zuma, she contacted us. The tracking chip didn't tell us your name, but we've been keeping an eye on things."

"Tell me about my mother." Gurlag said

Rosa, who had edged further ahead, walked backwards so she could look at Gurlag. "Easy there, kiddo. We don't want to repeat ourselves, so we won't say a word until we're aboard the ship. Then you can go gaga over the sight of our shiny buttons. Just don't press the big, red one. That one blows up the ship."

Gurlag's eyes grew wide. "What?"

"Rosa," Isaac said. Then, to Gurlag, "See that twinkle in her eye? She's trying to get a reaction from you. I've tried to guide her humor on the straight and narrow for years, but I suspect she's incorrigible."

Gurlag cast a glance at Rosa, then looked away a little too fast. She giggled. He felt his cheeks redden.

Isaac clamped a hand over Gurlag's mouth. "Look ahead but stay calm." Isaac whispered.

They stopped at the edge of the forest, where the tight-knit trees gave way to a field. A clunky, mechanical vessel rested in the middle of the field. How could that take them to the heavens? Its edges were rough, and it looked nothing like the oversized bird he anticipated. But he had never seen a craft made to travel heavenward, so he couldn't know what to expect. A sudden wave of disbelief washed over him. If it weren't for the fear of being taken back into captivity, he would have long since fainted.

A dozen Zuma crowded around the vessel. They were decked out in the regalia of the capital. The Zuma used their spears to try to pry open the vessel's door. They weren't making any progress against the reinforced frame.

The leader of the king's men clacked his pincers together to get the Zuma's attention. "The devil himself couldn't break into this ship. Grab the fuel. We'll torch it to the ground."

"Hey, you overgrown bugs, didn't your mothers ever teach you not to start a fight you can't finish?"

The Sun glared in his eyes. A cloud passed by and he saw Rosa. She held a weapon like the one Isaac had used earlier to knock out the Zuma guarding the tree Gurlag was in. She raised her weapon and pointed it at the captain.

The captain trotted over to Rosa. He didn't blink when Rosa centered her sidearm on his forehead. Gurlag started forward, but Isaac gripped his forearm and tugged him back. He glowered at the older man. "The king's guards won't tolerate her threats."

"Give her a moment." Isaac said. "If things go sour, I'll back her up."

"If things go sour, it will already be too late for her." Gurlag said. But when Isaac relaxed his grip on Gurlag's arm, Gurlag stayed put.

Gurlag struggled to hear Rosa against the rising wind. "You think I won't do it just because you were sent by his majesty, King Ralkor? I couldn't care less."

The Zuma captain reared onto his hind legs. "You don't frighten me, human. I would feed you to my family, but I don't have that luxury. King Ralkor ordered me to take my men and capture all humans we come across. He couldn't resist the price that the merchants pay for your kind."

The Captain lunged forward. Rosa fired a shot, but the Zuma knocked her arm up in time for the shot to stray into the air. The Captain tossed Rosa over an upper arm, ignoring her as she flailed her legs back and forth.

The Captain dropped back onto all four legs and turned to Gurlag. Gurlag looked around and saw he had, without realizing it, started to run across the field to meet the Zuma. He stopped in his tracks and felt his legs shudder. He wanted to free Rosa. He couldn't allow the Zuma to steal away the first woman he had ever met. But, at the same time, he was afraid.

"Don't stop there, Gurlag." The Captain said

Gurlag grimaced at the mention of his name. The Zuma Captain clacked its pincers together in pleasure.

"Yes, I know your name, human. We do our best to keep your kind isolated from one another. Only a couple of you are ever to be in a province at a time."

Gurlag never heard Medigo or his guards mention other humans. Against his better judgement, he found that the Captain had aroused his curiosity.

"How many others are there?" He asked.

"I'll tell you everything you wish to know if you come here." The Captain said.

Gurlag hesitated. Isaac had disappeared. It was up to Gurlag to save the day.

"The sooner you come here, the less I'll make you suffer." The Captain said, with a growing edge to his voice.

Hands trembling, Gurlag started forward. Rosa shouted from behind the Captain's back for Gurlag to stay put. Her voice sounded muffled. He continued forward as if he hadn't heard her.

Sunlight reflected off Rosa's dropped weapon. When he was close enough, Gurlag feigned tripping over it. He took most of the fall with his hand, but a little bit of grass found its way into his mouth. The Zumas clacked their mandibles together in laughter.

"What a clumsy human."

Gurlag spat out the grass. He bolted upright, grabbing Rosa's weapon in the process. He aimed it at the Captain's head as Rosa had. He squeezed the trigger as he had seen Isaac do and roared. The Captain's head exploded in a cloud of green mist. His body crumpled to the ground.

Gurlag shook a fist at the remaining Zuma guards. "Any of you uglies want some?"

The Zuma scurried away. Gurlag offered Rosa a hand. She smiled and took it.

"You're not too bad with that thing." She said, taking back her weapon. "Especially for someone who's spent most of his life with such a primitive culture."

Gurlag frowned. "They're not primitive. Just different."

Rosa shrugged. "Suit yourself. Where'd Isaac run off to?"

"Over here!" Isaac stood up from behind a bush.

"Where the hell have you been?" Rosa asked.

Isaac sighed. "I'm sorry, but the mission doesn't call for us to risk our lives. Both of our sidearms are low on juice. If those overgrown bugs had stormed us, we'd all be dead. No sense there."

A tear welled up in Rosa's eyes. "So, you left me for dead? You backstabber!"

Gurlag looked back and forth between the two as they spoke. What should he do? Isaac had proved himself a coward. Medigo would say that Isaac should be punished, but Gurlag was better than his master.

"We should leave you here." Rosa said. "How would you like that for a punishment?" Rosa tugged at Gurlag's wrist and led him towards the craft. He freed himself before they walked too far.

"No," he said. "He abandoned us, but that doesn't give us the right to abandon him."

Rosa glared at Gurlag until he looked away. "Then what do you propose? We can't risk him watching out for us. He'd sell us out in a heartbeat."

"It was a tough situation." Isaac said. "I said I was sorry. What more do you want from me?"

Gurlag and Rosa turned towards Isaac and spoke at once. "Shut up!"

Gurlag sighed. "Your weapon stunned the Zuma who was guarding me. Can't we stun him?"

Rosa shrugged. "Have it your way." She aimed her sidearm at Isaac and adjusted a dial on it.

Isaac's eyes bugged out. "Wait-"

Rosa fired her weapon. There was a spark of light and Isaac folded onto the ground.

Gurlag dragged Isaac's still form into the metal craft. Three humans dressed in the same ragged, slave cloths that Gurlag wore waited inside. Two of them waved at him. One of them was a woman a few years younger than Rosa. The other two were young men about Gurlag's age. One of the young men slept with a snore loud enough to make it near impossible for Gurlag to think. The other young man shook his companion awake. He quit snoring and opened his eyes to smile at Gurlag.

"Gurlag, meet some of your siblings." Rosa said, tying Isaac to a support beam at the center of the craft. "Some of Gurlag's siblings, meet Gurlag."

Gurlag didn't understand how he could share blood with any of the other three. The woman's skin was as pale as Isaac's, versus Gurlag's dark skin. Her hair was fiery red. One of the young men had a complexion much like Rosa's. The man who had just woken up was short and stout, compared to Gurlag's tall, lean form.

"I told you it would blow you away." Rosa said. She sat down behind a large screen. "Now quit gawking and sit down. We've got to get back to orbit"

The craft didn't fly like a bird. It shot straight up with enough power to nail Gurlag to his seat cushion. Gurlag, not the Zuma, was descended from the gods. The Zuma didn't have vehicles powerful enough to send them into the sky.

But if other humans could make such things, then he could make them, too. He was no god, and they were as mortal as he was.

Rosa spoke to them as she piloted the vessel. "When our ancestors saw this planet, it seemed like the perfect place to start a colony. The air was breathable and there was liquid water."

As if trying to plead a case, a light clicked on in her eyes. "You have to understand; our ancestors had no way to tell there was already a civilization here. If we'd sent probes to investigate this planet, it would have upped the price too much. So, we told each other how improbable it would be to find intelligent life."

"The craft we sent carried a hundred children, fifty males and fifty females." She continued. "You were to be raised by a robot, an artificial intelligence, until you were old enough to take care of yourselves. It would have worked, but the Zuma found you when you were a couple years old. They traded you off as status symbols amongst their elite. They destroyed the craft that brought you here and the robot that raised you. They gave you new names, names reserved for their pets."

Rosa paused and looked at each of them in turn. "We sent a ship to speak to King Ralkor, but he refused to listen. So, we took matters into our own hands. We sent every available craft down to the surface to help free you all."

Gurlag raised a hand. It all seemed too magnificent to be true. Artificial intelligence? A heritage not from the gods, but from another star, filled with people like him? No matter how fantastic the concept seemed to him, Gurlag clung to it as if it were his lifeline. No matter how bizarre Rosa's story seemed, he believed it. The

Zuma had told him he was an outcast. Gurlag needed to believe otherwise.

He waited for Rosa to acknowledge him before continuing. "If it's so expensive to send people from one star to another, how did you come to be here?"

Rosa smiled. "We learned to build better ships cheaper. No offense, my friend, but the science behind it takes years of studying to comprehend. I don't understand it myself, so I can't teach you."

Someday Gurlag would build star crafts, no matter how many years it took him to master the trade. He was capable of more than the Zuma gave him credit for.

There was the sound of a bump. Rosa turned around and made a curt bow in her seat. "We're docked. Thank you all very much. I'll take your tips as you head for the exit."

The door hissed and popped as it slid open. Gurlag's head spun. His stomach felt queasy. He ignored the sickness as best he could. He unclicked his seat belt and kicked off towards the exit. He couldn't walk. He could only float about, pushing off the walls and floor as best he could. It was all too much to believe. Yet, he did believe it because he trusted his senses and knew he wasn't dreaming.

The sight that greeted Gurlag once he floated into the corridor of the larger craft was duller than he had hoped to find. The walls were unpainted metal. The air didn't smell sweet and filled with the joys of tasty morsels, but bland, filled with little more than human sweat. Some heaven.

As soon as he moved about, he found that this bigger ship they had docked with allowed them to move more easily, no floating required. One by one, the other freed captives brushed past Gurlag and headed down the corridor.

"Where are you going?" Gurlag called after them.

The short, stout man glanced back over his shoulder. "Rosa said there's a viewscreen up ahead."

Gurlag hurried after them. Before long, they reached a vast chamber with a viewscreen as wide as a house. Gurlag gasped. A large crowd had already gathered to see the incredible sight before them.

The viewscreen looked out upon the stars. Which star had his ancestors come from and which ones were his race destined to conquer?

Rosa patted him on the shoulder. "You're taking this pretty well. There have been others freed who've broken down from the shock of the technological leap. It's as if we've taken you a couple thousand years into the future."

"It's like a dream." Gurlag said. "But I've never trusted the Zuma's lies about my origins. I'm ready to take pride in where I come from. I'm not ashamed anymore."

"Come on," she said, leading him away. "We picked out a list of names for you and the others we freed. I can show it to you if you'd like a name that comes from your people. From us."

"I'd love to do that." Gurlag's face brightened. It didn't matter what his name was going to be. All that mattered was that the name would be his to choose.

###

Derek Spohn's work previously appeared in Alien Dimensions #10 and #19. He graduated in December of 2020 from Old Dominion University with a double major in Spanish and Creative Writing. He is now an intern with the Muse Writers Center in Norfolk, Virginia.

amazon.com/s?i=stripbooks&rh=p_27%3ADerek+Spohn

Penthus
By Francis W. Alexander

If only LeBron Tate could get himself out of this hellhole and teleport back to the donut-shaped satellite that was Space Force headquarters. The Earthling did not want to be on this huge rock the agency had named Penthus. Having been born on Spaceport Gamma, he was not used to the gravitational effects of living on a terrestrial planet.

He felt a sharp sting in the middle of his back. "Keep moving, Slig!" the Cryon barked. It still irked him that this race of beings had attacked his ship and made the crew into slaves. They might be masters of the Mage who were the inhabitants of this planet, but they were not his masters.

As he trudged with Zygote and his other Mage work crewmates to the mines, his limbs aching, he thought about his predicament and wondered why he had volunteered to go on this trek to discover new worlds.

The rocky area he slogged through reminded him of the old movies of slaves working the mines in Roman times. The setting sun highlighted the cliffs on the mountains surrounding him. Patches of grass and plants, some of which he had never seen before, lie along the rock and boulder-strewn path. A mint-like scent was his only pleasure.

As he entered the mine, light beams and shards of light from the torches guided him to his work spot. LeBron followed the Cryon and was followed by Zygote and the other work detail.

As his eyes got acclimated to the light, he saw Commander Kuma

Bloom.

LeBron was elated to be possibly working in the mines with Commander Bloom. He hadn't seen her since the time one week ago when the Mage somehow rescued them. The Cryons had fiercely attacked his ship and things looked hopeless. One moment, the ship was rocked in explosions with life support slowly running out. The next moment, LeBron was in the care of Zygote and his fellow Mages. A day later, the Cryons had come, taken the Space Force crew from their rescuers, and placed them on work crews. He found himself with a crew of Mages and wondered if his other shipmates were suffering the same fate as he.

Perhaps, if he could approach the Commander, he'd get some information. Had she heard from the other crew members? What were her orders for them in these trying times? He grinned as he approached her. She weakly smiled back.

"Commander," LeBron said. He felt a Slight sting on the back of his head.

"Silence, Slig!" the blue-skinned Cryon barked.

"Your work is done," a pink-skinned Cryon said to Bloom. He grabbed her arm and shoved her into the other Mages, "Get to moving!"

"Dig!" the blue-skinned Cryon said to LeBron. To his left stood Zygote. The Cryon positioned himself to his right.

"I know," Zygote said to LeBron. "You are confused. I will tell you some things."

LeBron furrowed his brow and displayed the stinky face. As the Mage spoke to him loud and clear in spite of the blue Cryon standing so close to them.

"Won't they punish you for talking?" LeBron Tate whispered.

"The Cryons, as you call them, are cyborgs from a planet far from here. They call themselves xyloogechunufoos il DeUn. They are guided by what you call artificial intelligence."

We made a mistake," Zygote continued, "and made them crash on our moon. So now, we're helping them to leave."

LeBron thought about why he called them Cryons. They looked like crayons with their colorful wax-like skin and pointed heads. He also called them Cryons because their language seemed to omit the letter "a".

"Why help them to leave?" LeBron was confused.

"One," the Mage said, "we are nonviolent and have no desire to harm them. Two, like you, they will leave and forget they ever came here. And they will not come back."

LeBron shuddered at the thought of the Cryons coming to Earth. He thought about Meeshama, his crew's female cyborg. What had the Cryons done to her? Did she give them any information about Earth or the Space Force? Then, he thought about them talking when they should be quiet and why the Mage didn't answer his question.

"Why, at this minute," LeBron asked again, "are you not being punished for speaking? Why aren't they whacking me for speaking?"

"They don't know," Zygote chuckled, "that we are talking."

Why don't they know? thought LeBron.

"Because we won't let them," Zygote said.

It disturbed LeBron Tate that the Mages seemed to be able to go into beings' minds, both his and the cyborgs. He was disturbed more that they could keep the Cryons from knowing they were talking and yet had not gotten rid of the cyborgs.

Don't worry. You'll be home soon, LeBron thought. He knew that Zygote had to have placed that thought into his mind because he did not do it. He'd had no hope of ever returning home.

"Am I really here?" LeBron said. "How do we know you haven't put other thoughts into our heads?"

"You don't," Zygote responded.

LeBron Tate awakened with sore arms and legs. He was amazed the Cryons had not yet come and ordered him to work. After nine straight days of working, it looked like he was finally going to get a much-needed day of rest after working nearly ten hours a day.

He opened his eyes and was stunned to see Zygote looking down at him. Something about this alien was familiar, but he could not put his finger on what it was. All he knew was that the alien was freaking him out.

"Do you," LeBron asked, "always stand over a person while he's sleeping?" He looked at Zygote and had the feeling the Mage was floating rather than standing. As he saw it, the Mage were bipeds who stood on average six foot six, were dressed like savages and had powers.

"It's so sweet seeing you beings sleep." Zygote grinned with his thin slit mouth forming a u-shape. "And yes, I am familiar to you. Do you remember your childhood? Remember your imaginary friend?"

An image flashed in his mind. A memory. LeBron saw himself in that horrible room at the children's home on the Spaceport. Early that morning, he had awakened to the sight of a baby hovering over him. It widened its arms as if seeking to be picked up and then spoke. A pleasant feeling overcame him. He felt safe, unlike the times he did with the bullies in the place. The baby spoke and called itself "Zygote", a term he had learned in school. LeBron had a feeling he was with that baby now and his skin began to crawl.

"Let's go take a walk," Zygote said.

"Won't the Cryons have a problem with us fraternizing?"

"We are just ignorant natives," Zygote responded. "The Cryons don't think we can communicate with you."

"I… I don't understand."

"Let's take a walk," the Mage said, "and I'll tell you more."

Tired, he did not want to get up. He forced himself off what would have been a mattress made of straw and reached for his clothes.

As he left his hut, a structure made mostly of a bamboo-like structure and straw, LeBron emerged into a bright day under the warmth of a yellow sun. His hut was positioned in rows with others in an area bordered by high walls. He was glad he decided to go shirtless and sported the blue shorts the Mage had given him. The Mage appeared to live like primitives. He got the feeling they had been like that for thousands of years, like the Andamanese peoples on the islands in India on planet Earth.

"You will learn a lot today," said Zygote.

The day looked like it was going to be the best one yet. Yellow clouds hung sparsely in the turquoise sky. It amazed him that there were no birds flying overhead. Matter of fact, he hadn't seen any animals, only plants. The night was when most of the plants displayed their bioluminescent colors.

As the two walked, a green Cryon headed their way. Fear and apprehension suddenly gripped LeBron. He hated and feared the cyborgs. Just a couple of days ago one of them had given him a painful shock with its stunner because he did not move immediately out of a cyborg's path. He abhorred their arrogance and would fight them if he could. He wanted to smash the skinny thing. It might be robotic, but it looked awfully frail.

"It's quite a lovely day today," Zygote said.

"Yes, indeed," LeBron smiled weakly. He watched as the Cryon approached, walking at a fast pace.

"Slig," the Cryon barked, "you will move!"

I wonder what the Cryons would do if I struck this one? he thought. He chickened out and moved out of the being's projected path. Zygote did not.

"Slimy stinking Slig! You know not to be in the route of your conquerors." With a sneer on its face, the cyborg kept walking at the same pace, moving as if he were seeking to step on and squash the Mage.

At any moment, LeBron expected to see the scantily clad native spring out of the way. But the Mage stayed put. Sweat collected on the back of LeBron's neck, his sign of fear. He had done that since he was a kid, his own embarrassing bodily function.

LeBron's jaws dropped when the Cryon walked around the Mage.

"Sorry for the intrusion," Zygote said, "but I made him go around us and made him think we had moved."

"You have some strong ESP? How did they conquer you?"

"Yes," Zygote said, "you have lots of questions. You will get your answers soon.

"For now," Zygote continued, "We have what you would call apportation, biokinesis, psychokinesis, scrying, and what we call Statekinesis, which is the ability to change and control matter."

"Change and control matter," LeBron asked. "Is that shapeshifting?"

"More than that," Zygote responded. "We can make your synapses stop working. We can halt the electrical impulses in the robots or change their messages."

As the back of the Cryon got smaller, a question emerged in LeBron's mind.

"With your ESP, you should have been able to know that the Cryons would come."

"That's clairvoyance," Zygote responded. We don't have nor need clairvoyance. As I said before, the Cryons came, and we made their ship crash on that moon up there. As we were helping them to repair their vessel, your ship happened to enter our space. Although their starship crashed, their smaller ships were able to attack you. We kept them from destroying you. We made them think they had killed most of your crew.

"Do, you read our minds all the time?"

"No, we don't," Zygote laughed.

"How powerful are the Cryons?" LeBron asked.

"They are all run," Zygote responded, "by one hive-like being. It is what you call artificial intelligence. They are ahead of you earthlings by a million years or more.

LeBron also learned from Zygote that his galaxy is close to the Mage's galaxy while the Cryons' galaxy is two galaxies away, in an opposite direction.

LeBron spotted another Cryon approaching.

"Sligs," it said, "You should be working!"

LeBron looked at Zygote.

"Perhaps," Zygote said in jest, "there was a glitch in their programming."

"We," LeBron said, "don't get days off? Will they let me dress for work first?"

Arms aching, LeBron continued to dig. Somehow, it seemed he had been dreaming about a day off. He looked down at his trousers. They were the green khaki-like pants the Mage had given him along with his green t-shirt.

"Are you toying with me," LeBron angrily asked. Him thinking he was having a day off and then finding himself at work was not funny.

Suddenly, he heard a rumbling from above. Zygote shoved him and he flew into and landed on the pink Cryon to his right. Moments later, rocks and boulders fell from above and formed clouds of dust that moved towards him. There had been a cave-in.

Coughing from the effects of the dust, he thought about the Mage's strength. Had not Zygote pushed him, LeBron would have been crushed.

"Get off me, Slig," the Cryon said, "Get off, dirty slimy Slig."

LeBron rose off the alien and noticed it had tiny wires and bone protruding from its leg. There were still torches lighting the place, and they appeared to be the only beings in the mineshaft. He called out anyway.

"Is anybody else in here?"

"Shut up, Slig!"

"Hey, creep," LeBron said, "if we are going to survive, we'll have to work together."

"Work with Slig?" the pink cyborg said, "I think not. You work for me!"

LeBron saw some heavy boulders he was sure he could lift. He was tempted to smash the thing in the head.

"Slig will not voice to me," the Cryon said.

"Shut up," LeBron said. "You can't even move. You need me like I need you. Matter of fact. Try to rise."

The cyborg lifted its arms as if it were going to strangle LeBron. It attempted to rise on the broken leg and fell.

"I will crush you, Slig," the cyborg said as it made another attempt to rise. Leaning forward, it collapsed on its forearms.

"Infinite loop, infinite loop," LeBron sang as the Cryon repeatedly tried to rise. "Admit it, Pegleg. You can't move. Now let us work together for our survival!"

Although tired from working, LeBron moved alone to the wall of rocks and boulders that had fallen.

"Hey!" he shouted. "Can anybody hear us?"

"Slig will be severely punished for not shutting up!"

Lebron searched for an opening. "Pegleg, come help!" he shouted at the Cryon. He moved some rocks and stones from where he thought the exit might be. His not getting out of the mineshaft was added to the hopelessness of leaving the planet.

Surely, he thought, *with the technology the cyborgs have, they should be rescuing us by now.*

"Work, Slig!"

Exhausted, LeBron crawled to a pile on his right, making sure he was a good distance from the Cryon. He lay against the pile. Hopelessness was being stranded alone on Mars while Earth went through a nuclear war. He stared at the cyborg. His eyelids got heavy.

A thought burst into LeBron's mind. *You are a photon.* LeBron did not know if he were in a dream or not, but he felt himself being lifted, floating, and then flying. He began to travel faster and faster until hitting light speed. He saw streams of light stretching, then streaking past him. Dead ahead stood a supernova. He attempted to change direction. Couldn't.

Be calm, Earthling.

Zygote, LeBron thought. *Is this astral projection?*
Yes. Enjoy.

LeBron watched in awe as he approached what appeared to be a nebula. He wondered if his mind was playing tricks on him. Perhaps he was on drugs. He noticed himself being surrounded by a migraine aura with its pulsing colors. He'd had plenty of those in his lifetime. Fear began to rise within him. The aura's colors pulsed faster and faster as he moved.

Stars, galaxies, and comets moved past him. Any fear that had gripped him earlier was leaving. Everything was beautiful, the universe his comfort zone. An object blacker than the space around it, beckoned. A black hole. He plunged into the object. Around him wiggled dark waves and lines. As if shrinking, he fell into one of the lines and found himself being sucked by a point. The sensation of falling through a kaleidoscope of colors enthralled him. The beauty he was seeing could enslave him forever, if he had any say in the matter.

Present? he thought. This is what is presently happening *in a galaxy far far away. Welcome to the Cryon Empire.*

LeBron sensed himself zipping around like a fly as he moved along the thousands of waxlike figures that were the Cryons. They carried with them a bazooka-like object that spat out a substance, a short gamma-ray burst obliterating both three-legged foe and armament. The beings they spared were herded into groups. "Move, Slig!" LeBron traveled to another area and saw three-legged beings were hopping on the Cryons and ripping them apart arm by leg. More Cryons entered the scene and blasted all in their path be it Cryon or foe. He zipped to another area where the Cryons were enslaving and enjoying their foe suffer from the harsh work conditions.

"Keep digging, Slig!"

With arms and legs blasting pain, the exhausted LeBron looked down at his aching blood-stained hands. He saw various bruises on his arms, an indentation where the cave-in had been, and a huge pile to his right. It was a sign that he must have been digging for quite a while – by himself. He was sure Zygote had put the traveling and battle scenes in his head. But that wasn't helping him out of his present situation.

"Help!" he shouted. "We are alive! Is anybody out there? You cruel, craven, creeps!"

There was no sign that anyone was digging from the other side.

"Dig, Slig, dig! Get your superior out of here!"

To his right lay a boulder. Though tired, he thought of mustering all his strength to pick it up and try to flatten the cyborg's noggin. Besides, he wanted to see what the inside of the thing's head looked like. He knew that Meeshama's body had small wires that supplemented its veins and arteries. Like other cyborgs of its type, the brain was mostly grey matter.

"No talking, Slig! Work!"

If he had a conscience on both shoulders, the evil one on the right was winning. After moving to the boulder, he attempted to lift it. The object was heavy. He willed all the adrenaline and anything else within to help him muster the strength. LeBron lifted the boulder over his head and slowly moved towards the fallen Cryon.

"There's two in here," somebody said.

LeBron turned around and saw a beam of light enter the mine and highlight the cyborg. He dropped the boulder and collapsed to the ground.

"Wake up, sleepyhead," Zygote said. LeBron snorted upon waking.

"What happened?" LeBron yawned and stretched. "One moment, I was being saved. The other, I'm here."

"You've had a nice long rest," Zygote smiled.

"I thought you'd never rescue us," LeBron said.

"If it were up to them, they would have left you to die in there. We convinced them that there were more raw materials needed for their ships. So, they decided to clear the debris and continue to mine."

"They didn't rescue us?" LeBron said looking askance.

"They think you're dead. We dug into the area and gave them a temporary brownout. They could receive no information except to help us dig you out of the mine.

"How long have I been here?"

"Two of your Earth days. Come," Zygote said.

Muscles and joints aching, LeBron pushed the covers off, rose from the bed, and followed the Mage through the hut's entrance and out into the yard. He heard roaring and things breaking the sound barrier. Above him were Cryon saucers shooting up towards space.

"They are leaving," Zygote said.

"Leave…. How? Will they be back?"

"No," Zygote said, "We've programmed them to forget they've ever been here."

"You went," LeBron said and scratched his head, "into their hive mind?"

"From their empire, they'll see this area," Zygote said, "as null space. A region to be avoided."

"And what about us?"

"You don't have to go home," the Mage said, "but your presence is not desired here."

The Mage turned and swept his arms in the direction of a wall opening.

"I have to get my belongings." He ran into the hut and looked around. Only the bed was there.

He moved out of the hut and asked Zygote, "Where is my stuff?"

The Mage looked at him in response.

LeBron looked down and saw that he was wearing his uniform. He walked to the exit and spotted one of the crew's Elon Exploratory craft landing. He turned and looked at Zygote.

"Will I ever see you again," he asked.

Yes, Zygote answered with a telepathic thought.

"Specialist Tate," a metallic voice, Meeshama's, said.

LeBron turned and saw Commander Bloom walking down the steps of the craft, followed by the cyborg. He turned one last time to glance at Zygote. The Mage was gone.

There was no sign of a wall nor life, intelligent or otherwise. He shook his head in disbelief.

"We thought we'd lost you," the commander said. She placed an arm around the taller man and turned to move back up the steps of the ship.

"We're leaving?" he asked.

"Yes," she said, "there's nothing of value here."

"Plus," Meeshama said, "the star is getting ready to supernova."

Onboard the starship, there was a buzz of noise. Everyone was talking except LeBron. He was thinking about what had transpired on his timeline.

He looked through the porthole. Instead of seeing a bulging star, he saw Zygote. It then changed to a eukaryotic cell or the zygote he learned about in school, and then into a bulging star. He then turned and moved towards his sleep chamber. The hibernation would enable him to age for only one year. He felt relaxed, feeling confident it would be a smooth trip back through the wormhole to the donut-shaped satellite that was Space Force headquarters one hundred light-years away.

###

Francis W. Alexander is getting back into publishing fiction after a brief illness. His most recent stories have been published in Alien Dimensions and Outposts of the Beyond.

amazon.com/Francis-W-Alexander/e/B00SZ2XF6Q

Communications Barriers
By Daniel R. Robichaud

"Is everyone all right?" Captain Junji Hasan asked before he even managed to pick himself up. Of course, the crew was not all right. Something had slammed into the ship, throwing everything into disarray. A red alarm lamp made slow revolutions over the exit. Smoke filled the air near the empty forward view screen.

The crew sounded off one at a time until three of his four bridge crew had spoken. Only silence, then. Dr. Nimmons must have slammed his forehead into his station's display. The screen showed a nasty, bloody crack, and the doctor's own forehead showed the organic mirror of that impact.

"Status Assessment?" Hasan asked, righting his overturned captain's chair. The safety harness was all but useless now.

"Wormhole Drive is inoperable," helmsman Carlos Churro recited. "Sublight drives are functional, but a little punky." It was the helmsman's favorite description for anything that did not respond within nanoseconds of receiving a command.

As the helmsman tested his forward acceleration, Hasan came to understand his meaning. The rockets were activating, but lag times ran to seconds between command and response. He shuddered at the ramifications.

Einstein's supposition was correct: The cap on speeds in standard space was absolute. In the universe that relied on the three axes of length, width, and height, the speed of light was the fastest anything could hope to go. However, the subtleties of shifting outside the three standard axes into multidimensional space allowed ships to move further in less time, with no need for relativistic oddities. The Wormhole Drives wrapped vessels in cocoons and tore out of the space where such caps existed, into that as yet still mysterious region of wormspace. If they could not dig into wormspace, then they were stuck with the sublight engines, fuel hungry rockets that allowed speeds up to 0.25c. Without the wormhole drives, they had to hope for some kind of nearby satellite or system. Otherwise, the ship would be stuck slogging along at 0.25c, taking decades or centuries. They had maybe one year's provisions.

"I'm reading heavy trauma to the electrical harnesses along the ship's outer hull," Boatswain Shitaka said, adding to the imminent danger. "We're going to need a major overhaul."

"Please, tell me we're close to a CORE post," Hasan said.

"Unknown," Shitaka said. "I'm not sure just where we are. The ship's receivers are getting no hits from wormspace or sublight location transmitters. I don't think the shipping lane location transmitters have crapped out. It's never happened before. So, it's safe to say that leaves it as a problem on our end. It could mean damaged receivers along the hull, or signal loss between the hull and the comps. The harnesses are a mess, as I've said, so I'm guessing the latter."

Hasan asked, "Anything on comms?"

"Sorry, sir," Lt. Mahri Doona said. She tapped at her keys, flipping through various channels, and then shook her head. "Comm systems are unresponsive."

"Can't we send an SOS?" Hasan asked.

"It's possible," the frustrated comm officer said, "but the handshake is not responding. I've switched it on, but I have no idea if it is even transmitting."

Hasan slammed a fist against the arm of his chair. "Someone want to tell me what they think happened?" he asked, knowing the one person with the real answers was lying dazed on the floor. "I need a report on this mess."

"Nimmons reported an unprecedented wave of cosmic radiation was inbound while we were in wormspace," helmsman Churro replied. "It seems to have sideswiped us and thrown us back into sublight."

"Cosmic tsunami," Lt. Doona said with a sigh.

"I've never heard of such a thing," Hasan said. "Anyone? Cosmic rad wavs in wormspace?"

"We still don't know even a tenth of what can be found in multidimensional metaspace, Captain," Shitaka said. "Maybe even less than that. It's the great mystery."

"Understood," Hasan said. "But I've never been a fan of mysteries, only profitable conclusions. This ship runs under a trader compact, after all." He squeezed his fist tight enough that his nails drew angry red lines along his palms. "We can't just putter along blind and hope for a solution."

Suddenly, a gentle knocking sounded along the hull. It was the steady, slowing sound of a combustion engine's cooling cycle, and it was quickly followed by the groan of submersible or deep space vehicles experiencing extreme pressure gradients.

"Do we have some kind of hull breach?" Hasan asked.

There were only a few reasons for pressure gradients of that sort, and of those possibilities, only one or two reasons seemed likely given their immediate situation. If the pressurizing atmo inside the ship was bleeding into space through one or more rents, then the hull would respond.

Shitaka shrugged. "I can't tell, sir. But the communication lines from the breach sensors passes through some of the damaged harnesses."

"How long for a visual inspection?" Hasan asked.

"Given full range of movement and perception, it would take about twenty minutes," Shitaka said. "This case, it's more because I'll need to wear an environment suit per the regs."

"We'll all need to suit up," Hasan said. "Let's move people."

It was shipboard safety regulations to suit up in preparation for entering dangerous depressurization situations. The environment suits were bulky things, manufactured with as much mobility as possible given the multiple layers of protection designed to resist extremes of pressure, temperature, radiation, atmospherics, or other dangerous environmental factors.

The crew suited up, and when they were done Lt. Doona and helmsman Churro guided the unconscious Nimmons into a suit as well. With the environment suits on, the sounds along the hull were no longer audible. The suits had built in comms allowing the crew to communicate back and forth, but there was no appreciable audio from outside the suits.

"All right, Shitaka," Hasan said. "Perform as quick an investigation as you can. We need to know if this tin can is going to come apart, and then we need to understand our options."

"Affirmative," Shitaka's voice showed faint hisses of interference. Before taking his leave of the bridge, he used the analog gauge near the door to judge pressure gradient on the other side. A thumbs up said that the corridor beyond was not yet experiencing depressurization. That was a good sign. He opened the door and disappeared through, closing it behind him.

"Now, what can the rest of us hope to accomplish?" Hasan asked. The crew volunteered for various tasks.

Doona dragged a new monitor replacement kit from the electronics storage closet. That kit included each of the tools and hardcopy instruction sheets necessary to perform a hot swap for the damaged monitor at Nimmons' station. She applied the spanner to the four restraining bolts holding the damaged unit in place, cranking the simple tool around with deft motions on each of the restraining bolts. She then levered the monitor free of its rack mounting, giving helmsman Churro access to the quick connect/disconnect cabling. The setup allowed the crew to perform the switch without powering down that deck station's computer system. So, the last items Nimmons had up were still on display when the new screen went live. The two crewmen levered this unit into place on the rack and reapplied the restraining bolts.

"My goodness," Churro said. "Will you look at those readings?"

"Cosmic tsunamis," Doona nodded. She shook her head. "Those are definitely cosmic energy tsunamis."

"Those sound like readouts on his last known item of interest," Hasan asked, as he finished strapping the unconscious crewman into one of the emergency landing harnesses. With Nimmons secured, the Captain plugged in the automated diagnostics and analysis pack into output port on the left shoulder of the Doctor's environment suit. That information fed into the still active medical system. "Are any of his sensors communicating current data, or as they as blind as the rest?"

"I will attempt to access them," Doona said. She quickly tapped at some of the keys on the interface and shook her head. "No. No. No," she muttered while slowly proceeding down a checklist. "No. No— wait."

"Is that reading what I think it is?" Churro asked.

"It is," she replied, "Can it be real?"

"What is it showing?" Hasan asked.

"I think the Phlog barometer is damaged," Doona said. "It has to be. It's showing levels that say we're still in wormspace."

"There's no way we can be," Churro said, "not with the Wormhole Drivers offline."

She shrugged and gestured toward the screen in the ta-da gesture of someone confirming she did not make the sensors or station comps, only read the results they presented.

Hasan asked, "Could that explain the responsiveness lag between your controls and the sublight engines response?"

"Those engines should not function inside wormspace," Churro said. "The interlock wouldn't allow them—unless we *are* in wormspace. If the Wormhole Drive is reading as down, then the interlock will not register a conflict and will allow the sublight engines to activate." As he spoke, his padded digits performed a few mathematical equations in the air. "If that's the case, then yes. The sublight engines are running as soon as we give them the command, but the effect is limited. Nullified by the Phlog outside."

When the first engineers and scientist tore wormholes from tri-ax sublight space into multidimensional space, they discovered the region was not the perfect vacuum that existed in tri-ax space. Instead, it contained vast volumes of a protein rich aqueous solution. Although the concept of a hypothesized Ether-like liquid that filled the space between stars and worlds in sublight space was debunked long ago, one of the lead scientists dubbed the not-quite-void they discovered as the Phlog, a tip of the hat to that ancient, debunked term, phlogiston. Although essentially incorrect, the terminology stuck.

"I hope you're wrong," Doona said.

"Why?"

"Because—" Doona stopped talking and stared at the monitor for a moment before asking, "Did you see that?"

"What did you see?" both helmsman and Captain asked at once.

"There was a blip," Doona said. "From some of the other sensors. I wonder if they might not be overburdened."

"The flatline is not a flatline at all?" Churro asked. "But some kind of signal saturation?"

Doona said, "Yes."

"Can we set up a trigger to capture the readings if they blip again?" Churro asked.

"I will try," Doona said. She began to type away, making

occasional frustrated subvocalizations to let everyone know her lack of success.

"What were you saying before, Doona? About hoping we were wrong—"

"About being in Wormspace," she said, getting right back on track. "I hope not. Because if the interlock is letting the sublight engines run, then the SOS beam is the CORE Standard configuration that's optimized for sublight space."

Hasan saw where this was going. "And Wormspace needs tight beams, right."

"Right. So, we might be sending out SOS messages, but they won't get far in the Phlog medium."

"With the rains," Hasan muttered, "come the hurricanes."

"Captain," Shitaka's voice was downright ghostly, thanks to the interference in his comm signal. "I've got something strange here."

"Have you finished the hull inspection?" Hasan asked, glad to be involved in some kind of activity.

"Well, mostly," Shitaka said. "I can't seem to access airlock nineteen or the maintenance conduit on that side of the ship myself. But I've got a live video feed."

"What are you seeing, Shitaka?" Hasan asked. The only response from the Boatswain was static. "Shitaka, do you read?"

"It happened, again," Doona said. "Did you see the blip that time?"

"I did. You think it's maybe every sixty seconds or so?"

"Closer to ninety." Doona sighed. "I think I've set up a data isolating trigger. Now, we wait."

Time tolled by in slow motion, one second stretching past the next at a crawl. Hasan called for Shitaka a few times more.

"Captain can you hear me?" The interference made Shitaka sound far away. Not just three hundred meters across the ship, but entire kilometers off. A world away. "Captain?"

"I hear you, Shitaka. What's the situation?"

"Something's outside the ship," Shitaka said. "Something's out there and hanging on."

Hasan banged a palm on his helmet as though it might somehow adjust the comm to make the messages more sensical. "Say again?"

"Something's—"

Shitaka's comm went dead midsentence.

Doona said, "And there's the blip. Ninety-two seconds since the last—"

"What are those numbers?" Churro asked.

"The tsunami," Doona said. "They're the tsunami numbers." With a few deft button presses, she pointed toward the monitor. "See?"

"What is happening?" Hasan asked. "Is Nimmons comp fried or what?"

"The cosmic tsunami," she said. "The flood of energy that hit us?"

"Is another one inbound?" Hasan asked.

"Not if these readings are correct," Churro said. "I'd say it never left."

Hasan wished someone would start making some sense. "*What?*"

"It's wrapped right around us," Doona said. "A little cocoon outside the one the Wormhole Drive manufactured."

"Captain!" Shitaka called, as his comm came back online. "Captain! Can you read me?"

"We hear you, Shitaka," Hasan said. "Say again about something outside the ship?"

"There's something outside the ship," Shitaka said. "I got a visual read from a crawler drone. "

The crawlers were maintenance bots with electric-over-hydraulic functionality, contained sensor packages and processors and heavy-duty mechanical components perfect for allowing personnel to perform assessments outside the ship without having to perform a dangerous spacewalk.

Shitaka continued, "Something is wrapped around us, holding us tight. It looks like a rainbow of color, some kind of energy bubble. But it's preventing a pressure bleed out airlock nineteen."

"Preventing?"

"It's not any kind of energy signature I've ever—"

The comm went dead again.

Doona dryly reported, "And that's another blip. Ninety-nine seconds since the previous."

"These numbers are impossible," Churro said. "Why would a wave of cosmic energy and radiation stop and hang onto our ship?"

"Come in, Shitaka."

"I'm here, Captain. The energy outside. It's not behaving like mindless energy."

Hasan asked, "What are you saying?"

"I think it's trying to communicate, captain."

"*What?*"

"I think it's trying to communicate with us."

"How can energy be sentient?" Hasan asked.

Doona said, "That might make sense with these numbers."

After Shitaka returned from his inspection, Hasan ordered the active crew to assemble in the huddle room. It was a modest space with a table and chairs for ten possible occupants. Many of these were overturned following the earlier impact. But the crew put the space in order and then sat ready to participate in the impromptu meeting.

Although he wished he could override the safety code and have the meeting without the need for wearing the environment suits, regs were regs. They were stuck in the suits until they were out of danger.

"Let's entertain this notion and track it to a useful conclusion," Hasan said. "That some alien lifeform made of pure energy has attached itself to our ship after ramming us and damaging not only the area outside airlock nineteen, but the electrical harnesses, and various internal systems." The others looked at him and waited. "We need to establish some kind of communication. What are our options?"

"The drone registered different variations of EM radiation from the thing. These were not irregular or randomized, but regular adjustments over intervals between ninety and one hundred seconds in duration."

"Corresponding to the sensor blips Doona saw," Churro said.

"Do these EM variations correspond to any known form of communications we are familiar with?" Hasan said, already suspecting the answer to be a negative. His expectation was validated with silence and dark expressions.

"Actually," Doona said. "They do correspond to something. Even if there's been damage to the lines between my console's soft switch and the beacon, the system should have automatically activated the SOS routine when a cell death situation arose."

Hasan had hazy recollection of the term.

"The entire shipboard comp system was developed off neural network processes, effectively treating the ship's entire electrical system as one big brain," Doona explained. "When a human brain is threatened by something like stroke, damage to the brain, there follows a break in communication between healthy cells and the dead ones. This break in communications initiates certain protocols: namely, a programmed death impulse to generate enough scar tissue to prevent damage spreading further.

"The comm system has a series of checks with several critical systems. If the lines of communication fall, then a watchdog routine trips, forcing prearranged protocols including activation of the SOS beacon. That beacon fires off last known coordinates as well as a request for help every ninety to one hundred seconds."

"So, it's receiving our SOS?" Hasan asked. "And it's trying to respond?"

"It may well be," Doona said. "If we could rig up a receiver, we might be able to interpret the response. I doubt it would make much sense until we've had a chance to . . . decipher it."

"I still wonder about the why in this situation," Hasan said. "But I don't suppose we'll find that out operating, as we are, from a position of complete ignorance. Shitaka, can we convert one of the drones to be an audio receiver?"

"Better than that, Captain," Shitaka said. "We ought to be able to turn one into a complete audio transceiver: a transmitter and receiver. If our first effort is to hear what it's saying, then we might want to send messages later."

"We need to exercise extreme caution," Hasan said. "There are plenty of things in the universe that transmit comm frequencies that I would never want to blindly wander too close to. Black holes, for one, occasionally send out radio wave blasts. That doesn't make them friendly, however. They're still black holes."

They all agreed and went to work.

After four hours of intense work, Shitaka announced he finished a crude but effective conversion on one of the ship's crawler drones.

The ship's main comp could send commands to each of the drones. Unfortunately, the damaged electrical harnesses nullified this option. However, each of the crawler drones had a handheld unit for issuing commands, as well. The handheld units saw more use on terrestrial deployments than shipboard ones, but this was a special circumstance.

"Drone is deployed," Shitaka said. "Orders?"

"We don't know if the creature's transmitter or detector or whatever means it has for doing what it's doing is localized to any point," Hasan said. "So, let's start listening immediately."

As soon as he switched on the drone's receiver, a blare of noise passed through every environment suit's radio. Doona said, "Can you filter out background noise? Let's use low pass filtration."

Shitaka applied filtration to the data, and the result was profound. With the high energy noise eradicated, a pulsing signal emerged.

Doona counted off beats, and said, "That's definitely our SOS. Binary pulse trains that any CORE comm system will interpret as a call for help." Forty-five seconds later, the SOS came across once more.

"Is that the same signal?" Hasan asked.

A puzzled Doona said, "Yes, sir. It is."

"Didn't you say the SOS was deployed at ninety to one hundred second intervals?" Churro asked.

"It is," Doona replied. "I don't—

Fifty seconds later, the SOS message repeated.

"Of course!" Doona said. "The entity outside the ship is repeating the message back to us. It doesn't understand the words or the meaning, but it understands enough to know that we are not some lifeless hulk drifting in the Phlog. It knows we're . . . alive. Aware."

"That means it has to have encountered our kind of people before?" Churro asked.

"Or it has to have come into contact with our equipment," Hasan said. "There are AI controlled location transponders scattered along the shipping lanes in Wormspace as well as sublight space, right? They—"

"They communicate the same way!" Doona said. "So, whatever is outside our ship really *understands*. It's not just random energy, it's alive. It's had experience with our tech before." She breathed in awed silence for a while. "Captain, this is pretty big news. If there are more of these living tsunamis in Wormspace—"

"Let's not start speculating too much, Doo. Our necks are on the line here," Hasan said. "Hey Shitaka, can we send it a quick message? Something fast enough not to interfere with the SOS?"

"Like what?"

Churro suggested, "Hello?"

"Sure, using standard SOS encryption? I'll need a moment to convert it."

Before even half a dozen seconds passed, Doona recited the pulse train as a dozen or so binary values. "You can do that in your head?"

"I learned how back in Academy," Doona said, sheepishly. "It made tests quicker. And it makes regular routines quicker. SOS basic is an adaptation of CORE basic. Check my math if you want."

"I trust you. Let me program this."

"Send the message when you can," Hasan said.

After the ship's SOS passed through their radios, a new, brief message came across, and Shitaka said, "Message sent."

The response from the entity changed. It did not simply parrot the two messages the way it had been parroting the earlier SOS. Instead, it changed them.

"Well, that's gibberish," Doona said. "No, wait. It's not. It's—" She laughed. "It's a wormspace location transmission." She waited for the message to repeat to try to decipher it, but the entity went back to echoing the SOS, again. "We need to transmit the same 'Hello' message after the SOS, see if the entity will repeat that location transmission."

"Why?"

"I think it hears that," she said. A message beaming through the Phlog apart from our ship. Maybe it's trying to relay that information to us to . . . to help us out?"

"Will that help?" Churro asked.

"Sure," Hasan said. "If we know where we are, we might be able to figure out the best solution for our dilemma. Send a coded transmission tight beam to the relay, and have it pull in some rescue drones."

"But our tight beam transmitter needs an uninterrupted comm flow from the computer to the transmitter," Shitaka said. He then repeated the previous "Hello" transmission. "With the harness in as bad a state as it's in—"

"Shh." Doona recited the binary values as numbers, dialing them into a hand computer. She converted the values into meaningful information. "Looks like we're not far from Proxima Altair System."

"Then that's where we'll have to focus our tight beam."

"But sir!" Churro said. "We can't transmit!"

"Of course we can," Hasan said. "We've got a powerful transmitter surrounding the ship. If we give it the message in the proper configuration, then it will repeat it back verbatim. That high energy noise in the previous messages? The way it saturated the sensors at Nimmons' station? That tells me it's a *powerful* transmitter. And if it can echo the signals we send perfectly, there's no saying it cannot blast out a tight beam type signal pattern the way it does CORE standard."

Churro's voice got a bit of a whine when he started, "But Captain—"

"There's no reason not to try," Hasan said. "Is there?" No one formed a compelling argument, so Hasan said, "Let's do it, Shitaka."

Over the next hour, Shitaka and Doona generated the necessary message in the proper formatting and the correct frequency for the Phlog and loaded the tight beam to the drone. Before they transmitted it, however, Hasan and Churro had to isolate the power line feeding the SOS transmitter and cut it. When that pulse went silent, Shitaka commanded the drone to transmit the new message. The noise was shrill in their helmet radios, and worse when it was repeated verbatim by the energy entity outside. Shitaka repeated the process again, once per minute for the next three hours. He transmitted, the entity outside the ship repeated the transmission, and then they waited.

Then, something odd happened. The ship groaned and heaved. The transmission echoes ceased.

Hasan said, "I think the entity left us."

Shortly after, the rescue team arrived, latched onto the ship, and hauled it to Proxima Altair System for emergency repairs. The nightmare was over.

While they were grabbing a meal together in the Gateway Lattice station surrounding the ship repair yards, they got to talking about their experience. Of course, they were required to make official reports galore. A newly documented species was, as Doona speculated, big news. Especially since it was one of those rare creatures that could exist in multidimensional space.

However, when the crew got together over the meal, they did not repeat the dry interrogations they'd endured. Instead, there was a teasing of Nimmons for "sleeping" through the close encounter. Then, Hasan expressed his continuing confusion at the rationale for what they experienced.

"I think it's a case of an interstellar Samaritan," Churro said. "We had an accident. No one's fault. The entity didn't know us from anything. But for whatever reason it stopped it journey to make sure we were okay. It stayed with us until help arrived. Then, it carried on its way."

Unconvinced, Hasan shrugged and said, "I guess it's as reasonable an explanation as any."

###

Daniel R. Robichaud *lives and writes in Humble, Texas. His work has appeared in Spaceports and Spidersilk, G is for Genies, H is for Hell, Infernal Clock: Inferno, the May 2021 issue of the Flame Tree Press Newsletter, and parABnormal magazine. Forthcoming appearances include the Haunts and Hellions, The Howling Dead, Attack of the Killer ____, and Shark Week anthologies. His fiction has been collected in Hauntings & Happenstances: Autumn Stories as well as the Gathered Flowers, Stones, and Bones: Fabulist Tales, both from Twice Told Tales Press. He writes weekly reviews of film and fiction at the Considering Stories.*

consideringstories.wordpress.com/
amazon.com/Daniel-R-Robichaud/e/B00A7BIOVE

Sap
By M.P. Strayer

There was trouble brewing in 'V137'. Of course, I couldn't know how it would play out—with Mania, you never knew—but all the signs were there: irritability, malaise, chronic physical and mental fatigue. More and more he was tardy to his shifts. He was insolent. Indifferent. These were the symptoms I'd been warned about, in the seminar I attended after promotion to shift lead at the shop. These were the symptoms—so told the corporate psych appointed to speak at the seminar (a jolly, pink-skinned colonist who'd never skipped a meal in her life)—that signaled in our workers an imminent, spectacular, and often lethal breakdown.

The official term for the fits of psychosis suffered by shopworkers is *Dementia Sanguis.* But on Plant we just call it "Crimson Mania."

On paper it's my job to prevent the Mania from happening.

In practice I'm here to forestall it. And, when the inevitable collapse occurs, to minimize the damage.

I watched 137 come onto the line, late again. He said nothing as he passed the other donors, already plugged into their pods and awaiting the start of the day's business, went to the only unoccupied tank and eased himself back. His movements had the slow, careful quality of a person anticipating pain, like someone recently cured of some terminal affliction and still unused to it. The insides of the tanks were upholstered in a blue form-fitting gelatinous material that looked like padding but was in fact an aggregate of tens of thousands of microscopic syringes. As soon as he was settled the hatch swung shut over 137's body, so that only his head and feet remained exposed. He winced and faced forward. He hadn't said a word since clocking in.

Harlan, I thought. His name is Harlan.

That was something else. You were told at Orientation it was against spec for shopworkers to use their given names. Instead, you assumed an identification number assigned on arrival. But 137 had been insistent from the beginning. *My name is Harlan. I'm a human being, not a tool.* He answered to 137 if addressed by his superiors—like all of us, he desperately needed this job—but among his teammates he refused to respond unless called by name.

Harlan. I decided I would talk to him after his shift had ended. A bout of Mania was never a good thing, but with the Liaison scheduled to visit any time now an outburst could prove especially inconvenient.

I looked at the row of faces, looking back at me (all except 137), seemingly afloat above the metal hatches, pallid, beaded with sweat—then with a cheer I didn't feel I said: "Door's open, people. Let's give the suckers what they want."

In response they loosed a collective shout like a battle cry.

All except 137, who faced forward. Silent. Dour.

Plant is a moon orbiting the exoplanet BW 2213 w, first settled by the Venusix Corporation when interstellar imaging technology revealed within the satellite veins of a rare and valuable metal, one which enables certain machines on Earth to function more efficiently. There are twelve shops on Plant, and each shop contains a biome for the human workers it employs. Everyone who comes to Plant goes to work in either the shops or the mines, which were established during the Peaceful Trade Summits following First Contact, and new workers are shipped from the colonies on Earth on a per-need basis (which amounts to a more or less constant influx of people, as there is always need).

Humans cannot survive on Plant outside the biomes—if the atmosphere doesn't kill you, the indigene will—and a portion of every salary is used to cover the expense of maintaining room and board in alien territory. Most workers have families in the colonies they labor to support, sending back as much of their earnings as they can; and, as the process of transferring money from one solar system to another is costly—and to take a shuttle yourself even more so—

132

most people here have resigned themselves to spending the rest of their lives on Plant.

We must always remind our employees to think of it as service, never work, so advised the fat psychologist from the seminar. *And it is a noble service, we must remember—one that facilitates peace between humans and Mandrakes. In exchange our employees are provided with a means of caring for themselves and their loved ones, which is the very heart of dignity.*

Noble. Her exact word.

Unless you make the switch to management, the highest pay you can hope to draw as a shopworker is on the line, donating. This is because donors are integral to a shop's existence, but also because donors are most susceptible to Mania. No human who resides on Plant is immune to the effects, but the maladies of life as a donor are particularly acute.

When I came to Plant, I signed on as a donor. On arrival here I had nothing: no family, no assets: I hadn't cared, truly, whether I lived or died. All I'd known was that I could no longer bear to remain on the sun-blasted mega-slum that was Earth: mausoleum of everything I loved.

But it wasn't long before I saw the ravages of Mania with my own eyes, and it terrified me. My boss noted I possessed certain *empathetic* traits in regard to my fellow donors and, as my service record was impeccable, it was suggested I would make a good shift lead. As it happened, I agreed. So, when I was offered a promotion I jumped on it. It was known management had the highest life expectancy of any job on Plant.

I enjoyed my job, and I took it seriously. Indeed, as it was my duty to oversee the donors, so vital to our operation (in turn so important to our world), I saw my task of making them as happy as practicable for as long as I could as almost *righteous.* And, through the sheer blithe force of my naivety, I was able to stave off the Mania's advent within myself, despite the countless people I saw it consume.

I know now my contentment was rooted in ignorance.

Of course it couldn't last.

I led 137 from the line to the managers' office in back. Everything we passed—walls, ceiling, doors—was of clean blue-green metal. Now that he'd completed his shift, 137—like the other donors—had donned his black robe, and his bare feet left little ghost prints that swiftly evaporated on the smooth steel floor.

His knees quivered as he walked. When we were in the office with the door closed I sat him in a chair and connected him to the IV we keep for just this purpose. I saw his pallor darken. I waited.

When he'd recovered enough to speak, I said, "Talk to me Harlan. What's going on?"

"What do you mean?"

"I mean your performance is slacking. Not your ability to do your job—you're still one of our top donors, you know—but you've been late recently to almost every shift. And when you're here you snap at your co-workers. These changes are concerning. Has something happened we don't know about? Does this have anything to do with 093?"

V093 was our newest loss: a bearish and imperturbable donor who'd passed away on the line. He had not been in the throes of Mania, but there are other hazards to being a donor, and while death on the job is uncommon, it's not unheard of. I wondered if there was a link between 093's death and 137's attitude. Maybe, I thought. Hell, *probably*. But then—137 was insubordinate from the get-go.

"His name was James," said the donor quietly.

He would not look at me. I watched his eyes, far back in their sockets, rove the office. They came to a picture framed on a shelf above my head and paused. It was an antique photograph of my boss and his son, standing together with their arms around each other's shoulders, somewhere in the mountains, somewhere on Earth. You knew it was home because of the color of the sky. I wondered where exactly it had been taken… I had never asked my boss which colony he came from.

137 spoke. "Man, I just fucking hate this place."

"I understand."

He smiled. It was a cynical, weary smile, and there was no humor in it.

"I bet you do. That's your job, isn't it? To make sure we all know how much you understand? That you're one of us? You're here if we need you?"

"I *am* here for you, Harlan."

"Don't call me that. You have your specs. Use them."

"Okay, 137. Okay. Why don't you tell me what you hate about this place. Maybe I can help."

He scoffed.

"First of all, I hate that on Earth I had a name and here I have a number. I hate that the sky outside is always dark. And I hate that if I go outside, I'll die. I hate how everything here is made of metal or plastic. I hate that there's a rule for every single aspect of our lives."

"Those rules exist for your protection."

"Lotta good they did James, huh?"

"No system is perfect. 093 understood the risks of giving so much. And believe it or not he liked his work."

I was no longer amazed by my own capacity for pitilessness.

137 shook his head.

"No. He did not. What he liked was the comradery of the line. That's what you people don't get. And it killed him. He gave all he could to those fucking weeds and when he went the shop didn't even close for a shift."

All he could, I thought.

"Well," I said, "it sounds to me like this might not be the job for you. Have you thought about that?"

"Opposed to what?"

I spread my hands between us in a vacuous gesture, as if to say the possibilities were endless.

"I need this money," he said.

"There are other jobs."

"On Earth? Man, you been out here too long. There are no other jobs. Everyone in the colonies is trying to catch a ticket to Plant. Telling me to go home and try something else is the same as saying I should just go fuck myself and starve."

His voice was rising, his cheeks had flushed. Yes, there was trouble abrew in V137. I could see its advent in the glint of desperation flickering deep down in the darkness of his eyes, in his sunken face, his thinning hair and shaking hands. Mania. Soon it would have him, but in the meantime, I had a job to do and so did he.

"Tell you what," I said. "Why don't you take a couple shifts off? Head to R and R. Maybe you'll feel differently after you've had a chance to rest."

He shook his head again.

"I need this money. Can't afford to take shifts off."

"I'll talk to the boss," I said. "Maybe I can get you a little paid vacation. Would that work?"

"Sure," he said, but I could see he wasn't listening. He removed the IV from the permanent docking point in his forearm and stood from his chair. "Are we done?"

"Yes, 137. We're done. But get some rest. I'll let you know about that vacation."

"Sure."

He walked out the door.

I remained as I was. I thought about Harlan. I hadn't been there for his Orientation, so I didn't know the story of his life on Earth. I could always pull his file, but that was unnecessary. I already knew his story. I'd heard it many times. There were countless variations, but they all reduced to the same inevitable narrative. I could remember hunting through the foul hectares of the colony dump for edible scraps. The pang of shame, sharper than any hunger, as I set before my wasting wife a tin plate of blackened banana peels and called it *dinner*. Jhumpa. She had been the last of our family to perish in the unending famine. And I remembered that final night in the colony, before shipping off to Plant, sitting in the lightlessness of my empty hovel, at my bare table surrounded by empty stools. No, I didn't need to read 137's file to understand his motives.

The chairback where he'd sat was damp. I touched my fingertips to the moisture shining on the leather. The ends of my fingers came away wet. Looking at them I wasn't surprised to see my skin stained in a rusty film of red.

"I'm worried about V137. I think we should take him off the line."

My boss swiveled in his chair, frowning.

"Now? With inspection coming up? 137's got thirteen shifts before he's due a break."

"I know," I said. "But that's why I'm worried. I would hate for there to be an incident while the Liaison's here."

He considered. Watching him, I couldn't help but compare the man seated before me with his image in the photograph on the upper shelf. On Earth, my boss had been a hale young man, and his smile as he held his son was white and wide. Now he smiled seldom, his thistly hair was almost entirely diminished and his eyes, once confident and bright, had grown flat, insipid, and they seemed perpetually to be either worried or sad. As a General Manager with many years left on his contract, he bore the brunt of the responsibility for the shop's success or failure. And, as he was a good man, he was ever in the grip of one stress or another. Because of the amount of resources required to get new workers to Plant, not to mention supplies, shop managers are given monetary incentives—such as paid visits home—for pulling as much as they can out of as few of their workers as possible. This is not how the spec is written, but it amounts to the same. Ostensibly, such practices save on the costs of labor, but they hasten the Mania, and my boss was constantly torn between his need to meet corporate demand and his desire to keep his employees alive and well.

He said, "If you really think that's what's best. I trust you, 056. An incident while the Liaison's here is the last thing we need."

"There's more."

"What's up?"

"I said we'd pay."

His frown hardened. A good man, yes; but he could be *miserly*. Shops are given a budget for all manner of expenses relating to the workers and their quality of life—but whatever remains of it at the end of a quarter does not accrue or carry over but gets split between the managers as a kind of bonus. Ordinarily my boss wouldn't even deign to consider my request, but I thought in this case his fear of the Liaison might outweigh his greed. I was right.

"Tell 137 he's drawn ten shifts R and R on us. Ten shifts. But I better not hear one more complaint outta him for the rest of the quarter or it'll be your ass. Hear?"

"Heard," I said.

Blood. On Plant it's used synonymously with "sap." But on Plant sap is so much more than the living oil that powers our human machine.

Sap is the product rendered in the shops for consumption by the Mandrakes, the intoxicating and addicting effects of which were discovered during the short war between our species in the aftermath of First Contact. It was the creation of sap that led to the Peaceful Trade Summits. Sap is the brew of blood, marrow, hormones—basically, a complete sample of the bio-chemical infrastructure of a human being—leeched from donors on the line and served by tenders in the public sectors of the shops. It's the process of leeching this substance that provokes the Mania and, over the years, sap—and the whole vast web of industry by which it's contained: the shops, and the mines, and the corporation overseeing them—has become the single most important impetus of humanity's overburdened economy in the entire galaxy.

Sap. I stood on the line and watched as it was secreted from my donors, watched their faces as they gasped and cried out (the shops use a numbing agent to prevent donors from experiencing too much pain during their shifts, but this agent, like everything else on Plant, was strictly rationed and frequently in short supply), shouting words of encouragement back and forth as the pumps drained them away. It always got to me to hear the donors yelling their support for one another during our busiest hours. (We do not tell them to do this; it's just something they do.) The pumps have fail safes to ensure they cannot pull too much in a given shift, but the fail safes can be overridden and the flow of sap redirected from one tank to the next, as some donors are able to provide more than others, and sometimes the systems are imperfectly calibrated and the donors give too much anyway, as happened with V093.

James, I remembered, then pushed the thought away.

I would try to help my donors in the busy times by instructing the machines to stockpile quantities of sap during the lulls, which gave the team a slight reprieve when business picked up. Sap has a short lifespan, and this practice is very much against spec, yet every lead I know does it. But I couldn't allow it now, with the Liaison on his way. No. Until he concluded his survey of our shop we were operating by the books. And I was panged by the sights and sounds of the enterprise I directed. Looking at our newest arrival—a weeping young woman with curly dark hair and big gray eyes, fresh off the shuttle (her identification tag read V162)—I forced myself to hear the noise of her sobbing. Yes, the secretion hurt. I remembered the pain of it clearly. And I wished I could stop it. Knowing I neither could nor would. And as I had done in the midst of my conversation with 137, I thought: If you only *knew*. If you only knew what you actually gave…

I stepped away from the line. Stood where I could see through the observation window, into the shop proper, where the tenders ranged about with beakers of fresh sap, where the strange carnivorous beings known as Mandrakes drank and reposed. I looked into the semi-darkness of the feeding gallery and wondered when the Liaison would arrive.

I first learned about the true nature of the entity I work for after my promotion to management. It was at one of those corporate conferences shop managers are required to attend (a legal seminar, focusing on the liabilities inherent to the industry and the ways Venusix bulwarks itself against them), and my discovery happened quite by accident, but from that time onward I became aware of a certain irremediable *dimming* occurring inside me. I lost my self-assurance; could no longer meet my gaze in mirrors, in panes of polished metal. It was the irony of my life that the madness I had tried to avoid by accepting this job was now being quickened by my understanding of the job itself. My life assumed the texture of a lie, an absurd hypocrisy. I could sense poignantly that some fundamental aspect of my humanity was slipping away—drop by drop—loss after loss, shift after changeless shift.

I knew what my end would entail, the mechanism if not the details, and it felt inexorable, unavoidable, and my knowledge of the doom rushing towards me was only whetted by the sudden death of V093—known as James to 137, who'd considered the big man a friend—James, who, in his effort to alleviate the stress of his teammates, gave too much. I'll never forget that shift, when 093's eyes closed for the last time, and his chin lolled, and the alarms on his tank began to wail. I remember thinking that he was lucky. In a way, he'd been able to choose his fate.

It was shortly after 093's death that the trouble started with V137.

"All right fellas," my boss's voice scratched from the speakers in my helmet. "Ready?"

We were standing in the decompression chamber that divided the front of the shop from the back. I looked at him. I couldn't see his face behind the breathing mask.

"Yes sir," I said.

He looked at the Liaison, standing beside him. The tall faceless figure, anonymous in his suit and helmet, nodded curtly.

"Okay," my boss said. "Opening the doors."

With a heavy gloved finger, he tapped the password into the keypad on the wall. There came a pneumatic gasp and whooshing passage of atmosphere and the hatch slid open.

The physics of Plant are much the same as on Earth—it's the composition of the air that humans can't take—and as I stepped from the decompression chamber into the soft springy soil of the feeding gallery I looked as I always do when outside the shop's walls to the violent firmament roiling above, a churning whorl of deepest mauve and red-black clouds. There were no visible stars, no moon or sun. Beyond the far ramparts I could see the tops of trees, like stencils cut from the sky. I could not see the lights of the mine nearby, firing the undersides of the clouds—it's with the ore found in Plant's inner stratums that Mandrakes pay for the presence of the shops, and both shopworkers and miners are employed by the Venusix Corporation—but I envisioned the diggers, penetrating the skin of this mad jungled moon, down and down through the layers of rock, seeking that precious metal without which none of this would be.

The Liaison strode out into the gallery, my boss at his side. It was a slow time, and for that I was grateful. Sap acts as something of a sedative in the Mandrakes, but still I don't like to be around them. Surveying the floor I counted only five, and they appeared to be immersed in whatever it is sap does to them, sitting curled here and there like great glow-white rosebuds, yet oddly leonine, with their razor-like talons extending and retracting rhythmically in the lush, night-black soil.

I looked at these sleepy specimens, remembering excursions I'd made outside the shop's grounds, gazing in wonder at the tangled tracts of forest through the windows of an armored all-terrain vehicle. The Mandrakes I'd glimpsed out there bore small resemblance to those who came routinely to the shop—they were sleek as panthers, and they moved with a precise and liquid efficiency, flowing between the trees like mercury come to life. The weeds that frequented the shops were dense and sluggish by comparison; their vibrancy was lessened; it seemed they abandoned some essential component of themselves in exchange for the drinking of higher primates.

I recalled the corporate psychologist and how she'd described the work of the shops as *noble.*

I looked at the tenders parked behind the bar, idling at the wall of silver taps.

The Liaison was speaking with a customer.

In addition to enabling us to breathe while outside, the suits allow for limited communication with the Mandrakes. Amongst themselves, the weeds speak through a system of telepathy and chromatophoric changes; with us, psychic connection isn't possible, but the emissions of light that come from their bodies can be tracked, replicated and translated. I watched the Liaison's chest plate flash, saw a corresponding series of flickers from the skin of the Mandrake he was looking at. The Liaison's chest plate flashed again. I recognized the pattern as the weed asking for another drink. I saw the Liaison turn and gesture at the tender. The tender spun to the taps.

I imagined the drone of the pumps as they kicked on.

162, crying.

There came a disturbance at my back, not heard but felt—a brief palpable fluctuation in the atmospheric pressure behind me. I turned. I saw the hatch to the decompression chamber was open. And I saw standing silhouetted in the threshold a person dressed only in company shorts and an oxygen mask. Then I saw the knife.

It was 137. I don't know how I knew, but I did. I saw the system failure light burning above the bar, red and steady. I would learn later that he'd cut the lines from the taps to the tanks, spilling all that sap-in-progress in a scarlet tide across the floor. The red glow of the light glinted from the edge of the knife as 137 raised it into the air…

I had time to think: Too late… Then the donor drew the blade across his naked chest, and a curtain of blood unfurled down his front.

The breath froze in my lungs.

With the appearance of blood, a wind of change swept across the feeding gallery. From the peripheries of my vision I detected movement as all five of the Mandrakes swung their bulb-shaped heads toward the decompression chamber at the same time.

I saw a bulb open, revealing those awful recurving teeth. The swish of a pale white tail, like that of a housecat waiting outside a mousehole.

137 charged.

He barreled into the gallery, swinging his knife, and I dove to the side as he went by. The heads of the Mandrakes swung with him, tracking his course. He was going for the Liaison. I saw it then. Mania nearly always culminates in the suicide death of its victims, but an attendant murder or two was not unprecedented. So that was his plan. He would die himself, of course—an open wound in a feeding gallery was tantamount to a death sentence—but he would take the Liaison, this face of Venusix, this symbol of the corporation's interests and enforcer of those hated specs, with him.

I almost envied the poor bastard his audacity.

He charged. Spats of soil kicked up from the soles of his bare feet. Neither I nor my boss tried to stop him. What could we do? 137 had a knife. If one or more of us was cut, if more blood was introduced into the situation, all of us would be killed. We knew this.

He reached the Liaison and plunged the knife to the hilt in the tall man's breast. I imagined the look of triumph he must be wearing. Imagined it wilting into confusion when nothing happened. Confusion, then shock, as the nearest weed rose up behind him, gripped him by the shoulders and yanked him to the ground.

The Liaison removed the knife. Stood looking at it, as if it made a curious study. No blood flowed from the slit in his chest plate.

The Mandrakes in the gallery pounced on the jerking kicking form of V137, their pale hides pulsing, long tails whipping back and forth.

The shop was closed until the damage to the lines could be repaired. Once the Mandrakes finished feeding, they were ushered from the gallery, the front doors were locked, and the donors were told to return to their dorms.

V162, who'd witnessed the incident through the windows of the observation bay, asked if we could talk in private.

My boss and the Liaison were in the office, so I led her back to my personal quarters and took a seat at my desk while she sat on the lip of my bed, hands in her lap, looking at the floor as she spoke. She wanted to know about the Liaison.

"He's not human, is he?"

"No," I said. "He's a machine. You've seen them before?"

She nodded.

"He was built to serve Venusix," I said. "His purpose is to make sure we do our jobs properly. To ensure the longevity of the corporation."

"How many of them are there?"

"In Venusix?"

"Yes."

"Many. The whole Board."

She looked up.

"How do you know this?"

"I was at a seminar," I said. "About corporate law, the reasons for the specs, that sort of thing. There was an intermission, so I went exploring. I overheard a conversation between the Liaison and the Board. They were conducting a virtual meeting in one of the simulation rooms, and the door was open. They… They didn't know I was there. They're not infallible, you know. Even if that's what they'd have you believe."

"Does the boss know? That we work for machines?"

"Yes. All GMs do."

She fell quiet. She stared down at her thumbs, circling frantically.

"There's more isn't there," I said.

She nodded.

"You want to know about the Mania."

Tears welled into her eyes. She nodded again.

I considered where to begin. What to say. I thought about lying, as I had lied to so many others, so many times. But gazing at her then, so wan and thin with her swimming eyes, I was cascaded through my memories and my regrets, and I recalled the pain, the uncertainty, of my days as a donor (and for *what?*); I remembered the faces I'd seen come and go in my time as management—the emaciated, destitute faces—wrung by fear and grief—pared by thirst and hunger—gleaming, finally, with the lunacy of their ultimate extant moments. I thought of that meeting between the Board and the Liaison, that I wasn't supposed to hear, when I'd discovered that our labors on Plant were for the benefit of a corporation run by machines, for the benefit of machines, and also the horrifying reality of sap, known only by me, me, and how I'd hated myself for continuing my work, coward that I am, ever since. I thought of the colonies on Earth, and I saw Jhumpa's body vanish again into the flames of the crematorium, as I had seen the body of V093 swallowed by the incinerator here, as I had seen so many mutilated broken bodies burn, and I thought of 137—poor, misguided Harlan—disappearing into a swarm of frenzied weeds. I thought of my boss, who would likely die in this place, never knowing the truth as I did.

Perhaps.

162 waited, her thumbs circling. I looked at her for what felt like a long time. I asked her what she knew about sap.

"It's blood, isn't it?"

"Not just blood," I said.

"Well, I mean I know it's not just blood," she said. "How they explained it at Orientation is that sap is pretty much a blend of the stuff that makes a person. Blood cells, hemoglobin—but also elements like iron, calcium, oxygen. Carbon. Things taken…"

She paused. She bit her lip and squeezed her hands.

"Things taken from our flesh and bones," she said. "Our organs. But they told us blood was the easiest way for us to think about it."

"So, if the ingredients of sap are so prosaic," I said, "so common as you describe, why can't they just be manufactured? Why do we even need donors? The tenders are robotic, after all."

A frown creased her face.

"I don't know."

"C'mon, 162. Try."

"If I had to guess, I would say it's because it's too complicated. At least for us to reproduce."

"Exactly," I said.

"Sir," she said. "I don't understand. What's sap got to do with Mania?"

"What did they tell you about Mania during your Orientation?"

"Only that it's a potential hazard of our work here on Plant. That it's a type of psychological disorder and everyone is susceptible, and it must be safeguarded against."

"The Mania is an irretrievable loss of mind and sense of self," I said. "What you saw earlier, with 137… That was Mania."

She said nothing.

"It's triggered in part by the rigors of living on this moon. We're not supposed to be here. But here we are. Of course, this has side effects—most commonly depression. And for many that's all it is. But for donors the Mania is something else entirely."

"Why?" she asked. "Why should it be different for us?"

"Can you think of nothing?"

She thought. After a while she said: "It's sap. The giving of sap."

"Sap," I said. "Now I ask you: why would the giving of blood and minerals lead to violent insanity? Billions of people throughout time have donated blood and never suffered episodes like you saw in the feeding gallery earlier."

"I don't know," she said.

"But you already told me the answer. Because sap is not just blood and minerals, but *the stuff that makes a person.* And what is a person? What makes us different from the clay that composes us? How is it we're even having this conversation?"

Her eyes widened.

"It's the energy that animates us," I said. "Because a human being is more than just a collection of compounds. And it is this energy, the source of your very consciousness, that can be extracted but not fabricated, that makes sap what it is. It's for this the Mandrakes allow Earth's machines to plunder their world. This is what you're giving in exchange for the currency you send home, and it is the draining of this from your being that leads to the fracturing of mind known as *Dementia Sanguis*."

I took a breath.

"Your soul, 162. Call it whatever you want. But that's what it is… They're drinking your soul."

M.P. Strayer's work has appeared in numerous publications and anthologies, most recently Twisted Vine Literary Arts Journal, Aethlon: the Journal of Sports Literature, and The Loch Raven Review. Currently, he lives in Corvallis, Oregon.

Stone Cold
By Gustavo Bondoni

He pulled a knife on me, so I shot him.

The look of betrayal on the guy's face when he realized the gun in my hand was a modern Sig Sauer pistol was absolutely priceless. He wanted to tell me that it wasn't fair, that I had to play by the rules. But he couldn't, because he fell to the ground, dead.

I walked on. The cobbles ended a few meters further down the street, beyond that lay bare dirt, awaiting paving. The hijacked truck had to be nearby.

A sudden rush of air nearly knocked my hat off, and I looked up. A Carimin pod descended slowly to land in front of the theater across the street. Three of the aliens descended and walked inside, escorted by two guides.

I watched them disappear into the room looking like slightly elongated, even more elegant versions of the elves from the *Lord of the Rings* films, and sighed. The theater owner would be delighted. They could make a good year's revenue from the payment offered by the aliens. I checked to see what they were showing. *Tango Feroz*, a crappy movie from the 1990s which had nothing to do with Tango but the title.

Of course, the title would probably be enough for the aliens. They were obsessed.

But that wasn't my problem. I had a job to do.

When I got the text from Eliana, I was between jobs. The arrival of the aliens with their glorious technology and ready currency—

gold, tech, blue chip stocks from the exchanges of a million suns, you name it, they had it—had caused every war on the planet to suddenly dry up as the powers that were courted the visitors. As a private security consultant—and I'll thank you not to call me a mercenary—my employment opportunities dried up overnight.

So, I took the plane ticket, argued about the guns in my luggage with the airline clerks and headed back to Buenos Aires. Blood is thicker than water, and my little sister was in trouble.

At first, I liked the change that had come over the city. It certainly looked picturesque, and the cleaned-up old-style facades worked really well with the newly restored gas lights.

But then I realized what a pain was to have to take hundred-year-old taxis. It took forever to get anywhere… and that's assuming the stupid things didn't break down on the way. I'd heard that every single car in the world that dated from that era and wasn't owned by some curmudgeonly collector who refused to sell was being restored and packed in containers bound for Buenos Aires.

I'd even heard that some of the aliens were buying up old period-correct Ford taxicabs and shipping them back home.

But you couldn't believe every rumor.

The thing is, the aliens loved their tango. They loved it to the point where they would come to the city and insist that everything had to be perfect. They wanted the authentic experience, and nothing less would do. They would dance, they would watch the shows. Some of their females—they had four sexes, but no one was really certain what role the two that were neither male nor female played in reproduction—would actually pay huge amounts of money to be allowed to work as prostitutes in the tango cabarets. Historical exactness, not morality, was the key.

That's where Eliana's note came in. She'd put up a cathouse and had openings for a couple of exotics… but someone kept stealing the cobblestones she'd bought to pave her block with.

And the aliens wouldn't come to a place on a street paved with concrete. That wasn't authentic.

So, my job was to get the stones back.

Her job was to stop me. I could see it as soon as she began slinking across the street.

"Hello, handsome," she said, swaying her hips just enough to let the blood-red dress talk for her.

"Not interested," I replied.

"Everyone's interested," she shot back. "Especially you."

That got my attention. "Why me?"

"Because you were watching me even before I started to cross the street."

She'd been looking the other way, putting on her makeup with one of those tiny mirrors… oh. "You've got a camera on me… and the compact is a cell phone."

She shrugged. "The visitors don't mind, as long as it *looks* real. So how about it? You get a good time, and no one else gets hurt."

"I'm not planning on getting hurt," I said.

For a second, just a second, the streetwise charade faltered, and I saw the woman underneath wondering how the hell this had happened. But it lasted only a second. "You're really into the whole dockside tough-guy act, aren't you?"

"No. I'm actually a poet, but I lost a dare."

"Screw you. Get yourself beaten to death. I don't care."

She stalked away and, for a few moments, she was perfectly successful in her intention because I did stop to watch her leave.

Then I did something that would have gotten me fined by the city. I reached into the pocket of the overly tight suit, you had to wear in certain neighborhoods, and pulled out a tiny drone equipped with infrared cameras. Controlling it from the cell phone I'd also smuggled through the exclusion-zone barriers, I flew it into the dark patch of street ahead of me.

The idling engine glowed nearly white, even under sheet metal, and the three guys waiting for me were red patches in the dark. I let the drone drift about ten meters in the air and left it hovering there. I needed to make certain that it didn't go behind anything, or I'd lose it: every cell tower in the city center had been pulled down, so it only worked by line-of-sight.

Then, I memorized exactly where each of the bad guys were and closed my eyes—covering them with my palm—before activating the little flyer's other trick.

For a couple of seconds, the bright light actually shone red even through my hand. As soon as it was dark again, I walked purposefully to where the first of my recently blinded opponents writhed on the floor. A quick kick to the head silenced him and I moved to the next. A minute later, I was done, and no one had been permanently damaged.

Well, maybe they had, but they were still alive. It would have to do.

The truck was a Volvo, and it looked too modern to be correct for the era… but it had to be right. A drone was one thing, but there was no way anyone would be able to smuggle a modern truck through even the laissez-faire checkpoints between the rest of the country and the ever-growing Tango Exclusion Zone where the aliens accounted for ninety-five percent of Argentina's net income.

To my relief, the truck worked correctly, and Eliana was there to receive her cobblestones. A work crew immediately began placing them in front of her discreet establishment—only a red electric light above a narrow doorway indicated that this place plied its ancient trade.

I was restless. The night was warm, the conversation stale and, let's face it, a whorehouse run by your sister is never any fun.

"This place is going down the tubes," I said. "There are nearly eight million people living in a city that looks like a bad black and white movie set."

"You're just mad about the shoes," Eliana's husband Pablo, who also doubled as a barman and a bouncer, replied.

He was right. The fact that they were tight as hell was bad enough… but the platforms. Argh. I'd tried to get shoes that weren't tango shoes, and the proprietors had looked at me as if I'd asked them for a detonator suitable for a medium-yield nuclear bomb. Lips tightened, a furtive look around. "We don't carry that," they'd said.

And by 'they', I mean every single shoe store in the city. And you couldn't order them online because… well, because there was no internet in the tango bunkers of the early twentieth century.

"Besides," he went on. "It's not just here. I recently heard that an entire Swiss city died of starvation because all they have been producing for the past year is chocolate."

"You can't starve by eating chocolate. It has tons of energy."

"I know what I heard. But even they're better off than the French. The aliens apparently decided that what they wanted from France was actually just the champagne, so the entire industrial base has been turned over to that. It's even been rumored that people in Paris are actually in a good mood now."

"Then the aliens are good for something after all, it appears." I stood. "I need a drink."

"Booze not good enough for you here?"

"Eliana won't let me grope the girls, not even the alien ones, and they're paying for the privilege."

I walked into the night.

At first, I really don't think I knew where I was headed. I told myself I was just letting my feet choose the path.

But clearly, whatever intelligence my feet might once have had was strangled by the damned shoes, and soon I began to recognize the houses around me. I passed the theater—still showing *Tango Feroz*—and reached a patch of freshly laid cobbles. A small red light shone above the door.

I knocked and a guy with a huge black bruise along the side of his face opened. He did a double-take as he recognized me, but he let me in. The door shut behind me with an ominous click, but I didn't turn back to see what he was doing. I chose a table where I could sit with my back against a wall and surveyed the scene.

The place was nothing special. Black and white tiles arrayed in a chessboard pattern defined the dance floor, and the tables were pushed to the edges of the room. Thick clouds of cigarette smoke swirled above the dancer's heads. Two girls danced with men who were obviously patrons while another pair of couples were composed of just women. It was traditional in the houses to have people dancing even when the men didn't feel like it.

A three-person orchestra played the jerky tones the aliens had fallen in love with.

I felt the solid safety of the gun in my waistband. I didn't want to have to use it. That wasn't why I was here.

So I thought about the irony of the situation. There was a stage here whose intended audience was not even present. The aliens would come, the place was to their exact standards, and when they did, the proprietor could then walk away a wealthy individual. But in the meantime, the show had to go on, and the needs of the eminently rich visitors were deforming the very fabric of Buenos Aires society. Everyone moved to the rhythm of tango… and it was becoming a way of life.

Even I'd been sucked in. Was there anything more redolent of 1920s tango bravado than walking into the enemy's den looking for trouble?

Hell, I'd even been infected with the fatalistic attitude, I was waiting there rolling the dice that the right kind of trouble would walk over first, but not really caring if everything blew up in my face.

One of the dancers looked my way. I caught her eye. Her own opened wide in shock and she whispered something in her partner's ear. The other girl disengaged and the vision in red from the night of the cobblestones swayed over to my table.

"So, you want to die?" she said. "I have to admit that's interesting. Stupid, but interesting."

In better light, I could see the rings under her eyes. Turning an entire society into a tango-driven universe had a human cost that went well beyond the obvious. The roles available were very limited. And if you didn't fit any of the archetypes, then you would have to forego the riches.

She fit her archetype.

"You promised me a good time," I told her.

Her response was to roll her eyes. "You knew what I was saying."

"Of course. But can't I buy a little time now? I got paid for that job I did." Actually, I was a partner in little sister's cathouse, and the alien's gold had netted me a small fortune, growing by the day. But there was no need to tell her that.

"You don't have time for anything. You're about to die."

"You keep telling me that. It wasn't true last time and it isn't true now. Besides, these guys should be thankful. I could have hurt them when they were down."

"You killed Ramiro."

She didn't look too broken up about that.

"So? Was he a friend?"

"Not particularly. No one liked him much, but you know how it is. He was a bastard, but he was our bastard. Now we need to take out one of yours. It's one of those stupid guy things."

"Okay. Then can a condemned man ask a final question?"

"Depends on the question. I charge extra for the girlfriend experience, you know."

"What were you before?" I watched her face, but she wasn't giving anything away. "Before the aliens, I mean."

"I know what you meant," she replied. "But I'm not going to tell you."

"Suit yourself. Too bad I came all the way over here, then. I really wanted to know."

"Why?"

"There was something about you that night."

She snorted. "You are aware that literally every man who's spoken to me since I started this gig has said a variation of that?"

He thought about it for a moment. "It sounds about right. I couldn't stop thinking about you."

"Don't give me that crap. I know how I look, and I know where you can find a dozen girls who are prettier or younger or both."

"That's not what I was talking about. I mean that sometimes, you let your real feelings show through, not just the anger and the sassy front you use for clients. It looked to me like you're actually thinking about the stuff around us—and you're bewildered by it."

A second of the openness I liked in her ensued, but she soon clammed up again. "That's only logical. I think everyone's bewildered by what's happening."

She was wrong. Most people had simply shrugged and gone on with their lives, fitting into their new roles with the same bovine indifference they'd felt for the old ones. They just changed the stuff they complained about. After the first flurry of excitement, life had gone on.

I was about to tell her so when she spoke again.

"Anyhow, time's up. It was nice knowing you, I guess."

The doorman had gathered his friends, and all three were fanning out towards my table, knives drawn. Some people just didn't learn… or maybe they thought I couldn't shoot all three of them before they got to me. They were wrong, but I didn't want to shoot them. "Call them off before they get hurt," I told her.

She shrugged. "I just work here." Then, without looking away, she took three deliberate steps back, leaving the field open for whatever happened next. So stereotypical: the girl lets the men fight it out before celebrating with the winner. I thought she was falling into character.

Until she winked.

I pulled the gun out and pointed it at the guy who'd been at the door. "I don't think your friends will make it to the table," I said. "But I can guarantee one thing: you will never find out, one way or the other."

They stopped for a second.

And never started again. The bar went silent as the orchestra faltered. Every eye turned to the door.

More precisely, every eye turned to the figure entering through the door: tall, thin, almost human in appearance, but not quite.

The pause lasted only a second, and then the place came raucously alive again.

The doorman forgot I existed and rushed over to receive the visitor. The girl went back to her dance partner. The orchestra tried to pick up where it had left off, but that only resulted in a discordant jangle, so they started over on a new song. Someone actually brought me a drink and a cigarette.

I played my part. I bought a girl a drink, danced the dance I was entitled to, and generally played the part expected.

As far as I could tell, the alien was delighted, if the way it moved excitedly around the room was any indication. It was a male, that much was obvious by its clothes and build, but other than that, I knew nothing about it.

The guy—he was much too human-looking to think of it as a thing—paid a year's salary for a bottle of scotch, and then danced with all the women in the place. No one complained; that was why the joint existed. In fact, that was why the entire city looked and acted the way it did. Gold coins disappeared into bodices as he disengaged.

Finally, it was time to choose and, just my luck, he chose the girl with the red dress.

They disappeared upstairs and I stared bitterly into my glass, barely even bothering to keep my hand on the gun and glare at anyone not bearing alcohol who came too close.

But no one was paying me any attention. They were all waiting anxiously to see what would happen. If the girl was any good, they would all—well, the ones with an actual stake in the place—be rich when the alien returned.

The visitor came back and spoke to the doorman, who'd retreated behind the bar. I couldn't hear what they said, but the smile on the guy's face threatened to tear his face in half. I had to fight down a sudden urge to walk over there and punch him in the nose.

The girl came down the stairs. She wasn't wearing the red dress anymore. Now she sported perfectly normal jeans and a t-shirt. Well, they would have been perfectly normal a couple of years before.

Now, everyone stared at her uncomfortably. Anachronism in the presence of the visitors was economical suicide.

But the alien didn't seem to mind. They went through the door together, one of his arms protectively thrown over her shoulder. She caught my eyes for a second as she passed but looked away quickly. Or maybe I imagined it.

When the door shut, the place went dead quiet. I instinctively felt for my gun but when the doorman approached again, he wasn't carrying a gun. He was carrying a bottle of Dom Perignon and two glasses. He sat down at my table and poured in silence.

"I've decided to let bygones be bygones," he said.

"Is that so?"

"Yeah. You turned out to be lucky after all. Almost as soon as you walk in, our first Carimin shows up. Not only that, but he took a liking to one of our girls, says he'll take her out into the galaxy, show her the sights. And she was off like a shot."

"Yeah, I figured."

"No, you don't. If you knew how much he gave us for losing her…" He shook his head and drank, already giddy. "I don't get them, sometimes. Girl like that? I never expected much from her. She was never really into it, you know?"

"Yeah," I replied. "I know. Thanks for the drink." I stood to go.

"Come back any time," he said. "Drinks on the house, even if I sell it on. It's like lottery tickets, you know. Everyone wants the location where a big win happened."

I wondered if anyone printed lottery tickets anymore. It sounded so quaint in a world where all you needed to do was to wait for the aliens to pop in.

"I mean it," he called out happily as I reached the door. "Any time you want."

I touched my hat in his direction. It was the right thing to do. It was what the role demanded.

But I wouldn't be back.

Gustavo Bondoni is a novelist and short story writer with over three hundred stories published in fifteen countries, in seven languages. His latest novel is Test Site Horror (2020). He has also published two other monster books: Ice Station: Death (2019) and Jungle Lab

Terror (2020), three science fiction novels: Incursion (2017), Outside (2017) and Siege (2016). His short fiction is collected in Pale Reflection (2020), Off the Beaten Path (2019) Tenth Orbit and Other Faraway Places (2010) and Virtuoso and Other Stories (2011).

amazon.com/Gustavo-Bondoni/e/B004FRVMO2

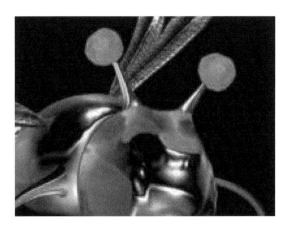

Crawdads
By Mark Silcox

Vice-Regent Carnehan slid a bowl of prickly spheroids across the table. "Do try these," he said to the cephalopod sitting across from him.

Ambassador N'yint-heppo's exoskeleton crackled faintly from within. He plucked at the offering with a slender foreleg. "New type of candy – how delightful!" A speaker affixed to the alien's chest was translating the polyrhythmic noises from his densely articulated body. The machine had for some reason provided the Ambassador with a dense Slavonic accent. The effect was half comical, half unnerving.

Carnehan guessed that the software must have been coded somewhere in Eastern Europe. Unless it was just somebody's attempt at a bigoted joke.

It was a quiet day atop the second-highest tower of the governmental palace. The Observation Room in which they were sitting was empty apart from the two of them. The small hexagonal space was ringed all around with heavily reinforced polymer windows. Carnehan loved both the privacy and the glorious vistas that the tower provided. He would come up here sometimes after a sweaty day in the city streets below just to gaze out over the sand-freckled landscape of the alien planet where he had now spent the majority of his career.

"The sweets are a classic flavor from the ancient cuisines of our homeworld," he told the Ambassador. "'Cinnamon,' we call it. Our chefs have been working hard to inject the flavor into comestibles suitable for your, ah…"

"Our eccentric digestive processes – of course." The Ambassador popped the tiny treat into his mouthparts, crunched, and rattled cheerfully.

The Vice-Regent smiled, grateful for his companion's frankness. Back in the early days of the settlement, even the most enlightened members of their two species had found mutual revulsion a difficult barrier to overcome. But these days, at least in the city, their gross physical dissimilarities were often a source of good-humored camaraderie. "What do you think of it, 'heppo?"

"Oh *my*, it's – yes, quite wonderful sensations, André! Delightful as that stuff you sent to the embassy last week – what was it called? 'Ansit?' 'Anoose?'"

"Star Anise. But cinnamon has been used much more widely by humans, often with a sweetener. I'm so pleased that you like it! The locally-brewed inebriant you shared with me last time was also…quite something. I took the bottle to bed with me after you were called away. Had myself some fascinating dreams that night."

A wheezing exhalation of mirth from the Ambassador's exoskeleton slowly turned into a crackle of regret. "Much embarrassed I could not provide similar gift for this visit. Disruption of trade routes has led to many inconvenient shortages." The alien glanced over toward the window closest to where they sat.

Carnehan gritted his teeth. He had been trying to distract his guest from the column of greasy brown smoke wavering above the horizon just a few miles past the city's outer edge. "An envoy came into town this morning and told me there has been a break in the combat. Not before one of your peoples' settlements was set aflame, as I've sure you've already heard. But the Regency has sent out human relief workers to help with the evacuation. I can assure you, we'll make a sincere effort to bring the vandals to justice."

The Ambassador helped himself to another couple of cinnamon candies, which he munched in rueful silence for a while.

"Is such a shame, André," he said at last, "to continue with these assurances to each other. Of course, I know Regent's administration is different from these outer-colony humans. Why must they set off bombs over even very tiniest of trade disputes? Bickering about movement of water, or price of nutritional algae! And of course, you know our government is not these silly rural peddlers, pushing your settlements to brink of starvation with stupid price-gouging."

A friendly concession seemed to be in order. "Your people can hardly be blamed when they set steep prices for commodities. Everything they're selling was yours alone for centuries before our ships landed."

The alien emitted a distinctive creak of chitin that Carnehan had learn to construe as a suggestion of mournfulness. "So many years ago. And now, the fools must surely know how human munitions could turn all our burrows to vapor."

Carnehan stood up abruptly. "Come on, 'heppo – let's not brood. Let's go take a look at a few of the artworks we've just unloaded from last week's cargo hauler. There's an exhibition of new synesthetic arrays touring the outer colonies this year. Not all of the sensory couplings will be accessible to you, but the ones involving scent, color, and touch…"

But the Ambassador was still in his chair, gazing out at the signs of faraway battles. "On walk here today," he said, "I passed through one fully integrated neighborhood. One of very first that was built in years after final *détente*. You remember those days, don't you, my friend?"

Carnehan nodded slowly. "I do." This was not the conversation he had wanted to have today. There were important topics the two of them needed to get around to discussing. He was anxious to prepare the Ambassador for upcoming visit from the colony's wealthiest sponsors, who were traveling here all the way from Earth. "I was deputy chief of the Curfew Squad back then. We expected to be walking the streets breaking up fights for months after the treaty was signed. But things settled down amazingly quickly. It was the making of my career, in some ways."

"And mine," said the Ambassador. "I made many promises on behalf of your species. Would have got me dismembered, perhaps, if not upheld." A soft inner rasp, intimating gentle laughter.

The aliens didn't normally express solidarity through physical contact, but Carnehan risked placing a hand on his old ally's upper carapace. "These foolish skirmishes will peter out eventually, 'heppo. You've read about how badly things went on other worlds my species has visited, during our earlier days of adventurism. There are species on worlds we've visited out there that have sworn oaths to exterminate all of humanity. What we've achieved on this world is fragile, but we must think of ourselves as fortunate."

The next delicate squeak from the Ambassador was not translated by the device fixed to his chest. Carnehan found this one oddly difficult to parse. Perhaps it was just the transfer of exotic gastric chemicals through the Alien's interior.

Both of them turned upon hearing a whisper of movement from the elevator shaft at the center of the room. A low-level Regency staffer stepped out and dropped into a bow when he caught sight of their visitor.

"Good grief, Yashomoto. I did ask not to be disturbed." The Vice-Regent was irritated first, then worried. Had there been even *more* bloodshed and vandalism out in the exurbs? The last thing Carnehan wanted was for the Ambassador to hear about this from one of his own personal flunkies.

"Apologies, Vice-Regent. But you *did* also put us under standing orders to come straight to you if we should receive another surprise visit from…"

"Oh *blast!*" Carnehan couldn't help himself. "It's Tyrone, isn't it?"

"Yes sir, I'm afraid so."

N'yint-heppo's eyestalks twitched back and forth with obvious bemusement.

Carnehan smiled thinly. "Sorry about this, 'heppo. It's just my aunt's stepson, dropping by unannounced for a visit."

The alien tapped the translation device at the top of his thorax, signaling incomprehension.

Carnehan remembered how his guest's vocabulary lacked equivalents for certain familial concepts. "I believe the corresponding term in the language of the burrow is 'lateral birth-debtor, twice-deferred.'"

"Ah, yes." The Ambassador relaxed.

"Tyrone is a dew harvester out at the southernmost edges of the colony. He 'drops by' whenever he's running errands in the city and gets bored. He leans *very* heavily on family privileges. Well, Yashomoto, I suppose I can visit with him after we've spent some time in the museum. Just bring him up here and give him a piece of fried dough or something to munch on while he waits, would you?"

"Sir!" The chastened staffer returned to the elevator, which descended with a muted *whoosh*.

"My own family is also often…troublesome," the Ambassador offered.

"Most of mine were quite happy to stay on earth playing music, or taking drugs, or otherwise spending away my grandfather's inheritance. But Tyrone has what some might call a 'sense of adventure.'" Carnehan sighed. "It's too bad he's also a drunkard, an ignoramus, and a religious fanatic."

The Ambassador wriggled a few of his lower arms: a mild startle response. The aliens were notoriously big on filial piety. But Carnehan couldn't resist the temptation to vent. These unannounced visits from his country cousin always seemed to shake loose hard and unwelcome thoughts from deep inside him. He cursed to himself a few times quietly, making sure the giant crustacean couldn't hear.

A few minutes later, they were both standing in the embassy museum's private viewing room, their heads enclosed in delicate polymer bubbles. They breathed in and out deeply as a fist-sized, elaborately involuted nanotech sculpture shivered before them in midair.

"How lovely!" said the Ambassador. "The scent reminds me of coastal air; how it smells in spring, at far edge of Southern continent."

"We really do need to send another expedition there," said Carnehan. "The economists tell us there's nothing worth harvesting for export, but I'm sure they're being hasty." He consulted the exhibition catalog in his heads-up display. "Are you ready to sense the next piece? It's from an artist's collective on Ganymede. Apparently this one also makes its very own music."

N'yint-heppo creaked assent. Carnehan clapped his hands to summon the curator, who walked in from an adjoining room carrying a transport crate under one arm. He whistled a high note at the dancing sculpture, which instantly disintegrated and shot up through a metal grate in the ceiling.

"So many new things I have seen, since your people came to my world, Vice-Regent!" The speaker on the alien's chest went up a notch or two in volume, signifying intensity of feeling. "And to think how foolish spawn in outer territories still want to dicker about price of water! How long will it take my kindred to forget quarrels and appreciate of all you can offer our humble world?"

Carnehan felt that now was the ideal moment to come to the crux of their interview. "I have expressed similar hopes to some of my family's oldest friends back on Earth. They've told me that they wish to send a new trade emissary with the next convoy."

Before them, the next sculpture had escaped from its crate and begun performing slow, rhythmic convolutions. Their transparent helmets filled up with strange fugues and wordless melodies. The Ambassador began to sway a little back and forth in a childlike way.

"The Regent has already given them his approval," Carnehan continued. "If we're lucky, certain investors on my homeworld will eventually send further resources our way."

"K-k-k-k, so pretty, this one is."

"There's just one small thing that I must ask of you, to prepare the way for their visit."

"What is that, my friend?"

Carnehan was speechless for a moment as a muzzy, floral scent suddenly overwhelmed his senses. As he gasped and swallowed, trying to form the words for his vital request, he heard the elevator door at the back of the room whisper open. It was only just loud enough to be audible over the weird, atonal melodies that were playing for the pair of them.

He turned to see Corporal Yashomoto stepping out of the elevator, followed by his cousin Tyrone. The former looked deeply nervous and distressed; the latter was wearing his usual loose, sand-flecked outdoor clothes and self-satisfied leer.

"*Yashomoto*! I explicitly told you not to bring him here! What on Earth are you…?"

"Sir? I'm sorry, but didn't you say…"

"Ah!" said the Ambassador. "Is this your honored relative, André? An unexpected, but charming surprise." He scuttled forward a couple of feet, his mist-clogged helmet swaying back and forth atop his knobby carapace.

"Oh, sweet lord a'mighty!" screamed their visitor. "It's a *crawdad*!"

Carnehan looked on helplessly as his cousin staggered backward, then pulled a small metal gadget from the front pocket of his ragged trousers. A tiny red dot appeared on N'yint-heppo's chest, and a trail of smoke issued from the front of the Ambassador's carapace. This was followed with a sudden burst of diverse crackles and hisses from every part of his body. The translation device interpreted these noises as "Ahhh! Oh God – such pain. Such pain I am in! I cannot…"

Then the ambassador exploded. A chunk of shivering orange meat bounced off Carnehan's chest, and a hot splash of the alien's inner juices caught him on the side of the face, scalding his cheek.

After the last piece of the alien's flesh had slid to a stop and the fog of choking steam had cleared, the first audible sound was a quiet sob from Yashomoto. Then Tyrone came back to himself, clapped his mouth shut, and strode across the slippery floor toward the Vice-Regent.

"Jus' what the *hell-on-earth* has been going on here, cousin?" he demanded, waving his miniature weapon above his head. "How did that crawdaddy git itself up in here? Don't you know that them creatures are…"

Carnehan reached back behind his right shoulder and slapped Tyrone once, very hard, across the face. While his relative was still recovering from the impact, he reached out to pluck the lightgun from Tyrone's hand and slipped it quickly into his own back pocket.

"Yashomoto!" he barked.

"*Sir!*" The corporal held up a trembling hand. "Sir, I *swear* to you, Sir, what I thought you meant was to bring him to wherever…"

"That doesn't matter now!" Carnehan tugged the ridiculous spherical bulb off his head and dropped it. The scent of burning meat almost overwhelmed him, but he swallowed hard and forced himself to breathe deeply. "Call down to the basement and summon a Protocol K team, *now*! Enter code 377 on the elevator so nobody else wanders up here and sees this mess. Then go down and help the team carry up their cleaning equipment."

"Sir!" This last acknowledgement came out as a choked whimper.

The Colonel departed. Carnehan leaned forward and established a steely grip on Tyrone's shoulders with both of his hands.

"I…I…" his cousin stammered.

Another less aggressive slap to the face got him to quiet down. "Tyrone! Listen up, now. It's all right. You've made a colossal fuckin' mess, like you always do, but it's all right. As long as you do *exactly* what I tell you. Understand?"

"But…André! Why were you in here with that…just talkin' to that, uhh, that *thing*…like there was nothin' wrong with…?"

"*Because* – you stinking dumbass – because we…" Carnehan breathed in heavily again. He knew that he needed to keep his cool for at least the next few crucial minutes. But that was not going to happen if he started up one of his little political debates with Tyrone. His cousin lived in a part of the colony where there was minimal interaction between the two species, and the religious cult he belonged to regarded the more integrated society of the city as a farrago of barely imaginable perversity.

Carnehan pointed over at the polymer crate the museum curator had dropped on the floor just after the Ambassador exploded. "*Sit!* I'll get back with you in a moment."

To the Vice-Regent's very considerable relief, Tyrone sat down, clasping his hands between his knees in a gesture of temporary subordination. Perhaps the gruesomeness of what they had all just witnessed had caught him a bit by surprise as well.

Carnehan pulled an earpiece out from under his shirt and typed a long code into the nearest wall interface. "Beckwith, I have a Code-Y. Can you talk?"

"Yes, sir!" came an immediate response. Beckwith was his spy inside the alien embassy. An Earth-trained linguistics professor making a study of ancient alien runes, but also a tough, reliable character.

"We've had a mishap here. Ambassador N'yint-heppo is, ah, deceased."

A low moan at the other end of the line.

I know, I know, thought Carnehan. *Calling this a 'Code Y' is a little like calling the Proxima-B Genocide a 'friendly disagreement.'* "I need to know what path the Ambassador took to get here. He mentioned passing through at least one integrated neighborhood."

"Let me think a moment, sir…I'm pretty sure he was headed northeast when he left, through Quadrant C. So…he almost certainly would have been in what the crawdads call 'Inscription Town,' on account of all the graffiti. I can double check."

"Do so. Get back to me if there's new intel."

Carnehan knew the part of the city his agent was talking about – a chaotic, ramshackle slum where inter-species brawls broke out as often as anywhere else in the colony. Perhaps – just *maybe* – the plan that had formed in his mind about eight seconds after he saw the Ambassador explode had a passable chance of working.

Four muscular security staffers stepped out of the elevator, followed by a queasy-looking Yashomoto. They all wore heavy polymer gloves, and the tall one in front was pushing a giant mop and bucket.

"Mother Earth, what's that putrid smell?" the bucket man remarked. "Did the crawdads have an orgy up here, or…oh!" His air of indignation gave way to a horrified grimace when he caught sight of a chunk of the deceased Ambassador.

"Gentlemen, there has been a diplomatic incident here. I need you to completely clean out this space. Not just until it's spotless, but until the air is purged of any and all chemical indicators of what happened. Have any of you ever dealt with crawdad corpses before?"

Two of them nodded.

"Good – so you know how difficult it is to totally eradicate the smell. We have a solvent that we keep in bright orange bottles in the sub-basement; it's labeled 'Purgation-4.' Yashomoto, go back down and bring up as much of it as you can carry."

They all saluted, and were about to get down to work, but Carnehan help up a hand. "Just a second: you." He pointed to the big man. "I'm giving you special orders; come over here."

Tyrone had been getting a little restless. He was drumming on the crate with his hands between his legs and shaking his head back and forth with an attitude of forced nonchalance.

"Stop making that goddamn noise and *listen* to me now, cuz," Carnehan snarled. "You're going to help out with this shit too."

Tyrone was about to make some sort of protest, but he bit his lip when he saw the look on his relative's face.

"When that bucket over there's filled up with dead alien, the pair of you are going to wait 'till nightfall, then heft it over to Inscription town. Cover it with foil so it looks like you're lugging a piece of machinery or some damn thing."

"Um, but sir...the smell?" The tall Protocol man has a surprisingly soft, submissive voice for such a lug.

"That whole locality stinks of crawdaddy puke. There won't be much of a whiff left one you guys splash a gallon or two of Purgation on the outside of the bucket. Dump out the whole mess in the quietest alleyway you can find, then get the hell out of there. Don't come back to the palace for at least two days. If anybody looks suspicious or stops to ask you questions, just act like you're on Curfew Squad."

"How do we do that?" Tyrone asked.

Carnehan sighed. "In your case, just keep on acting like the surly dickhead you already are."

Tyrone grinned at this. He was the sort of guy you couldn't really insult; anything you said that sounded critical was interpreted as a merry jest. *At least he seems to be up for the challenge*, Carnehan thought.

The other Protocol men were setting an impressive pace with the cleaning. Yashomoto was mucking in too, after some initial squeamishness; he slid a chunk of one of the Ambassador's forearms along the slippery floor with one foot, then carefully lifted and folded it so that it fit into the waist-high receptacle.

Carnehan was just about to reassure himself that absolutely nobody else would have to know about this whole ghastly affair when he had a sudden, abominable thought.

"Tyrone! Get over here." His cousin loped across the floor, which was getting increasingly sticky as the greasy alien viscera started to evaporate into the dry air. His shoes made a crackling sound as with each step he took on the gluey tiles.

Carnehan leaned in close. "When you first got up here," he said, "before you pulled out your little weapon, did you see another person?"

"Oh, yeah! The short-assed guy in the fancy jacket with the transport crate under his arm! Say, where'd that fella get off to?"

Carnehan's eyes almost rolled backwards inside his skull. *Think, think…*

"Do you want to keep this for any reason, sir?" said one of the Protocol men, holding up the dripping remnant of N'yint-heppo's translation device between two fingers.

"Mm…best to destroy it, I think. Just in case the Ambassador was recording our conversation."

What to do about the curator, though? During the two years the man had been assigned to the planet as a middle-rank cultural envoy, Carnehan had come to know him passably well. Major El-Amin was a shy but articulate aesthete who had difficulty digesting the local food, but who had also enriched the lives of everyone at the colony. His taste as a collector was subtle and sensitive, and he exhibited patient eloquence explaining new trends in the arts back on their forever-yearned-for homeworld.

In Tyrone's eyes, a light was slowly dawning. "Uh oh. I think I sort of see the problem, cuz. I guess if that other guy saw what happened here – you getting all friendly with that crawdad like you two was some sort of kin, and then later, when I…" He stuck a thoughtful finger into the corner of his mouth. "And if he ever *told* anybody, that could sure create a world o' trouble! Maybe you'd better send someone to, uh…*deal* with him." A look of slow cunning crept over his features. "Maybe *I* could even…"

Carnehan turned away, leaving Tyrone to the cumbersome grinding of his mental gears. He walked over to the nearest window.

Outside, the alien sun was setting. The smoke from the horizon had mostly dissipated, while the rest was being swallowed by the encroaching dusk. Closer to his tower, members of the Curfew Squad were walking about the streets lighting torches – one of their more benevolent functions. In the circles of light that they cast, Carnehan could see a few itinerant members of both species leaving their houses and burrows to taste the evening air. It was a curiously calming tableau, and it had the effect of smoothing out some of Carnehan's inner waves of panic. He turned back around to face his cousin.

"You will go nowhere near the curator. I'll have him confined to his quarters for the next few hours. Then, when he's had a chance to reflect, I'll visit him and carefully explain the situation. He's a commissioned officer in the Regency Occupation Force; I'm sure he can be brought to an understanding. We're not animals."

###

Mark Silcox has had other stories accepted for publication in The Dread Machine, Sci Phi Quarterly, Perihelion SF, Leading Edge, Heroic Fantasy Quarterly, Write Ahead/The Future Looms, and KZine, among other venues. His novel The Face on the Mountain was published in 2015.

amazon.com/Mark-Silcox/e/B01F2KS4JQ

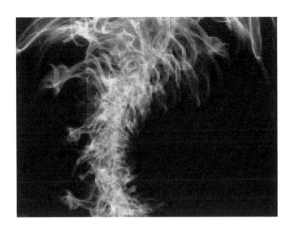

The Fleeting Glimpse
By Allen Ashley

Maybe mere survival was success enough for thirty years of off-Earth colonization. Life here on Antalar 4 had proven somewhat more difficult than expected but the settlement was growing and thriving, with Antalar-born residents now outnumbering the original settlers. And somewhere up there the starship *The Fleeting Glimpse* that had brought everyone and everything here – people, technology, seeds, materials, spares, knowledge banks – still orbited. Some said it held further spares that had never been transported down. Some said it held the corpses of those who didn't survive the Fold jump through hyperspace. The best estimates from here on the rainbow soil suggested the ship could stay in orbit for a hundred years before plummeting. That was a hundred Earth years, and that had been a bone of contention back in the early days. To Ryssa, born on this world that orbited one and a half suns and carried with it two orbiting moons, it was patently obvious that all time should be measured in local units. That was the astrophysical reality they all had to cope with on a daily – twenty-seven hours two minutes – basis.

It was natural for each successive generation to want to push forward with new and better ideas. That was how human society kept evolving and expanding. Although that expansive jump that had brought the explorer-colonists here had somewhat stalled lately. The plague five years back had been a tragically negative factor, but they were recovering now. Still, their domain encompassed only about a hundred square kilometers of this planet's surface. Like they'd reached a comfort point and not felt the need to push much further.

The recent problems with the functioning of the Fabricator had only exacerbated matters.

- We do not perceive self as parts. We are one. Except that glow ball is where we started and where we will return. Love glow ball. Glow ball is us.

- You are cold. You hardly register.

- What are these terms invasion and settlement? Ownership is not thing. We are owned by glow ball and time of leaving, being, and returning.

Technically, Antalar's companion star, although tiny and russet, wasn't a red dwarf. It was comparatively small and as the fourth planet passed close to it, the perturbations and effects included a severe reddening of the sky. Best guess was that this was a former planet now flaming up through proximity to the star and also heightened volcanism caused by a catastrophic event such as a collision.

This time was known as the reddening or the burning and even sheltering inside one wasn't safe from the rougen-ray output. The original settlers had nearly perished until Dr Wang had discovered the benefits of symbiosis with the worm-like sylpha. Now everybody had one of these gentle creatures lodged beneath the skin. As the sylpha grew, it usually settled around the abdomen, causing a new ridge of reddish skin to form. The visual effect made it seem as if each person could be unscrewed at that point and separated into top and bottom halves.

Ryssa was in the council meeting, absently rubbing her belly and reminding herself to increase her fruit sugar intake for the benefit of the beneficial symbiote. Chief Arken was droning on through his usual list.

"Nkana reports that solar cells and water filtration are operating at maximum. Once the burning is over, we may need to expand the quarrying activity. And with three pregnancies, we certainly need to breed or acquire more sylpha."

Johan rose to speak, his one-piece Fabricator-produced polycloth coverall artfully opened beneath the neck to reveal much of his muscly chest. Ryssa had grown increasingly wary of the young deputy leader, having turned down his amorous advances on a couple of recent occasions. Now he said, "We should remind everyone of the need to maintain population control. We're already close to resource capacity."

"Maybe you should have considered that before you procreated with Helvira."

Ryssa grinned at her friend Canton's interruption but Johan looked daggers at his rival. "Get with the program," he barked. Then, lip curled unattractively, he added, "Of course, there is an issue that settlers are living much longer than anticipated."

Arken, an original arriviste, cut in, "We'll live as long as our own nature and this planet's reserves allow us to, thank you very much. OK, I'm calling a halt for today. Tomorrow we'll reconvene to discuss the study of the flamers and also the reported faults with the Fabricator."

Ryssa heard Johan mutter something about authority always dragging its feet. As she left the chamber, Canton lightly touched her arm.

"Want to share the evening meal?" he asked. "It's only the usual buck cutlet and clamber fruit. But I'll sprinkle it with rock salt."

She smiled. "Wow, I haven't had that in… a day. Let's chow down."

Seated on a fabricated chair in the living unit, Canton said, "Arken and the other Earthies reckon bucks breed like rabbits but have the protein content of caviar. That's not a useful analogy to those who've never encountered Earth fauna."

"We hit lucky with this herd," Ryssa answered. "They must have a predator somewhere up the food chain. We need to anticipate something clawed, fierce and toothy when we explore more of this world."

"You make me feel like a caveman worrying about a sabretooth."

"Now who's using Earth analogies!" She wiped her mouth. "If the burning eases, then I'm on fruit-picking duties tomorrow, but should finish early. The crop's a little slow and thin this year."

He looked pensive. "You may have wondered why I haven't been around much lately. I've been studying the flamers."

"Aren't they dead-end in terms of communication? They're not even carbon-based, from what we know. Beings constantly on fire but never burning up? It's like they've fallen in from a different reality, Can."

"That's what makes them fascinating. Besides, this is their place. We're intruders even if we have managed to stay mostly on separate paths for now. Listen, Rys, Arken gave me a special mission and I've been reaching out to the flamers. I let them touch me."

"No, you must have sizzled."

"The flame was cold. Or at least cool. I'm using memory bank capacity to contrive a compatible language."

"Wow, and I'm plucking jadenberries off a branch. Some people have all the fun."

*

- What is fear?

- Caution. This we call non-interference. Paths need not cross. Until necessity.

- We are fire, we are flame, but we are control. We will not burn you. See how insubstantial is our passage across the surface of this world. We are creatures of air.

- World may not exist. Only a flicker state. Glow ball we will return to is only real world.

Arken had a gaggle of Antalar 4-born youngsters gathered around him. They could just as easily have been sat in front of the learning machines, but he liked to play the wise old man role.

"Late Earth technology gave us incredible advances. The Fold Drive that enables a starship to jump across the empty vastness of space so long as it rematerializes not too close to any astral body. Because nothingness can be folded up and passed through with the right approach. And then there's this, kids: The Fabricator. It sprung out of the thinking behind 3D printers and it takes in ore here and can be programmed to turn that into furniture, clothing, tools, all sorts of things we use every day…"

Ryssa took a look at the group's faces and couldn't decide whether they were fully attentive or glazed over. Probably they'd rather be kicking and throwing balls around in the open space a hundred meters away. Children had jobs and duties as well, of course, along with being educated in the colony's ways. No doubt Johan would be keeping an eye on their development and roping them into more tasks as soon as their young muscles could cope with them.

It was hot in the orchard, the effects of red time or burning time still hanging on. She rolled up the sleeves and waist area of her top coverall, produced by the Fabricator from synthesized fabrics. She wished she could take a break and go swim in the stream that wound its way past the jadenberry bushes but the run-off from the nearby quarry had caused raised acidity levels lately. She had no way of checking and didn't want to add chemical burns to the tingling that Antalar's double sun system caused on her exposed skin.

Shielding her eyes with her forearm, she saw one of the indigenous flying creatures lazily circling off to the west. No-one had ever caught one of these animals and a debate raged as to whether they were birds, reptiles or some other genus. Ryssa had scanned the memory banks and formed the opinion that the closest correlation was a pterodactyl from the pre-human era back on Earth. But it was just another example of how much there was still to discover on her home planet.

Yes, it was *her* home planet. Arken and all his off-Earth fables were old history. This was her time and place on Antalar 4. To make a human mark.

Nkana was crouched over the innards of the Fabricator, seemingly immune to the late evening bugs gathering in the purple sunset. Ryssa coughed politely.

"Oh hi, Ryss. Hey, fresh fruit for me?"

"Sure. How are things with the machine?"

"Still finickity. Johan was talking about fabricating some weaponry to go and deal with the flamers. He's also trying to double ore consignments but that won't make any difference."

"He's the dumbest dope on the planet. With the biggest mouth. Bigger than the Fabricator's intake hold."

Nkana smiled. "The problem is the equalization leveler."

"Maybe I'm being dumb now, but can't the Fabricator fabricate a new one?"

"We've yet to find merecadium in the soil. Spares are empty. Maybe there's some left on the starship."

Involuntarily, they both raised their gaze to the darkening sky. A powerful telescope would have afforded them an opportunity of determining where *The Fleeting Glimpse* was orbiting; there were no telescopes to hand.

"Dr Chan would have known what to do," Ryssa stated.

"Sure thing. There's a lot of her bio-logs saved in the memory banks. You could take a look when you get the chance."

Early next morning, Ryssa stood in front of a screen as it fired up. The solar cells were often shielded during the red time. Now that daylight and temperatures had returned to what passed for normal here, everything would soon be running at pace.

"Please enable implant."

Ryssa vigorously rubbed the side of her neck. She noticed that the sylpha housed in the ridge around her midriff squirmed as if also roused to heightened attention by her action. She waited until the creature was quiet and still once more.

Then she let her eyelids flutter and began absorbing information at an increasingly rapid rate. Around her, other colonists busied themselves with daily tasks, either socially required or through personal choice. A light wind soughed through the often iridescent vegetation over to the west. The smaller of the planet's two moons appeared briefly on the horizon. When the clouds gathered and delivered a light dousing of tepid rain, Ryssa didn't deviate from her task.

Until an almost sub-vocal: "Yes, that's the solution. But I'll need Canton."

"No-one disagrees that we need to expand our dominion," said Arken, "but all in good time."

"Now is that good time," Johan replied. "We should be mastering this landmass and then the continents beyond. And the seas. We owe it to our children. Honestly, old man, what have you been doing for the past thirty years?"

"Building a Garden of Eden. Taking this second chance."

"That's exactly it, nobody takes any chances. We need a reward system that encourages people to work harder, to do more."

"We left those ideas to fester back on Earth. Money is the root of all evil."

"And evil is live backwards. We need new strengths for a new world. *My* world."

Ryssa wondered why she'd never sought out the shuttle before. Sure, it was located half a day's walk from the settlement on a plain of barren rock. It was the largest artefact and the biggest habitation she'd ever seen. On a surface level, it was in a state of disrepair, but once she operated the door mechanism and let herself and Canton inside, the place was a marvel. With slightly musty air, of course. She closed her eyes, let the download from the memory bank guide her movements. Incredibly, lights came on across the control console, a motor hummed and then thrummed beneath their feet. Things seemed to be in working order despite years of neglect.

"Do you remember playing *Sleepers* in the trees when we were children?" Canton asked.

"I'd forgotten until now. Actually, I was just thinking that it's a good job there's no weaponry onboard or that bully Johan would be after it."

"You really think you can pilot this thing?"

"I've absorbed all the necessary knowledge. Now, strap yourself in because there's going to be something called gee force. Like massive heavy blocks pressing on your body."

"I hope our sylpha survive. I hope *we* survive."

Ryssa was onto the final stage or pre-launch checks when Canton pointed at the windscreen and said, "Cut everything. There's a bullet storm on the way."

The sky roiled purple and fist-sized hailstones clattered against the hull like an off-key symphony for dangerous percussion. Ryssa was slightly annoyed by Canton's caution. The shuttle had survived worse than this over the years, surely?

She fired up the thrusters. The craft lifted… hovered… slumped bone-jarringly. She swept her hand across the controls, a one-woman conductor of an electronic orchestra.

A voice broke the silence.

"Hello, shuttle? Do you receive? This is Hargreaves aboard *The Fleeting Glimpse*. I read that you are active. Come in, please."

Ryssa squeezed her eyes shut, desperate to recall how to send signals. Canton's jaw had dropped open but then he started mumbling about "recorded messages" and "ghosts". What the double sun were they?

"I've been mostly asleep," the voice continued. "Fault in the system. Thirty years down the drain. I got left behind, mistaken for expired. I've only been up and about a month or so. Earth calendar. What's your position, shuttle? Copy."

"We're coming to rescue you," Ryssa squealed. "And we need merecadium."

"Oh I've got some of that. Not edible. Unlike the corpses… Just joking. What's your ETA?"

"I don't even know what that means. We can't get off the ground."

"I was third back-up pilot. Brain and memory are still alive even if the body's rotting. I'll try and talk you through procedures. Stay online, guys."

- *Flamers are love, friendship, camaraderie. See how we have learnt your vocabulary even though we cannot speak or hear in ways you understand.*
- *Speech and thought are illusions. Communication is present in non-linguistic forms at all times.*
- *Oneness real. You are cool shadow echo of our existence that encompasses all existence.*
- *Peace.*

As the thrusters powered up once again, they lost contact with the mystery voice. The shuttle had only gained minimal altitude. Suddenly they were surrounded by a mass of balls of fire.

"We're burning up," Ryssa screamed. "We're gonna die here."

"No, look, it's the flamers. They're buoying us up like we're floating to the top of the water. Except in this case, we're heading up into the atmosphere."

And they were. The ride was slower and less stressful than Ryssa had anticipated. The flamers were like fragments of clouds, breaking up and reforming in new patterns as they lifted the craft up to the edge of the stratosphere. It was all so dreamlike that she felt her eyes closing. But their cold brightness still penetrated her brain. They were non-corporeal creatures carrying her away to a sleepers' paradise of soft sweetness and joy –

"Shuttle, this is Hargreaves. Guess what, folks? I've got the tractor beam locked onto you and I'm taking over from here on in."

Canton pressed the response button. "What is a tractor beam?"

"Oh Christ, I'd forgotten you'd revert to primitive. It's like a fishing line reeling you in. No? A lasso – a coil of rope catching an animal or pulling a tree log."

"I think I get it."

"Well, don't you worry yourself. I'll talk you through the whole process from this point onwards. Approach, docking, airlock. God, haven't spoken so much in decades. It's just great to have something useful to do after all these years."

The weightlessness. The nausea. The head pressure almost unbearable. The metal clang of docking. The inertial jolt of stopping. The hiss of air exchange. The unsteady disembarkation. The shock, the anticipation.

The first of their generation to accomplish such a feat. The sense of everything being so new, uncertain, dangerous…

The smell made Ryssa gag. Clearly, Hargreaves had become unfamiliar with several aspects of basic hygiene. Or else he was saving all his water for drinking only. The man had something of a silvery hue as if the optima-advanced liquid nitrogen that had preserved him in a sleeping state until recently had replaced his blood and other bodily fluids.

"This is all a little incredible," Canton began. "We knew the spaceship was still here – one of our knowledge banks regularly tracks the low orbit. But to find a living person… You are living, aren't you?"

"Been awake nigh on four weeks now," Hargreaves smiled. "Earth time measurement. Got dry stores and water to last me a lot longer. I guess I somehow got left behind when McCabe and the rest headed downside."

"McCabe died ages ago," Ryssa answered. "Arken's in charge now."

"That rascal? Probably re-programmed the computers to ignore any maydays from me. Still, I suppose I've been up here floating above you all like an old-time god."

"We don't have religion."

"Make you kids right on that. And I was effectively absent. God is dead, like Nietzsche said. Who? Oh, an old Earth fellow, had a lot to say for himself."

Ryssa smiled. "We've got plenty of those sorts."

"Hmm. But what's wrong with your waistlines? Did you have an injury?" The couple pulled up their tunics, explained the necessary symbiosis. The sylpha had survived the rigors of the journey but the ridges looked a darker shade of red, quite badly bruised. "Well, how about that? As we head through the galaxy, the definition of what constitutes a human starts to change."

"Is that a bad thing, Hargreaves?"

"No, lady, it's just a thing."

Ryssa had noticed that Hargreaves' face was starting to grey over, like the evening clouds were obscuring the double suns.

"I don't feel too good," he stated. "I'm going to need to sleep for a bit. Thirty years and still –"

"Where's the merecadium?" Canton interrupted.

Honestly, her boyfriend had no sense of history unfolding and involving them all right here and now. Still, maybe urgency was the paramount factor at present. She absently stroked her neck, wondering if there were any programs she should access while she had the chance.

Hargreaves gave directions and added, "I've only geed up this part of *The Fleeting Glimpse*. Where you're going will be a weightless zone. Grip the… grip the side rail and use the handholds. If you… feel yourself floating, just go with… don't panic."

"We had a bit of that on the way up. No issues, old man."

During their absence, Ryssa located the button to unlock the portholes. She'd been too shocked and busy on the shuttle flight to really take the opportunity to drink in the incredible vista. There was Antalar 4 floating below her like the most fabulous, fabricated children's ball. She could see seas, mountainous regions, a massive, forested area to the north and, occasionally, flashes of bright light that probably indicated groupings of the flamers, their inscrutable but newly acquired friends.

Ryssa relaxed into the view. How many people got to look down on their world, whether they were from Antalar-4 or Old Earth? This was a privilege and an experience that cut deep into what Arken might have called a soul or a spirit when he was on one of his rambling schoolmaster trips.

She wondered what her parents had thought and experienced at this point. They had died five Antalarn years ago when the water mite plague had taken the lives of many of the original settlers, including McCabe and Dr Wang. It had been a tough half decade resetting the colonization plan under Arken's leadership.

Canton settled silently at her side, the enormity of their achievement starting to hit home.

"Did you…?"

"All in this box. It was a wild ride. Where's the old guy?"

"I'm right behind you," Hargreaves croaked. "Couldn't let you leave without saying goodbye. I'm, uh, ready to assist you on your return." He paused and Ryssa saw his face shimmer like a reflection in a pool, broken by a thrown stone. "Listen, I can reverse the polarity on the tractor beam to give the shuttle a little push away. Get you to the top of the stratosphere. Then you can let your programming kick in."

"This tracker beam sounds like the sort of weapon Johan would love to get his hands on," Canton mused. "We'll leave that bit out of our recount."

"Wise."

Ryssa cut in with, "You must come back with us. We've lost Dr Wang but there's a lot of medical expertise down there. We haven't had a single fatality for four years."

"I wouldn't want to skew those statistics, my dear. I'm in no fit state to travel. Except round and round in a low-flying tin can above this beautiful new world."

"It is beautiful. I'm going to appreciate it more now. And forever. Thank you for that, Hargreaves."

"I feel a little like Moses. Granted sight of but not access to the promised land."

"Moses? The name's familiar from the history bank. Some sort of hero."

"And now it's your turn, Ryssa."

"Not heroic at all. I feel more scared than I did on the way up here. Now that I know what is involved."

- *Glow ball is great and we are one. All come to glow ball in time which is no time.*
- *Flame burns but not harm. Enriches, encompasses, invites in.*
- *Welcome.*

Later, in the shuttle readying to depart and make landfall, Canton said, "What is it with old timers and all that promised land nonsense?"

"I think it makes sense to them. I suppose it's what's got humankind out this far into the galaxy and will keep us spreading our metaphorical wings. Come on, I'm dreading this bit but... let's go."

####

Allen Ashley is based in London, UK and is President of the British Fantasy Society. He has recently had work published in print or online in "Sein und Werden", "BFS Horizons" and the anthologies "Terror Tales from the Home Counties" (Edited by Paul Finch, Telos, 2020) and "Time We Left" (Edited by Terry Grimwood (The Exaggerated Press, 2020).

allenashley.com
*amazon.com/s?k=%22allen+ashley%22&i=stripbooks&ref=nb_sb_*
noss

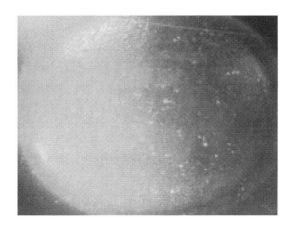

Earth Space 2071
By Neil A. Hogan

Minisode 1: Inclusion

Scientist Shaun Smith, encumbered in a spacesuit, floated outside the alien sphere, waiting for entry into what had been jokingly referred to as the 'interview room.' The greenish ovoid shape, bigger than most office blocks, undulated and then a slit appeared, glowing from within. Smith was sucked inside and, with a rush of something he couldn't quite see, the slit closed behind him.

This was it, he thought. The greatest job interview in the Solar System. Ambassador to Earth for the new gas ball aliens. Like most with ADHD, he was a polymath—the ideal type to be able to deal with an alien culture. He was confident that his intelligence would get him through the interview.

Around him was a well-lit space full of floating green balls of various sizes, shades and patterns. Some were in clumps like bubbles, others were separated, moving in all directions. He stared at them, fascinated.

For a moment his momentum continued to carry him forward, before the gravity of the situation caught up with him. He hadn't considered the ovoid would have a mass.

So much for intelligence.

As he fell towards the curved floor, he struggled to activate his thigh thrusters. He was sure that breaking the membrane would cause a major diplomatic incident.

The thrusters weren't strong enough to take him back to the

center, but they did slow his descent. He landed gently on his feet, and found the membrane to be like springy leather.

One of the balls drifted down to him. "Follow me," said a bubbly voice through his translator. The ball, with a puff of gas, floated back up to the center.

Smith looked after it, incredulously. "How?"

Maybe he could jump? He bent his knees then pushed off with all his strength, adding his thrusters for good measure, but just got a third of the way before the mass of the shell pulled him back down again.

"I don't believe this," he said, frustrated. Then, to his surprise, several balls came closer to him, making cooing noises. They stuck to his arms and released gas, lifting him up to the center far above. When the pull of gravity equalized on all sides, the cooing balls left.

"Why would they send a youngling?" asked the guide.

"I'm not," Smith replied, confused.

"Stuck to the barrier, not yet able to use your vents?"

He must look like a baby bird. "Our planet's gravity means humans never evolved self-powered flight. We use machines instead."

"Are all humans deformed like you?"

Smith frowned. Diplomatically he said, "We all have this disability."

"Ah. Pity for your race," said the ball. "Continue to follow, poor, helpless thing."

Smith grimaced. Disabled, and now the ball had started infantilizing him. The interview hadn't even started yet.

This did not bode well.

His guide indicated three other balls then said to them, "Keep the human Sphere-centered. Birth defects suspected." It flew up and the new balls spun forward towards Smith, juggling around each other. Smith's eyes widened when he realized each one was wider than he was tall.

"Greetings, human," said the foremost ball.

"Greetings." Smith struggled to remain facing them and found himself drifting away. He fired his thrusters to get back.

The second one said. "Forgive us for laughing."

"I didn't hear anything."

"It's not aural!" The second ball turned to the third. "What is your laugh frequency?"

"400 terahertz. Yours?'

"10,000 terahertz."

"I'm sorry," said Smith, understanding the wavelengths. "Humans cannot usually perceive infrared and ultraviolet."

"A handicap!" said the second ball.

"You can't see us laugh?" said the third.

"No. Our eyes only perceive the visible spectrum."

"Then your visible spectrum is different to ours," said the second ball. "Another disorder that humans have. Not something we have any way of compensating for."

The third one moved to the front. "After work, we meet near the center, absorb waste gases and make jokes. If you can't join in the fun, it may be detrimental to successful negotiations, project allocations and possible promotions."

Smith rolled his eyes. He had the same problem on Earth when he couldn't join the team for Friday night drinks. But what was it they did? "Absorb waste gases?"

"Oh yes," said one of the balls. "Inhaling tubes of hydrogen sulfide is very popular."

Smith shuddered. "I'm afraid I'm unable to due to, er, allergies."

The balls looked at each other.

"Health problems," said the first ball.

"Not eligible for immigration," said the second.

"Perhaps a temporary work visa?" said the third.

The third ball came forward. "Are you crippled? Are your vents spastic or blocked?"

"Vents?"

"Yes," the three balls turned around to show three tiny holes at its back. "We use these to move around the Sphere," said the first ball. "If you're near the end of your life, the vents don't work. Our policy is we hire beings for their skills, but if they can't even make it to our central workspace, well…"

"Older iterations of us are unproductive due to their obstructed vents, and will decay soon," said the second ball. "Best ignored and forgotten. Like most countries on your planet, we don't hire past a certain age due to increasing mental and physical disabilities. Those that are still cognizant are assigned to Sphere-door control."

Smith raised an eyebrow. "Could you grow vacuum tubes for the elderly so that they could work in the center?" he asked without thinking. "Sorry, cultural reaction. We believe everyone can benefit society in their own way and that the only thing that holds them back is being included. So, we make allowances for mental and physical disabilities where possible. For the position with your good selves, I will have something appropriate made to assist me to get to the center."

The second sphere rotated forward. "You need to interact with a wide variety of us across the vast expanse of the Sphere. The job description does say 'some travelling involved.' You need to meet the criteria to be offered the position."

"I understand."

"We have studied their debilitated," said the third ball to the second. "When their legs don't work they use a contraption with wheels. However, these vehicles damage infrastructure. Screws and other parts of the device stick out and cut into the barriers of their living spaces."

"Your device would damage our barrier," said the first ball. "You must be trained to live here. We understand you have a single vent and a flexible spine."

Smith shrunk further into his suit, feeling invalidated. "My major was in flatology, so I'm more aware of how humans emit gases than most. Unfortunately, I don't have control over the gases that my 'vent' emits. Certainly, it might only happen once an hour, and usually unexpectedly."

"You will attend the new iterations' training courses," said the first ball. "And upskill for this position. We also believe if you are lighter you will pass the course. A body of 20kg as you measure weight would suffice."

Smith had already started sweating at the idea of having to take his pants down and fart his way across the inside of the sphere. There was no way he could reduce his 80kg, plus suit, to 20kg. "Unfortunately, my colon does not create as much gas as your good selves, so propelling myself would be impossible. Our scientists are experts in developing soft materials that cannot damage the membrane. Please let us show you."

The central ball nodded. "Very well. Let's not dwell on all your disabilities. We must find a way for the abnormality of a human to live with us so that we can exchange knowledge."

"I have a solution," said the third ball. "When we are near death, we reproduce from ourselves. The older self dies, and the newer self takes over the older self's positions and responsibilities. My deceased earlier iteration's body has not yet become part of the barrier. You could use that."

"You want me to live inside one of you?" Smith almost choked.

"Yes." The ball indicated further away where a wall of balls had appeared to watch this meeting with the human. "Also, being inside, you could avoid the stares."

Smith shook his head. "I couldn't do that. I would, well, throw up."

"Do you have any mental issues that might preclude you taking this position?" asked the second ball. "When the iterations die, the younglings absorb the organs and bacteria then play inside them for a while before the body is taken to the barrier for reabsorption. If younglings have no trouble…"

"The barrier?" Smith became horrified, then overwhelmed as his ADHD struggled to cope with the reality.

"Oh, yes," said the third ball, gleefully. "The membrane barrier is made up of billions of all our old bodies."

"I need to… I…have to think. Think over…." said Smith, shuddering. "Can we end the interview here?"

The first ball came forward. "Very well. Your guide will open an exit for you. Thank you for coming."

Smith blinked, his thoughts coming back into focus with standard responses. "Thank you for the opportunity."

Cooing sounds accompanied him as he followed the guide ball back to the vent. Several balls had made an airlock-like section for him and parted as he approached, then closed around him. The vent opened and Smith was pulled out into space. He turned and saw, to his horror, the balls quickly fill the hole and turn black.

Old balls had sacrificed themselves to not only help him leave, but probably to help him enter too.

He could not work there. His 'disabilities' would prevent him from being included in everything. He was trapped being a human and trying to be anything more than that would just be constantly degrading.

He now felt what people with disabilities must feel. It was, ironically, dehumanizing. He hailed an uber shuttle and headed back to Earth.

Minisode 2: Rejuvenation

Sunday 16th August 2171.

It was today.

Victor Horatio Allowishus III half-opened a rheumy eye on his hissing ventilator. The thump, shhh, thump of the device, echoing in his private palliative-care ward, had been his only constant companion these past few years. Soon, it would turn off. A penance for his 170 years of wasted research.

As CEO of the largest interplanetary medical and pharmaceutical supplier in the world, he had utilized everyone and everything under his command. But, even after all this time, there still wasn't a cure for aging. Now, here he was, at the mercy of nursebots and the occasional faux-obsequious visit from long-suffering board members, counting the minutes until it was over.

But what had woken him?

The echo from the nearby corridor of a shambling patter of sneakered feet, and the swish of a lab coat -- his long-time business partner, and deputy board member, Cecil, had returned. "News?" Victor's voice caught as the white blur moved into the room.

"Sir." Cecil approached his bedside. "A solution has been found."

Victor felt hope begin to fill his biomechanical heart. "I knew my company would find an answer," he gasped. "Though, this is cutting it a bit fine! Solution compound or solution answer?"

"A bit of both, actually, sir."

"Well?"

"Well, firstly, it isn't from our company. Secondly, I don't think you're going to like it."

Victor wished he could read Cecil's expressions rather than have this dialogue, but he'd lost that skill a long time ago. He squinted at the nearby clock. Reddish numbers revealed how close he was. "Don't fuck with me, Cecil. I've got less than an hour to live. Just tell me."

"I need to show you. Happy 200th birthday, by the way, sir."

"Yes, yes." He'd forgotten he'd chosen this date for a reason. 200 orbits around the sun. He squeezed open the other eyelid and a double-blurred image of Cecil appeared. He closed it again. "Hurry up, man. How?"

Cecil unfolded a tablet from his pocket, and a hologram activated, shining blue across the sterile hospital bed.

Victor peered at the image again. "Oh, a DNA helix. Isn't that my design? I don't need the research."

"Marketing for the Obsidians, sir. Let me flick through." Cecil swiped away several images then settled on one of fertilized eggs showing XX chromosomes and XY chromosomes, and a little arrow indicating the male activation gene.

Victor grimaced. "My body might be practically dead, but my brain and memory are very much alive and present. I'm not looking for an infodump, Cecil. Get on with it."

"I need to show you this image to be sure you're clear on this, sir. It is an incredibly exciting development and will have wide-reaching ramifications." He pointed at one side of the image. "The Obsidians showed us. The inactive X chromosome, hidden in males."

Victor frowned again. "Impossible. Only females have an inactive X chromosome."

"It's been in pieces the whole time," continued Cecil, showing another image. "Hiding, folded up in every twist of noncoding DNA, hidden by insulation barriers. We never believed it was there so never looked. We can push the proteins to reassemble and transcribe it, and, ahem, activate the, ah, other side of you." Cecil put the hologram away.

Victor's mind reeled. How had he not discovered this before? He'd been playing with DNA ever since the first gene-editing system had become available in 2009. In all that time, he never thought there might be a jigsaw hidden away in the helix. Even the A.I.s and their combination equations were focused on creating something new, not assembling something old.

But there was something that didn't quite make sense. Many somethings. His mind struggled to think of everything at once. If the X was expressed, then the Y wouldn't be. Is that right? His mind was suddenly full of questions. Why was this told to him with no time to research it. Could he trust Cecil? The board? Who were the Obsidians? A rival company? His fear of his company being taken from under him, even at this late stage, immediately focused on the potential enemy.

"Cecil! Who, the fuck, are the Obsidians?"

Cecil balked, then rubbed his hands together. "Ah. I thought you'd been updated. Sorry, sir. New trading partners from beyond the Solar System. In a nutshell, a society of all-female aliens."

A moment to take it in, then Victor smiled, thinking about the economic possibilities. Well, half a smile. He'd lost the use of his left side long ago. "Big buyers, I hope?"

"We've developed a great trading relationship. We're at a similar level of medical advancement, but with different techniques, so we've exchanged skills, methods and equipment, then added the adapted works to our catalogue."

Victor blinked. An alien solution. And at this last minute he knew what it meant. "You've set me up to be the first, right?" Victor drew a ragged breath. "Are you insane?"

Cecil shrugged. "We've done extensive testing on rats, monkeys, and with human organs. It definitely works. And, as you just said…" Cecil pointed a finger at the clock.

If he said no, he would die in about 45 minutes. That was the agreement with the board. He had no choice. "How do you know this is going to work for me?"

"My assistant will know for sure." Cecil then shambled out of the way.

"Assistant?" Victor heard a faint buzz against the floor, then she flickered into view. Tall and purple, wearing long, writhing robes, like knitted mineral shavings, that reflected his drab hospital gown. The buzz was her personal biome protection field pushing against the tiles under the soles of her feet.

"Obsidian," said Victor, awed. "You have a solution for me?"

Her long fingers extended to almost touch a barren section of skin amongst the forest of wires attached to his skull. Terranese language filled his ears.

"A rejuvenation is possible," her translator burbled. "All memories have been retained."

"I'll still be me, just younger?"

"The same biology. Yes."

The remaining hairs rose on the back of his patchwork neck. He half-grinned as he heard the beep of his heart speed up. But then his mind began to put the pieces together. "What's the catch?"

"No catch," said the Obsidian. "A necessity."

"I'm listening."

"We are all equal. You must be, too. For the safety of humanity, and the galaxy."

Victor squinted, then regretted it, shifting back into the pillows, taking a breath. "What do you mean?"

"Not patented. Not exclusive. Available for all. No elites."

"That's it?" Victor was incredulous. "Save my life as long as I agree you can save other lives?"

Cecil moved closer, again. "We will do it, sir. She will give us the technology on the condition that if anyone else wants it, we only charge what it costs. No profiteering. Even some of your more vocal, unionized, staff, if they want it."

Victor pondered. "If it doesn't work, I'll die, and won't care. If it does work, I'll live, and be too happy to care."

The Obsidian's head swayed from side to side, then she buzzed away from his bed and back down the corridor. She'd got the answer she had wanted.

"If this is successful, are there others wanting the same operation?"

"Millions. Governments are standing by ready to subsidize if needed. So…"

It was so much to take in, yet there was something missing. There must be catch. Other side? Same biology? What was he missing? Then it hit him, and he almost shrank back into the bed.

Impossible.

"I know the real catch, Cecil. The only way I can use the reassembled X chromosome to rejuvenate this husk is if it replaces the corrupted Y. That means no longer being completely male."

Cecil nodded. "It's more than that. It's a complete rejuvenation. You'll be 100% female. Every aspect of the male side of you will dissolve to help create the female side. Everything."

"I'll even lose… Goddammnit."

"You'll have a completely new body with all memories intact. Completely you. Not a robot body or a clone. 100% you, just with different hormonal responses and, er, functions."

Victor's face went a whiter shade of white.

"But you know the alternative," continued Cecil. "If you don't, the company will go to your granddaughter, and your body will be podded for the tree cemetery."

"Cecil. The board is full of codgers and curmudgeons. What will they do when I tell them I changed my sex to live longer?"

"Well, women do live longer! Past 300, these days."

"Oh, for God's sake."

"Victor, just think about it. You'll be doing the entire Solar

System a favor. Shareholders have been lobbying for a new leader for years now. The company needs stability, run by someone with experience."

Victor began shaking at the idea of discarding itself, even though his body was arthritic, prone to blood clots, and looked like dried chicken necks cobbled together. He knew he'd miss it. He sighed. "I honestly don't think I'm strong enough to be female."

"What if becoming female will give you that strength?"

Victor closed his eyes. He could still end it. He could leave this mortal coil and go onto the next life, or wherever humans go when they die. Everything would turn off in about 30 minutes. It might not be quick, but it would be over.

Steeling himself, he opened his eyes again. If the soul were eternal, another few hundred years with a different body wouldn't really make much difference. "Perhaps being a woman would mean I'd feel a bit stronger in this lifetime?" he ventured.

"Yes, exactly. You'll be one of the tough girls."

"And it would be a new experience."

"Yes, sir. Absolutely."

Victor decided. At the very least, it could make a great research paper, or even a memoir. "Well, what are you waiting for? Let's get this started."

"We can start the regenderation process immediately." Cecil reached over and placed his hand against the clock. The red figures disappeared. "I've disarmed the timer."

Victor gave the slightest nod before falling further into the pillow, his mind whirling. He'd be a young woman with old male memories. He wondered if he would just end up staring at himself in the mirror for hours.

The first thing Victor saw, when she awoke from her induced coma, was how focused everything was. No more glasses or magnifying plates.

She was lying in a long plastiglass tube that revealed the operating theatre around her.

She felt more alive than she had in years.

She pulled at her hair and looked at it. Clean, fresh, and alive.

She felt her face. Smooth, with no wrinkles.

No pain. Her thoughts were clear. She even smelt better. Amazing.

It was almost like getting a new vehicle. What should she do next? Check the oil?

She closed her eyes and extended her senses.

Blood rushing in the ears. A heartbeat steady and strong under her breasts. Fingers and toes that opened and closed smoothly, without a twinge of arthritis, cramp or gout. No pain when stretching. She could even lift her arms above her head, with no tightness in the shoulders. She marveled at the pleasure of it.

A trundling sound to her right, and she turned to see vats of old skin, bone, hair, dissolved organs, and liquids taken away, probably to be burned. For a moment she felt what amputees might feel when they lose arms or legs, never to see them again. Though, with this process, her own body had rejected 'him'.

That body had carried her through 200 years. She would never see it or even see reminders of it again. For a moment, grief tore at her stomach and a tear came to her eye. She shook her head, refocusing on the moment.

They had told her of the procedure just as she went under. She had grown from the brainstem, the spinal cord, then the lungs and heart outwards, discarding the unused parts of the old body like a cancerous growth. All the excess material and toxins had sloughed off, dripping into ready-made catchment funnels while she was unconscious.

They'd washed her, styled her hair, given her some new clothes, and now she had trouble believing she'd ever been Victor Horatio Allowishus III.

But enough of this. She was eager to get back to directing the board on new projects she had in mind. She would promote the treatment through the Solar System. Make humanity young again. She would be lauded a heroine. Millions, maybe even billions of men would want to do this, and she would be their savior, their queen. What would the world be like if all the men decided to become women? A new golden age? She almost floated at the thought.

Then Victor coughed as the smell of a spicy cologne assailed her senses before Cecil had even entered the room.

"Welcome back," said Cecil. "Great to see you're awake."

Victor blinked. Cecil looked a lot bigger than she remembered.

"Firstly," he began. "A message from your granddaughter. I went to visit her this morning. She says she's glad you're not passing the business onto her. Really glad. I actually have it in writing."

"Thank you. Soon as I'm discharged, I'll go and visit."

Cecil gave a slight shake of the head.

She stared at him for a moment. Her skill at reading people had returned. Memories flooded back of corner-of-the-eye expressions from Cecil that she had missed in her old body. Words he spoke that were on the surface, friendly, but underneath… Then again, it was probably something more obvious, like that grin he was desperately trying to conceal. "Alright. Out with it."

"Actually, there's been a slight complication, I'm afraid, Victor."

A sick feeling began to churn in Victor's empty stomach. "What kind of 'complication'?"

"Well. The regenderation activated your female side successfully, but at the point where the parts of the X chromosome had finally become completely dormant. It's quite funny, really."

Victor raised an eyebrow. "I think you're the only one that's laughing."

Cecil snickered. "I'm afraid you're genetically about ten years old."

Ten years old. Victor frowned. But she could make it work. It wasn't a huge problem. Hire some assistants. Buy smaller furniture… she wasn't one of the smartest people in the Solar System for nothing. "Cecil, isn't that great news? I might even get another 290 years! This isn't a problem for me, I assure you. If the board can accept a rejuvenated version of me, they can surely accept how I look?"

"Well. Yes. In a sense." Cecil finally released his grin. "The Solar System quickly accepted the rejuvenation solution, and many centenarians have signed up. Thanks to your sacrifice."

Victor narrowed her eyes. "And?"

"Well, it's a new procedure, and the laws are going to take a while to catch up." Cecil leant closer. "As your DNA now registers you as being ten years old, you can't be a CEO. In fact, you can't be a board member at all, anywhere."

Victor's face went white as the full force of this piece of information hit her. "WHAT?" She gasped, throwing herself back against the glass tube with a thud. "WHAT?"

"We have our legal people working on it, but it doesn't look good. Well, it doesn't look good for you." Cecil chuckled. "You need parents and guardians for everything until you're at least 16." He stepped back from the glass tube. "I'm so sorry. Really, I am."

Victor felt her eyes fill with tears. She tried to fight against it but had forgotten how. "This is so idiotic!" she yelled. "I'm CEO of the largest interplanetary medical and pharmaceutical supplier in the world! Half the Solar System works for me!"

Cecil's face became hard. "I've discussed it with the board, and we agree with the laws. In fact, we're going to send you to planet Saturn, all expenses paid. There's a great vegan family for you on Titan Base, with all the mod cons. Hydroponic farms, play areas. Completely unionized. You might want to change your name. How about Victoria?" This time Cecil did laugh. A deep-throated, villain-like laugh.

Victor now understood. All this time while she had been stuck in the ward, Cecil had been moving his pieces into position. Staying alive meant her company couldn't be willed to her granddaughter. Being too young to be a CEO meant the position would go to the next most experienced. And there was only one that could take her place with no argument.

Cecil.

Victor smashed her fists angrily on the hard glass as tears streamed down her face. "You're a fucking bastard. You planned this from the beginning."

Cecil stood confidently, no longer shambling, or sycophantic, reveling in the moment. "Language, please, young lady. You're talking to the CEO of the largest interplanetary medical and pharmaceutical supplier in the world. Have some respect."

Victor pushed her face against the glass, glaring at him. The betrayal. The treachery. If she ever got the chance, she would kill him.

"And Victor," said Cecil.

"What?" she screamed.

"Bedtime is at 8pm."

Minisode 3: Flash Ships Ltd

Space twisted, shuddered, then ripped apart as Flash Ships Ltd.'s experimental craft tore back into reality. The triangular ship shot forward, momentum from its previous suborbital position above Earth throwing it further into the Kuiper Belt.

Inside, Captain Bruce Malper saved the target drone's recording of their arrival, unhooked his belt and checked the oxygen levels. "AI. Record. 11:47am AEST. Sunday 12th April 2071. The first human test of the interplanetary flash drive is a success." He straightened carefully in the confined space, brushing off cables that had gathered near him, and checked stats. "Pluto's orbit confirmed. 7.5 billion kilometers in 7 seconds."

"Incoming!" yelled a muffled voice from his helmet.

Immediately he was slammed back into his seat as the craft shot EM pulses from his corner. A bright burst of plasma blasted past the front metal glass, almost blinding him. "Commander Wei. What the hell was that?"

His chunky fingers struggling with the hybridized old and new technology, Malper pressed a spring-loaded button on the outside of his helmet to activate the quantum-entangled mind-view signal. External cameras broadcast an image into his mind in x- and gamma-rays, but the object it showed was almost too impossible to believe. "I don't believe it."

He felt Wei link and add more data. A new image flowered open in his visual cortex with an analysis of the energy blast. Wei's alpha waves were like a cool breeze across his brain, their interaction in this mental space calming him quickly.

"Particle stream?" began Wei's thoughts. "The kind that a…"

"…that a compressed mass like a black hole emits," finished Malper. "Yes."

"Ten Earths in a cricket ball." Wei turned the mass around in their heads. "The magnetic field is strengthening. It's going to fire again. Two thousand kilometers away means three seconds to impact."

Malper gripped his chair as the ship's EM pulses changed their course again, the plasma blast going wider. "You know, I was worried we'd materialize inside Pluto. This is a lot worse. Exiting."

His tiny control station filled his vision again as the image of the compressed mass faded away. "Any suggestions?"

"Return to Earth."

Malper turned in his seat and peered around the central cylindrical flash engine, hoping to catch her expression. He could just make out Wei's back at the end of the tiny corridor that branched off to the left. "Wei. Seriously? It's taken three years to get this far."

"If the next particle stream hits, none of this will matter." Her voice had a slight edge. "Instant vaporization."

They couldn't end the mission this quickly. Then he remembered, she wasn't an astrophysicist. "Look. We must have arrived above it. If it's like a black hole, well, they only stream at the poles. Set an EM course at 90 degrees and see if that works. Just make sure we don't get caught in its gravity well."

"Yes, sir."

Malper sighed, then jumped as a large metal tail snaked around from the right corridor and gripped the handhold next to him. "Shinky! I'm already jumpy. Could you have knocked first?"

"So, you are alive!" Two of her exoarms gripped the bulkhead and slowly pulled the rest of her human body into the confined space. "I've been trying to contact you guys for hours."

"Hours?"

"Joking. A few minutes, though. My corner of the ship is closer to the black hole, so time is slower. The hybrid system couldn't connect."

Malper rubbed his face. "That's all we need. Will it affect the flash drive?"

"I don't think so. Let's just get out of the area."

"Flash engine?" asked Wei.

"EM drive," said Malper. "Set course for Eris, or Arrokoth. Anywhere."

They felt the EM pulses increase and held tighter.

Shinky tapped Malper's control panel. "Found this. That thing out there is not a natural mass. Human-made. Well, alien-made?"

"What?" Wei bounced out of her chair and launched herself like a diver down the tight corridor. Malper frowned at this, remembering his bulk, and how the only exit he had was up. "Aren't you supposed to be driving?"

"I engaged the autopilot."

Wei reached past Shinky and zoomed the image further. "So, the plasma bursts are deliberate. It detected something large and high speed, then fired."

Shinky pointed with an exoarm at the edge of the image. "There's even a bloody force field around it." She tapped the screen with a claw, and it showed another graph. "And a signal being broadcast. It might be networked to something, or somethings."

"I don't like the look of this," said Malper. "What if there are more of these out there?"

"I know, right?" said Shinky. "They could be here to stop us from leaving. Imagine millions of these things hiding in the outer Solar System. If the deep pockets hear about this, that's it for interstellar travel, and my career. I'd be just another disabled body again."

"Well, we're not going to let that happen," said Malper. Then he saw that Shinky had started looking alarmed at her heads-up display. "What?"

"Black hole thingy? I think it's started chasing us."

"No. No. No," said Malper, seeing the projected trajectory on his panel. He groaned. "Goddamnit! Commander Wei. You're right. Turn off the EM pulses, and the autopilot. Shinky, prep the flash engine. AI. Abort all testing programs."

"Yes, sir." Wei quickly dived back to her station.

"On it." Shinky's exoattachments scuttled her back down her corridor.

Malper shot out a drone to record their departure for the shareholders, then activated the flash drive. As it powered up, he deleted every record of the mass. The last thing he wanted was the company to think the Solar System was under lockdown.

Flash engine microwaves poured through the ship, increasing its frequency to 300,000 cycles per second. Outside, reality shattered, and the triangular shadow disappeared, just as a bolt of magnetic plasma blasted through now empty space.

Publications featuring **Neil A. Hogan's** *work include Plague Stories: Essays on Life in a Reshaped World, by Bowen Street Press. Outside in Makes It So, and Outside In Boldy Goes by ATB Publishing, not to mention every issue of Alien Dimensions. His most recent novel is The Robots of Atlantis, published by Space Fiction Books. He has a short story paying homage to Stanislaw Lem's writing style, in a volume due out later in the year. Of these minisodes, a previous version of Rejuvenation appeared in Hoganthology, and Flash Ships Ltd first appeared on the AntipodeanSF Radio Show in 2021.*

NeilAHogan.com
amazon.com/Neil-A-Hogan/e/B006K5UA68

You might also be interested in

Hoganthology

In this 800-page (5" x 8") collection of over 47 of Neil A. Hogan's stories you will discover ancient space battles, alternate dimensions, sentient dark matter, dinosaurs, robots, galaxy movers, planet-sized aliens and more.

Expect many twists and turns along the way. These stories throw you into many universes of an SF craftsman - mad, mind-bending, marvelous and always alien.

Available in digital and print from Amazon

You might also be interested in

The Robots of Atlantis

The Stellar Flash crew and the Saturn Space Station X-1a team have been getting ready for an expected robot uprising. Afterall, there's one every few years.

But, the Array on Saturn Space Station X-1a, the final solution to a major robot takeover, has been compromised, and humanity is, well, in disarray.

The Stellar Flash ship, humanity's defense against an invasion, is nowhere to be found.

And an ancient Entity from Atlantean times has appeared, intending to take back her planet.

Where and when has the Stellar Flash gone?

Will Admiral Heartness and her team repair the Array in time?

And how did Captain Jonathan Hogart end up in Atlantis, 13,000 years ago?

Available in digital and print from Amazon

Special release. Where it all began!
Celebrating the Third Year of Alien Dimensions.

Alien Dimensions

Science Fiction, Fantasy and Metaphysical Short Stories Magazine 1-3 box set

(Updated for the 2019 re-release)

Download it from Amazon today!

Are you a writer?

Would you be interested in writing a short story for a future issue of Alien Dimensions?

If you've got an idea for a story set in space, in the far future, with aliens, then you're already halfway there!

Check out the detailed submission guidelines at:
www.AlienDimensions.com/submission-guidelines
and see if it is something that interests you.

Many thanks for your interest in Alien Dimensions

P.S. If you thought this issue was worthwhile, can you give it a review and/or rating on Amazon? It would be very much appreciated, and more reviews means more Alien Dimensions! Many thanks in advance.

Printed in Poland
by Amazon Fulfillment
Poland Sp. z o.o., Wrocław
26 March 2022

332a57ba-48b9-4b3a-9634-5f8353e91d10R01